THE LEGEND OF NIMWAY HALL

1940: JOSIE

LINDA NEEDHAM

BIG SCRUMPY PRESS

THE LEGEND OF NIMWAY HALL
1940: JOSIE

*USA Today bestselling author Linda Needham
brings you the fourth story in a series of romances
touched by magic as old as time.*

*A courageous young woman is just managing
to keep up with her family's vast, wartime farm
when a handsome Lt. Colonel takes command of her home.
A private war ensues between them,
and the couple soon learns that resistance is futile
when it comes to love in the heat of battle.*

World War II has come to Nimway Hall, and with it an endless series of wartime challenges that its lady and guardian, Josie Stirling, must overcome. As passionate and courageous as each of the guardians who have come before her, Josie is fiercely determined to defend her family's ancient and beloved estate from all possible threats. But with the recent evacuation of Dunkirk and the bombs of the Blitz raining random terror all across Britain, even the once-pastoral manor farm of Nimway have become as dangerous as any battlefield.

Loved and respected by everyone in her circle of care, Josie is knee-deep in evacuee children, Land Girls, the local Home Guard, a much-reduced estate staff, two cranky tractors and her widowed father she has just rescued from the London Blitz. Her days and nights, and even her dreams are chock-full of wartime charity fund raisers, meeting the strict requirements of the Ministries of Agriculture and Food, organizing knitting circles, leading her local WAS, tending the acres of orchards, the mill, and fields of grain. And even with every tillable square inch of Nimway planted in crops for the war effort, her beloved Balesboro Wood is being threatened with destruction by the Timber Commission.

And to add to her problems, not only has the military requisitioned an entire wing of Nimway Hall, they've sent the most arrogant officer in the entire army to command the unit and impose his orders on the finely-tuned workings of her estate. A man as arrogant as he is handsome. Not that Josie has time in her life to notice!

The very last post Lt. Colonel Gideon Fletcher ever wanted was to be holed up in the wilds of Somerset, in an old manor house, far from the front line. But he was seriously injured on a secret mission early in the war and has recovered just enough to command of a team of Royal Engineers, commissioned to build Operational Bases for Churchill's new Secret Army. Once a highly respected intelligence officer, Gideon resents his demotion to the "Home Front" and has little respect for the so-called civilian army he's been assigned to recruit and train. War is waged by soldiers in the field, not by farmers and factory workers.

A sentiment the contentious lady of Nimway Hall disputes at every turn. She seems to believe that her work for the war effort is as critical as his. Though the woman's opinions are seriously wrong-headed, she is as beautiful as she is devoted to her people and he can't help admiring the firm and resourceful way she manages the estate. Can't help noticing her fiercely green eyes and the sun-blush of her cheek. Not that he should be noticing such distractions. Not now. Not with a war to win and contact to make with a secret agent named Arcturus.

As the war between the sexes heats up, so does the ancient magic of romance. Josie and Gideon may not be looking for love, but at Nimway Hall they'll soon discover that love has come looking for them.

Fourth book in the series. A historical novel of 75,000 words, entwining romance, mystery and the magic of love.

Praise for the works of Linda Needham

"Trust Linda Needham with your heart–you'll never regret it."
Lisa Kleypas

"Linda Needham has the ability to mix laughter with tears to touch a reader's heart." — *"Romantic Times"*

"Ms. Needham has a knack for drawing her readers from page 1, and not letting go even when the story ends — " *New and Used Books*

THE LEGEND OF NIMWAY HALL
1940: JOSIE

THE LEGEND OF NIMWAY HALL

1940: JOSIE

Copyright © 2018 by Linda Needham

ISBN: 978-1-940904-04-7

Cover design by Big Scrumpy Press, LLC

Big Scrumpy Press, LLC, North Plains, OR, USA

Contact: https://lindaneedham.com/contact/

❀ Created with Vellum

THE LEGEND OF NIMWAY HALL

A love invested with mystery and magic
sends ripples through the ages.

Long ago in a cave obscured by the mists of time, Nimue, a powerful sorceress and Merlin's beloved, took the energy of their passion and wove it into a potent love spell. Intending the spell to honor their love and enshrine it in immortality, she merged the spell into the large moonstone in the headpiece of Merlin's staff. Thus, when Merlin was far from her, he still carried the aura of their love with him and, so they both believed, the moonstone would act as a catalyst for true love, inciting and encouraging love to blossom in the hearts of those frequently in the presence of the stone.

Sadly, neither Merlin nor Nimue, despite all their power, foresaw the heart of Lancelot. A minor adept, he sensed both the presence of the spell in the moonstone and also the spell's immense power. Driven by his own desires, Lancelot stole the headpiece and used the moonstone's power to sway Guinevere to his side.

Furious that the spell crafted from the pure love of his and his beloved's hearts had been misused, Merlin smote Lancelot and seized back the headpiece. To protect it forevermore, Merlin laid upon the stone a web of control that restricted its power. Henceforth, it could act only in response to a genuine need for true love, and only when that need impacted one of his and Nimue's blood, no matter how distant.

Ultimately, Merlin sent the headpiece back to Nimue for safe keeping. As the Lady of the Lake, at that time, she lived in a cottage on an island surrounded by swiftly flowing streams, and it was in her power to see and watch over their now-dispersed offspring.

Time passed, and even those of near-immortality faded and vanished. The land about Nimue's cottage drained, and the region eventually became known as Somerset. Generations came and went, but crafted of spelled gold, the headpiece endured and continued to hold and protect the timeless moonstone imbued with Nimue's and Merlin's spells...

Over time, a house, crafted of sound local stone and timbers from the surrounding Balesboro Wood, was built on the site of Nimue's cottage. The house became known as Nimway Hall. From the first, the house remained in the hands and in the care of a female descendant of Nimue, on whom devolved the responsibilities of guardian of Nimway Hall.

As decades and then centuries passed, the tradition was established that in each generation, the title of and responsibility for the house and associated estate passed to the eldest living and willing daughter of the previous female holder of the property, giving rise to the line of the Guardians of Nimway Hall.

THE GUARDIANS OF NIMWAY HALL

Nimue — Merlin

Through the mists of time

~

1720: Moira
(to come)

~

1750: Jacqueline
by Stephanie Laurens — available now

~

1771: Olivia
(to come)

~

1794: Charlotte
by Karen Hawkins — available now

~

1818: Isabel
by Suzanne Enoch — available now

~

1839: Miranda
(to come)

~

1862: Georgia
(to come)

~

1888: Alexandra
(by Victoria Alexander; to come)

~

1926: Maddie Rose
(by Susan Andersen; to come)

~

1940: Josie
by Linda Needham — available now

CHAPTER 1

"*H*alt there, miss! Stop your vehicle and present your identification card."

Not believing her eyes, Josie Stirling leaned her elbow out the driver's window, nudged her aviator glasses down to the end of her nose and glared at the freshly-minted young soldier who was barring her van from passing through the entrance gate to Nimway Hall. "Who are you?"

The soldier straightened, saluted. "Sapper Mullins, miss, of the Royal Engineers."

Bloody hell, the invasion and occupation of Nimway Hall by the Royal Engineers had begun nearly a month before the schedule that she had confirmed with the War Office only last week.

"How long have you been standing at this gate, Sapper Mullins?"

"Posted here this morning. Six a.m."

"By whom?"

"My commanding officer, Lt. Colonel Gideon Fletcher. He ordered me not to let you pass, miss, without you show me your papers. If you please."

She didn't please. Wasn't pleased at all and wouldn't be pleased until she had it out with the arrogant colonel who seemed to think it was within his charge to forbid her entry to her own home.

"What's my registration plate, Sapper?"

"Your what?"

She pointed to the front of the van. "Affixed to the bumper. The metal plate with the numbers. What does it say?"

"Ah." He stepped to the front of the van and bent down to give the plate a good look, placing himself in great peril had she been an enemy agent rather than a friendly, if irritated, one. "YC2346."

"And the make of the van?"

"Looks to be a Bedford—"

"A 1938 Bedford PC delivery van. Tomato red. Her name is Bess. Easy to recognize. Do you note any other distinguishing markings on the vehicle? Say, scrapes or dings, perhaps bold lettering on the side panels that might identify her as belonging to Nimway Hall?"

Mullins stepped around to the driver's side of the van, pressing his backside against the bramble hedge in order to read, squinting at the gilded advert on its tomato red field. "Says... Nimway Hall, Balesborough, Somerset, Farms & Orchards, by Royal Warrant to His Majesty King George, since 1673."

"That's me, Sapper Mullins. I am Nimway Hall. That's my house up on the hill. You're standing in my gateway. Now let me through." She'd been away four days, and, by the looks of things, all hell had broken loose in her absence.

Mullins shook his head slowly as he sidled around to the front bumper again to block her way. "I still gotta see your papers before I can let you pass. Miss—"

"Miss Jocelyn Regina Stirling, owner, manager and guardian of

Nimway Hall, and if you don't step aside and let me though this minute, I shall run you down, flatten you like a digestive biscuit. I suggest you memorize my face, my van, my registration plate and my ire, so you never again make the mistake of stopping me at the entrance to my own home. Do I make myself clear?"

The sapper's face bore the pinched look of the soon-to-be-strangled but he held his rifle pike-like and parallel to the ground, clicked his heels together and tipped his chin to the sky. "Miss, by orders of Lt. Colonel Gideon Fletcher, I am standing here to protect you from an invasion force—and from your good self—during these dangerous times on the home front. I will see your identification papers as I have been instructed to do, or I will gladly die in the attempt."

"The boy seems to be honestly trying his best, Daughter." Josie's father had emerged from the back of the van where he'd been napping on his old upholstered chair for the past hour, surrounded by boxes and chests of his most prized possessions. He slipped between the front seats into the passenger seat and tapped her arm with his own identification card. "Be kind."

Josie ignored the card and her father's famously charismatic smile and glared out the windscreen, past the stonework gate posts and the old gatehouse, up the long winding drive lined with ancient ash and beech, toward the forecourt of Nimway Hall just visible on the rise. So close and yet so bloody far.

"They weren't supposed to arrive for another month, Father. I'm not ready to be invaded by anyone."

"I wasn't ready to abandon Stirling House to Hitler's bloody Blitz, either, dear girl, but you convinced me of the folly of staying a day longer, and so here I am, at old Nimway—bless its mystical heart—with all my worldly treasures stuffed into the back of this rattling old van."

"Bess isn't old."

"Nevertheless, you need to give the nice young sapper our identity cards immediately, and I need to pee."

Out of habit in these days of rationed petrol, she'd turned off the ignition the moment she'd stopped Bess at the gate. Now she turned the key and the van rumbled to a start. Glaring at her father because she knew he'd make good on his threat to water the hedgerow, she reached into her jacket pocket, stuck her and her father's ID cards out of the window with a stiff arm and wagged them at Mullins.

"Make no mistake, Sapper, I submit my card to you under protest, and only after your assurance that you will never stop me again."

"I shall take up the matter with Lt. Colonel Fletcher."

"You do that, Sapper." If this Colonel Fletcher yob was like any of the other officers left behind to defend the realm against a Nazi invasion, the man was gray, grizzled and pushing seventy. Fought heroically alongside Baden-Powell in the Boer Wars, was under siege in Mafeking, where he was starved, stabbed, and escaped capture on the strength of his wits alone and hadn't stopped elaborating on his war stories to anyone within earshot since the Armistice. From buck private thirty years ago, to Lt. Colonel in the Home Defense Forces today, Fletcher was just the sort of old soldier to press his authority beyond the limit of his orders and abilities.

Let him try.

Mullins examined both ID cards closely, flicking his attention from Josie to her father to the cards and back again, as though there was any more information in the documents than their handwritten names and addresses and the pre-printed identification numbers. He raised his eyes, his nervous gaze moving past her to her father.

"Before you ask, Sapper Mullins, this man in the seat beside me is my father. Until this morning he was living in the heart of London where, nightly, the bombs of the Luftwaffe have rained down around him. For his safety, I fetched him home to live with me for the duration. We shall register his change of address with the proper authorities in short order. And if you dare hold us for another moment I will make sure that your time here at Nimway Hall is the stuff of your nightmares. Now stand aside."

Josie snatched back the cards and gunned the engine. Bess gave a victorious pop and the Bedford leaped through the gates, missing Sapper Mullins only by the swiftness of his reflexes, and throwing her father back against the seat.

"Who the devil are those hooligans, Josie Bear?" Her father was pointing out the passenger window as she motored up the drive. "They're plowing up your perfectly good badminton court!"

"It's September, Father; we're planting winter wheat. And those young women are members of the Women's Land Army, hardly hooligans." Relieved to see the rows of rough furrows being turned up in Nimway's once expansive front lawn, she paused to exchange a wave with the four young women. Maureen on the tractor, Francie and Trina standing on the cross bar of the harrow, keeping their eyes on the spinning disks just below their boots, churning up the ground, and Patsy directing them toward her from the far end of the field. The rows weren't as straight or deep as when she herself drove the tractor, but pound for pound, the women were a net benefit to the farm and generally easy to manage.

With any luck, a moderate winter, and a healthy crop of wheat come spring, along with the other one-hundred acres of arable fields now planted on the estate, she might not be forced by the Ministry of Agriculture to clear-cut her beloved Balesboro Wood and plant barley or turnips. Losing Nimway's legendary wildwoods to an unreasonable wartime requisition was as inconceivable as it would be heartbreaking.

If she'd learned anything in her twenty-three years on this earth, it was that if she wanted something done correctly, completely, with the highest standards, and in a timely manner, she'd best do it herself. Best that this crusty old Lt. Colonel Fletcher understand her mind straight away.

Gravel sprayed as she pulled Bess into the forecourt of the Hall below the wide steps and four columns that held up the portico. She yanked on the brake, set the gear lever into park, killed the engine, threw open the heavy door with her shoulder and stepped out. Winnie came bounding up the hill from the stables, her wavy black ears bouncing, the flag on her tail curled over her topline, wagging like the wind, Josie's haying gloves flapping in her mouth.

"My Winnie dog, how I missed you!" She dropped to her knees and retrieved the gloves. "Thank you, girl! Come along with me." She gave the dog a skritch on her chest and a kiss between her deep brown eyes. She fetched her leather satchel and gas mask box from behind the driver's seat then slammed the door. "As for you, Father, your room is ready; first floor, the old nursery in the east wing, as you requested. The library is also yours, for as long as the Ministry of Mayhem allows us to keep the books on their shelves and not have to use them to heat the hall. Now, you'll have to forgive me, you need to pee and I need to find the colonel."

She was the current guardian of Nimway Hall and he was little more than a squatter. The sooner he realized that, the better they would get along.

"Go easy on the frail old fellow, Josie. Wouldn't want to shock him into heart failure."

"I think I'll risk it, Father." She lifted Bess's bonnet, used her handkerchief to yank out the engine's rotor arm, wrapped it and jammed the wad into the pocket of her dungarees, then ran up the wide limestone stairs, Winnie loping happily at her heels.

Despite everything, she was happy to be home at last. She thumbed the brass latch, applied her usual shoulder to open the thick oaken door and—

It didn't budge. The latch hadn't clicked either.

The front door of Nimway Hall locked? Never in her life! She tried again, harder this time, met the same resistance, regrouped with a muttered curse then pounded the door with her fist.

"Hallo, in there! Mrs. Patten? Mrs. Lamb? Someone's locked the bloody door! Let me in!" Winnie braced her paws against the door, whined and barked in agreement.

Three more resounding thumps before the door gaped open just wide enough to reveal the face of another young soldier who stepped into the slight opening. "Your business, madam?"

"Correct, soldier, Nimway Hall is my business. My house. My front door. You're standing in the foyer of my great hall. Now step aside."

"Can't ma'am, until I see your—"

"Where's this colonel of yours?"

The young man blinked. "In his headquarters, last I saw, madam. State your name, and if you wait here quietly, I'll tell him—"

"Thanks awfully, but I'll tell the colonel myself." Josie took a step back then rammed the door open, tucked her identity card into the startled soldier's breast pocket and brushed past him into the vestibule, with Winnie at her side. "Come along, girl, we'll find this colonel and—"

"Ma'am you can't just—"

"Bloody hell—" Josie hadn't taken but a few steps when she was stopped in her tracks by the most shocking and shameful sight imaginable. What had once been her family's crown jewel, the great hall of Nimway, had been reduced to an enormous storage closet, the magnificent floor piled with crates and sheeted furniture, ages old palms and exotic ferns abandoned in their urns.

Even the grand staircase was stepped with boxes and crates, the landing stacked with ladderback chairs, the bannister over-hung with blankets.

"Begging your pardon, Miss Stirling, here's your ID. Welcome.

I'm Sapper Lewis." He haltingly offered the folded brown card as though certain she would command Winnie to bite off his hand. "You see, I wasn't told to expect... I didn't know... shall I show you to Colonel Fletcher?"

"No need, Sapper Lewis." Judging by her mother's displaced piano in the far corner under the stairs, the sheeted shapes of gilded upholstered chairs and two matching sofas pressed against the wall, the ormolu mirrors and her grandmother's collection of marble busts teetering on inlaid tabletops, the tinpot colonel was holed up in Nimway's celebrated conservatory. "I know just where to find him."

Josie snatched the identity card from the sapper and followed Winnie along the path of sheeted obstacles—Mrs. Patten must have had kittens when the solders started manhandling the Chippendale!

As she approached the double sliding doors leading to the dining room, she wondered if Fletcher had cleared out the enormous table that could seat forty when fully extended, and replaced it with a tank.

Well, good. At least the table remained in place, its length reduced shortly after the war began to accommodate half its original number. The evacuees from the Blitz, Land Girls and various other itinerant lodgers who called wartime Nimway Hall home.

Colonel Fletcher and his men added another ten mouths to feed, according to the requisition from the War Office. The only possible saving grace was that if she fed the soldiers from the kitchen of Nimway Hall, then by law, Fletcher must turn over his unit's ration books to her. Which would then allow Mrs. Lamb to pool the rations and stretch the portions of protein and fat into a more extensive menu.

Winnie skirted the table and led Josie past the fireplace facade with its two life-sized, scantily-clad marble figures of her many-times-great grandmother Charlotte, which had been scandalously live-sculpted by her as many-times-great grandfather, Marco.

Josie turned as she hurried past. "Wish me luck with the colonel, Great-Granny. Though, he's the one who'll need it, once I get through with him!"

The door from the dining room to the butler's pantry stood wide open into the connecting corridor, the perfect sound tunnel to amplify the rumble of male conversation coming from the conservatory beyond.

Near shaking with anger at the colonel's presumption, Josie stalked down the corridor, intending to launch into a blistering tirade, but reached the doorway to the conservatory only to be stopped again, struck in the heart by the wartime alterations inflicted upon the elegant salon that still smelled of soft candle-light, sweet pipe tobacco and Shalimar.

Winnie nuzzled her damp nose into the palm of her hand and Josie gave the soft muzzle a fond caress, clearing her head of the mist of memories and directing her focus where it belonged: on the enemy.

On the four men at the center of the room—officers of various ranks, by the pips on their tabs—heads and elbows bent over the middle of the rare 17th century rectory table, which they had obviously abducted from her library.

The gilded chairs that had once lined the room when it was filled with music had been replaced by a half-dozen tall metal filing cabinets fitted between the two north-facing Palladian windows, their shutters and blackout curtains shoved open to fill the room with afternoon light.

Smaller tables had been stolen from other parts of the Hall, and were now loaded down with typewriters, telephones and in-baskets, pencils and inkstands. Two drafting tables sat beneath the southern windows. Three large clocks had been fastened to the wall above a bank of equipment with dials and gauges and long runs of wires strung every which way, making grandmother's conservatory resemble Churchill's warren-like headquarters under the Treasury building at Whitehall.

And in the far corner of what remained of the conservatory, near the wall of French doors that had once spilled open to the cool evening air, freeing music and laughter out onto the stone terrace, to roam the lawns and down to the lake, was her great-grandfather's massive oak desk, now decamped from its home in the east parlor.

Doubtless now claimed by the venerable Lt. Colonel Fletcher. Whose ancient reflexes were so finely-tuned that he hadn't noticed she'd been standing in the doorway for the past minute.

"This field, to the north—"

"Water table too high—"

These soldiers, supposedly trained in stealth and defense, were still bent over their large document as she approached, so involved in the heat of their discussion that she was able to wedge herself between two of the men and ask, "Which of you is Lt. Colonel Fletcher?"

She looked pointedly from man to man, surprised that they were younger than she'd expected. Handsome, crisp, welcoming. Until she found herself looking into the iron blue gaze of the man standing directly across from her. A gaze fierce and feral, that lit fires deep inside her, leaving her breathless, wordless.

The man straightened, squared his broad shoulders until he seemed as tall as a tree. "Miss Stirling, I assume."

His statement was curt, polite, and sliced through her reverie like Excalibur through stone, a thunderous splitting of her world, between 'before this day' and 'all the days afterward.'

"Yes," was all she could manage.

"Lt. Colonel Gideon Fletcher," the man said with an aristocratic nod. "Delighted to meet you... at last."

Dear God, this colonel was no grizzled veteran of the Boer Wars! He was thirty at most, though threads of gray ticked through the coal dark hair at this temples. A canted, serious brow dipped above those piercing blue eyes, jaw squared off in a strong, clean-shaven chin, lightly limned in the deep blue-black shadow of a beard. He was taller than the other men, lit from the side by the westering sun streaming through the windows, striking his broad-shoulders and glinting off his hair.

And his mouth—it was quite perfectly shaped, full and firm, a wry smile tucked away at the corners.

"Miss Stirling?"

Josie blinked at the man, embarrassed to the bone for falling so far into his gaze, nearly swooning like a schoolgirl. "Yes, Colonel. I would have been home when you arrived, but you're here a month beforehand and I was in London."

"So I understand."

"But you made yourself at home in my conservatory, not the accommodations agreed upon in the original contract."

"You may not understand, Miss Stirling, given your protected vantage point out here in Somerset, but orders change quickly during wartime."

"Do they, really—" you bloody, arrogant blighter, she wanted to add.

"We have settled in nicely as you can see, with little enough trouble—"

"What a relief," she said, with a smile, hoping he caught her sarcasm where she'd aimed it.

"Now, Miss Stirling, if I may introduce my staff officers—" he gestured toward the three men exchanging easy glances around the table. They were handsome, physically fit and well-heeled, as though each had graduated in recent years from the Royal Military College at Sandhurst. "Second Lieutenants Easton and Crossley, and Lieutenant Durbridge; you're likely to be seeing them about, along with a few other members of our patrol. We are ten in total."

Josie gathered back her composure as each man offered a polite greeting before petting Winnie—who seemed quite taken with the lot of them—and stepping off to other parts of the room, until she was finally standing across the table from the colonel, who had stealthily gathered the large document and was rolling it into a tube.

"Yes, I've already met a few of your men—Sapper Mullins in particular. He stopped me at my own front gate. Refused to let me drive through with my van unless I showed him my identity card."

"And did you show Sapper Mullins your card?" Fletcher asked as he slid the document into a large metal cylinder and screwed on the lid, all without taking his eyes from hers.

"I informed the young man that I own Nimway Hall and that I needn't show him anything in order to enter my own property."

"And—?" Fletcher frowned, his gaze hardening. "Did Mullins then allow you to pass through the gate without checking your identification?"

"He did not! Even after he planted himself in front of Bess and I threatened to run him over."

"Who is this Bess?"

"My van."

"But you didn't."

"Didn't—?" What a dreadfully confounding man!

"Run over Sapper Mullins."

"Of course, I didn't!" How dare the arrogant man accuse her of such a... ah, then—that tucked away smile again—he was taunting her. "Because, Colonel, I didn't want to bloody the front of my van."

"Good. I shall write up Sapper Mullins this evening." He slipped a propelling pencil from his breast pocket and made a brief note on a card.

Josie felt a guilty twinge, that she might be over-blowing the incident. "Do you mean to punish the man?"

"On the contrary, Miss Stirling, I shall commend him for his bravery in the face of danger." He tucked the pencil back into his pocket and the card onto a stack of loose papers in a wire basket at the end of the table. "Now if you'll excuse us, Miss Stirling, you can't have known that you interrupted a critical planning meeting, and that we are very busy with the war."

"*You* are busy with the war, Colonel?" The insult struck her like a slap to the face. "And I'm not? *We're* not? Is that what you're implying?"

That dark brow of his quirked. "I don't believe I understand your—"

"You don't understand? That you and your staff are meeting here in my conservatory, living under my roof, eating my food while the rest of us at Nimway Hall are merely out in the fields plowing, planting, bringing in the harvest, milking the cows, making cheese and jam, knitting socks and scarves, turning my badminton lawn into field crops so that your lot can plot and plan the war—"

"Miss Stirling—" he glanced across the room at his staff, who ducked their heads and begun busying themselves at various, unconvincing tasks, before turning back to her with those cool blue eyes. "Perhaps you and I can discuss the rules of engagement later tonight. In the library?"

"Oh, do we still have a library, Colonel? I've been gone four days, surely you've had time enough to remove the books to the cellar and install a munitions factory."

He let her protest fall to the tabletop between them. "Shall we say ten o'clock, then?"

The colonel best learn who was in charge of Nimway Hall. "Half-ten."

Josie threw him a look that she hoped was haughty, turned abruptly to leave, feeling the man's gaze following her as she and Winnie strode toward the door, completely unaffected by the man, by his rudely imposing size, the conceit in his tone, least of all by the suspicion in his scandalously blue eyes.

∾

Try as he might, Gideon couldn't drag his attention away from the woman who was striding so imperiously toward the door, her lithe shoulders erect, head held high, the black dog prancing beside her, eyes raised in homage.

From the day they had driven into the forecourt of Nimway Hall, everyone on the estate had seemed mad about their mistress, dazzle-eyed with deference, near swooning with admiration over their Miss Josie. In spite of the glowing reports, Gideon had expected the lady farmer to look a bit more, well... like a farmer: fingernails cracked with dirt and wear, horse-faced, cheeks parched from too long in the sun, thick shoulders and a sturdy gait.

Miss Jocelyn Regina Stirling was anything but, her skin like peaches, with a spray of golden freckles across her high cheekbones, her limbs lean and athletic, blond hair out of sorts but silken as it escaped its bounds. And as she paused for a moment in the doorway and turned her implacably green gaze back to him, he drew a silent breath and set his jaw against her, accepting her challenge and dismissing his attraction as having been too long without a woman.

Without the right woman.

The very last thing he needed in the midst of this backwater posting was to waste precious time doing battle with the contentious lady of the manor. By all measures, the sort of woman who'd stick her nose into his business at every chance. He couldn't let that happen, wouldn't—not if he was to guard the most secret element of his mission, one known only to himself.

"That girl knows how to fill out a set of dungarees, Colonel, if you don't mind my saying, sir."

"I do mind, Crossley." Minded the direction of his own thoughts even more. "And you're a better man than that. Miss Stirling is the lady of Nimway Hall and will be treated with respect at all times. As will every person on the estate. I didn't think I had to actually say that to the lot of you."

To a man, they were younger than himself by at least five years, each graduating from one Oxbridge college or another just in time for war to be declared and their particular specialties seconded into the Royal Engineers. Good lads, fine lads, if a bit rowdy when not attending to the work of the moment. And at the moment their work was to site and build a secret Operational Base somewhere on or near the grounds of Nimway Hall, to then recruit and train members of Churchill's newly-formed secret army of Auxiliary Units who would occupy the base as a resistance force against an invading German army—all without the locals learning the existence of those units or the location of the base during or after completion.

"Let's begin where we left off before Miss Stirling arrived, gentlemen," Gideon said, rolling out the large sketch of a map he'd concealed from the doubtlessly observant Miss Stirling. Her downward glance had been brief, but how could she not have recognized that the map on the table in front of them contained every detail of Nimway Hall and its grounds known in advance by the War Office. Stretching westward from the three farms of the lower fields, eastward up the hillside and through the ancient woods, north beyond the lake to another two farms and south to the boundaries of Balesborough village, with the eccentric Hall, its extensive stables, the old barn and scattered outbuildings at the center of its beating heart.

Surely she noticed, just as she surely must have noticed him staring at her with as much naked interest as Crossley had so crudely described. Just as surely as she was, even now, plotting some offensive against his command of her fiefdom, a battle that would endure for as long as Churchill's Special Operations Executive required the use of Nimway Hall, whoever was posted here —which looked to be for the duration.

"Easton," Gideon said, trying to shake off the woman's influence over his thoughts, "you were reporting on the local topography."

Easton returned to the table with Durbridge, drafting compasses in hand. "As I was saying, sir, the site that we choose for the Operational Base must be well-drained–this is Somerset, after all—and, because the excavation must be done by hand, quickly and in secret, it must be free of rocky outcroppings and occlusions."

"We could hope for another badger sett like we dug outside of Minehead," Crossley said, taking up a ruler. "Cut through that hillside of tunnels like a sword through butter."

"Unfortunately for us, Crossley," Gideon said, "hoping won't get the job done." He hadn't yet been assigned to the Royal Engineers at the time; he'd joined the group as its leader only a month before and still felt like a fish out of water. He'd supervised the construction of exactly one Operational Base in that time, but as his CO had said when he offered the posting, it was that or nothing. Better than sitting around the war on his backside, warming a desk at Whitehall.

"What about using the ruins of that old tithe barn below the escarpment?" Durbridge asked, pointing to the ruins on the map.

"Too central and an attractive nuisance," Gideon said, making a note beside the barn. "I watched for a time this morning and saw the evacuee children playing there, chasing rabbits."

"Also true about both cattle sheds, sir," Easton said, "abandoned, according to the groundskeeper, until after the war, but a playground for the children."

"That," Durbridge added, "and we can't have a dozen men disappearing inside a cattle shed every night and not reappearing until the next morning. Someone would notice."

"Miss Stirling would notice," Gideon said. And he must do everything in his power to keep the woman out of their business. "The same is true of the stables, busier even than the dairy barn. We might look at the farms and the outbuildings to the west. Though they are doubtless just as busy and exposed. Anything else come to mind?"

"The grist mill," Crossley said, leaning in close to read the tiny print. "Says here it's in ruins. Worth a look. You remember, Durbridge—that first base we constructed just outside Exeter. Sited it in the gear room below the floor of an abandoned mill."

"That was a brilliant find," Durbridge said. "Removed the shaft and the workings, added plumbing, electricity, field phones, built an escape tunnel, supplied it, disguised the entrance with that trapdoor, trained the Aux Unit and Bob's your uncle."

Gideon caught an anomaly that had been hiding in plain sight, tapped the map with the point of his finger. "What about this rectangle here? Looks to be in the woods on a slight rise east of the Hall. Whatever it is, it's been unused long enough not to warrant a note."

"An old saw mill?" Durbridge removed his spectacles and bent down to inspect the rectangle. "Would make sense. Plenty of wind on this side of the hill to turn a blade. We may be in luck. May not have to sap like moles this time round."

"Good then," Gideon said as he rolled up the map. "I'll check out the mysterious rectangle tomorrow afternoon while you survey the farms again and walk the perimeter. Decide who does what."

"Durbridge and I will check out the farms," Crossley said, heading back to his drafting table with a bit of a strut.

"And the farmers' daughters, if I know you two," Easton said with a laugh. "Sir, if anyone asks, do we tell them we're on a walk-about?"

"Since we're headquartered here in Somerset, gentlemen," Gideon said, "our official cover should work for anyone asking. That we're part of the Defense Chain Operations Task Force, surveying and siting the Taunton Stop Line."

Crossley snorted. "Well, if that mouthful doesn't choke the locals, nothing will."

"Divide and distract, Mr. Crossley," Gideon said, "one of the pillars of tradecraft. Learn that lesson and you'll soon be able to hide in plain sight while you carry out the most critical of missions in broad daylight." Just as he was doing.

"Truth is, sir, I thought by now I'd be using my Master's in Civil Engineering to build bridges and cities, not hidey-holes for the SOE."

"This war has altered everyone's plans, Crossley." He'd orchestrated his own post-graduate studies for just that purpose—as a career military officer, specializing in gathering intelligence. But the best-laid plans....

"Sir, what if we meet up with Miss Stirling in our progress?" Crossley asked, his judgment of the woman on point. "She's bound to object—what then? What do we tell her?"

"Be respectful, obtuse, and then send Miss Stirling to me." Gideon took a step away from the table and winced. He'd been standing too long, took a sharp breath. "That goes for all of you, gentlemen. Be respectful—"

"What, me too, sir?" Easton asked, "I'm a happily married man. Going to be a father in a few months! I'd never!"

"Of that, I am certain, Easton." As certain as he was of Crossley working his charm on every woman in his path. He checked the wall clock. "Two hours until dinner. We'll work the remainder of the day outlining tomorrow's canvassing and setting up a grid. You need to log your routes in advance, then report the details of your findings when you return tomorrow. Include the names of any locals you might meet, notes on their attitudes, any resistance to your authority or undo curiosity about your presence."

He purposely left his derby-handled cane hooked over the edge of the table and steeled himself for the walk across the marble floor toward the large old desk in the corner. If only to see how far he could travel without resorting to the limp that had plagued him since he first rose out of his recovery bed. Nearly four months ago, it was. Long past time the blasted thing should have healed and set him free to return to combat.

He managed a strong, regular stride for a dozen feet, and in his progress attempted to avoid a waste bin, mis-stepped around it, then over-compensated. A white-hot pain shot through his knee as he caught himself, straining tendon against bone, tasking his knee beyond its limit to hold him upright without grabbing the back of a chair.

He could feel his staff watching his struggle to steady himself. Even more galling was their pretense that they hadn't noticed his humiliation; that they weren't each wondering how the devil a man who couldn't walk across a marble floor without the aid of a cane was going to manage a trek through the woods tomorrow in search of the mysterious structure on the map.

Same damned thing he was wondering about himself, same reason for welcoming such a challenge to his injured leg. No one would be watching his progress, judging him, assessing his worth to the war effort. A measured walk at his own pace, through a late September woodland in Somerset, that most bucolic of English counties, the jewel of England's southwest, known for its lazy streams, its apple orchards, its cheese from the caves of Cheddar and scrumpy. A simple stroll compared to the terrain he'd covered in the struggle that had claimed the lives of three of his comrades, nearly cost him his own life and left him with a debilitating wound in his leg that cramped his back and stretched his patience.

Gideon worked his way to his desk and gripped the arms of the chair, positioned his leg straight in front of him and lowered himself onto the seat cushion, holding back the groan of relief because he'd heard himself groan too often.

Had suffered humiliation under his mother's care while he remained delirious with fever—*I love you, Son. You'll come through this.*

His sisters' unfounded encouragement—*You'll be up and fighting again in no time, Brother, dear.*

Watching helplessly while the soldiers being evacuated from the beaches of Dunkirk were landed at Ramsgate Harbor.

The surgeons, his doctors—*You need to let your body heal on its own, Gideon, or you'll never return to a normal life.*

He couldn't imagine what kind of life that would be, so he'd worked even harder, vowing to recover in record time. *You're over-doing it, Gideon. You'll do further damage.*

And when he approached his Commanding Officer—*Yes, Gideon, I see that you are able to walk across the room with a cane. But you can't return to lead your unit. You know already that it was disbanded after Norway, the men redeployed to other units, on other missions.*

"Besides," his CO had said, over-kindly, "until you're at full strength, you would be a danger to fellow agents on any operations behind enemy lines."

"I'm not begging, sir," Gideon remembered saying, "but I've got to do something for the war effort. I'm a soldier. I should have been helping evacuate Dunkirk. Instead I was sitting with my mother on the lawn like a derelict from a long ago war, no more helpful to my comrades than the bin man. Please, sir, give me a job. Anything."

Though he realized now that he hadn't truly meant 'anything.'

"The map's all set, Colonel," Durbridge said, bending over the long table, "ready to mark out the grid."

And here he was, a month later, mired in the banalities of the home front, living the life of a country squire, nanny to a pack of eager of school boys playing at soldier, the unwelcome guest of a most beguiling woman who needed taming.

CHAPTER 2

"Winnie, my girl, it's going to be a bloody, long war if that man thinks it's his job to command Nimway Hall!" Josie left the conservatory in a blazing fury and continued past the butler's pantry and the door to the dining room, pushed her way out the service door, finally popping into the clutter of the great hall, which only started her blood boiling again.

"Come, Winnie, let's see what those barbarians have done to the library." She dodged through the maddening landscape of sheeted furniture, took a deep breath and slid open the library door.

Fortunately for the colonel, everything seemed to be as she'd left it, acres of books shelved safely in the bays that ringed the enormous room, island of tables and chairs, floor lamps and statuary. The pair of Chesterfield sofas still faced each other in front of the ornate fireplace in the main part of the library, in sharp contrast to her own favorite alcove with its pair of wingback reading chairs still flanking the carved wooden fireplace.

The shutters and blackout curtains were open and with the lowering sun sending sharp rays across the room, she didn't see her father at first, then found him two steps up on the rolling ladder, peering down at her from his perch, a book open in his hand, like a bird about to take wing. Winnie sat at the base of the ladder, smiling, tail sweeping the mahogany floor.

"See here, Josie Bear," he said, "Mr. Tennyson hasn't moved from this spot in all these years." He waved a slip of paper at her. "My own bookmark, placed here by me for your mother.

> 'Light, so low upon earth,
>> You send a flash to the sun.
>> Here is the golden close of love,
>> All my wooing is done.'"

Sudden, hot tears rose in Josie's throat, stung her eyes; the rich sound of her father's baritone, the memory of her mother gazing into his eyes. "'Marriage Morning,' I remember. Mother's favorite."

He sighed. "And mine."

What a surprising joy to have her father here at Nimway! She swallowed the knot of sorrow and scratched the top of Winnie's head. "You seem to have settled in, Father."

"Reluctantly, my dear girl. A bird in a gilded cage." He stepped down the ladder to the floor carrying the book of Tennyson.

"Where would you be tonight then, if not for Hitler's bombs altering your plans? Sitting in your study at Stirling House?"

"On a Tuesday night—" he considered, with a dear and familiar tilt of his head. "At my club, the Garrick, though the place has been stripped of the art that once hung on the walls, the most valuable stored along with the treasures of the National Gallery deep in some Welsh mine or other. The rest scattered among the country houses across the land, windows draped in mourning black. Once the bombs began falling last month and the sirens began to wail, we'd all flee from the luxury of the Garrick to the tube station—quite an unsavory place. After a week of that nonsense I started staying at home—as you found me, reading The Times, listening to the wireless, indulging in my wee dram."

"Until a bomb dropped three blocks from Stirling House and I insisted you come live at Nimway. I'm so thankful that Aunt Kitty is living safely in Hollywood."

"Now, there's an oxymoron!"

"Have you been up to see your room? Is it to your liking?"

"The young man who helped unload the van is delivering my entire wardrobe upstairs and, as you can see, my treasures are sitting there in the corner, still in the boxes. As they are likely to remain until I feel like unpacking."

"I can't guarantee that Mr. Tennyson and his comrades won't be conscripted for the war effort, but unless and until then, the library is yours. Please make yourself at home, Father." She kissed him on the cheek and gazed up into his handsome eyes, still bright behind his grief over her mother.

"I am home wherever you are, my little love."

Why ever did she allow this dear man to hole up in London, all alone in his family's rambling old house? Her mother had warned her that he would probably need tending after she was gone. But what power did a ten-year old have over a parent, when her own world was dark and falling apart at the time? She stayed behind at the Hall with her Aunt Freddy and Uncle Anthony after her mother died, let her father return to London without her. She saw him often afterward, quick trips and summers, but they hadn't lived in the same house for all that time. How could thirteen years have passed so quickly?

"Then we are together for the duration, Father."

He smiled so fondly down at her, she felt tears prickle the backs of her eyes again. "My dear girl–'til the end of time."

The service door at the rear of the library burst open, launching Mrs. Lamb's rugged frame toward them. "Ah, there you are Miss Josie! I heard you was home from London, thank the good Lord for not letting one of those bombs fall on you!"

"The bombs did fall every night, Mrs. Lamb," Josie said as she was swept up into the older woman's arms, "just not on Stirling House."

She'd felt no small amount of guilt that the bombs had fallen on other neighborhoods, with thirteen dead and hundreds left homeless, nothing more to their names than the clothes they had worn as they fled to their assigned shelters.

"Lord keep them far away from us, Miss Josie." Mrs. Lamb straightened Josie's shirt collar. "But now that you're safely back with us, ther's summat needs doing 'bout feedin' our newest so-called 'lodgers'. 'Course, I don't mean you, Mr. Stirling—" Mrs. Lamb nodded and blushed like a girl "—chuffed I am to see you back here again, after all this time. But it's them soldiers' ration books I'm needin'. Tomorrow is shopping day in the village. I have to register the lot of 'em with the butcher and the grocer before I can buy for 'em."

"Have you asked Colonel Fletcher for the ration books?"

"Did so. But he said I wasn't authorized. That he'd wait to hand them over to you when you got home. Said it politely enough, and with a charmin' sort o'smile." The woman's eyes sparkled under the steely gray spray of hair fringing the fashion-ably functional scarf they had all begun to wear. "And I must say, that fellow's right easy on the eye."

Not so easy on the pulse, Josie thought, but would never say. To anyone! At all.

"Thank you for trying, Mrs. Lamb. I'll take care of the ration books myself. You go along to the kitchen and I'll be right there. We'll go over the shopping list for the week's menu, then I've got a dozen things to check on before I can stop to eat."

"Then you'll be too late for dinner again. Can I make you a plate?"

"I'll come by the kitchen when I get back, Mrs. Lamb," Josie said, thinking again of the two hours of work ahead of her before her meeting with the colonel. In the library. At half-ten. "But I know Father's hungry, I can hear his stomach from here."

"What's that?" her father said with a broad smile as he handed Mrs. Lamb his own ration book. "You don't like my singing, Josie Bear? But thank you Mrs. Lamb. I'll be delighted to have one of your delicious home-cooked dinners after taking most all of my meals in the Garrick for the last decade."

Mrs. Lamb screwed up her face. "Cabbage stew again tonight, sir, with bread, butter and fresh elderberry jam, sweetened with Nimway's own Top Drawer Honey. I'll fetch it for you here, sir." Mrs. Lamb bundled out of the library, her elbows swinging left and right like a drill sergeant's.

"I'll need the library at half-ten, Father, for my meeting with the colonel. Best conducted in private, though I can't guarantee that our conversation won't be heard by everyone in the Hall."

Her father smiled that famous Stirling family smile, raised his chin and began to recite with a twinkle in his bearing:

"The gingham dog and the calico cat
  Wallowed this way and tumbled that—"

"Father, please don't—"

"Employing every tooth and claw
  In the awfullest way you ever saw—
  And, oh! how the gingham and calico flew!"'

She narrowed her eyes at him. "Am I the dog, or the cat?"

"You needn't tell me how the meeting goes, Josie Bear— *I'll get my news from the Chinese plate!*" He laughed broadly at his own cleverness. "But just now, that shelf of Mr. Tennyson awaits!"

He pointed up the ladder then ascended in a charge so agile it surprised her and, by Winnie's barking, delighted the dog.

～

"Imagine, Miss Josie, their Royal Highnesses havin' to plan those fancy state dinners 'round these very same rations th't we do our own suppers: just so much meat and butter and sugar."

"But how very like the Windsors, Mrs. Lamb, to lead us by example." Ration books guaranteed everyone, of every class, including the Royal Family, the same access to the critical nutrition that would keep the country healthy during the war. Nimway Farms and Orchards provided a wealth of food, not only to the people who depended on the Hall, but to the local shop and the air station at nearby Yeovilton.

"Bet that nasty Mr. Hitler eats high on the hog."

"Actually, I understand he's a vegetarian." Mrs. Lamb blinked, waited for an explanation. "Vegetables only. Doesn't eat meat."

"Who tol'ya that?"

Who, indeed. "Someone in London during one of the air raids. Probably just gossip. Nothing else to do down in the tunnels while the bombs are falling above. That and play cards."

"What a mad world is this one, I don't mind sayin'."

Josie left Winnie in the kitchen, awaiting her dinner, and started up the backstairs to check that all was right in her father's chamber, reached the first landing and found the bean-thin Mrs. Patten waiting at the top.

"There you are, dear— just in time to sort out our mattress troubles." Without waiting for Josie to catch up, Mrs. Patten strode off down the corridor leading to the guest chambers, chattering all the way. "I've put three men to a room as we had planned. Those three rooms along the front range, and the colonel billeted on his own in the Buttercup Suite in the west wing. Gives him a sitting room for an office and a bed chamber. Said he needed privacy for his work."

Don't we all. "Thank you for adapting to the change of schedule, Mrs. Patten. I'm sorry I wasn't here at the time. But there's nothing for us to do about it—the War Office requisitioned this wing and the Buttercup Suite for whatever use they felt necessary at the moment. Commandeered the conservatory without a warning. Who knows, next week we'll be billeting POWs in our attic."

"Heavens, you say!"

Seeing Mrs. Patten's distress, Josie tried to wave away the woman's concern. "Only joking, Mrs. Patten, a bit of dark humor." That only seemed to deepen her worry lines. "Come then, show me the mattress trouble."

"See, Miss Josie. There aren't none. No mattresses at all."

Josie entered the first guest chamber and realized what the housekeeper meant. None but the thick felt mattress on the elegant hundred year-old tester in the middle of the room.

Incongruously, three rope-sprung wooden camp beds that had been constructed here at the Hall by the talented Mr. Broadfoot with the help of the Land Girls, were arranged along each of the remaining walls, with blankets folded neatly at the foot of each bed, and sheeted pillows at the head.

"These fellows slept on the floor the last two nights. So did the fellows in the other two rooms. Said they didn't mind. Were used to sleeping rough and glad to have a roof over their heads."

"Well, I mind. I've a letter on my desk from the War Office confirming the mattresses will arrive here early next week, along with extra linens. Not a word about the men arriving early. But I'll ring the supplier and see if I can speed up the delivery. If not, the colonel's men will just have to keep roughing it."

She suffered a fleeting twinge of conscience. After all, these were His Majesty's soldiers—even the arrogant colonel who was stuck like a badger in her conservatory. They deserved the best she could give them.

"What about Colonel Fletcher? Is he also sleeping rough?"

"On the floor as well, just like his men. Though he's got a perfectly good mattress on his bed."

Not wanting to credit Fletcher with a jot of devotion to his men, Josie stepped out into the corridor and realized what was missing from the usual chaos at the end of a long day. "Where are the children? It's nearly bedtime."

"Ran off to the lake after their dinner in the kitchen." Mrs. Patten flicked her feather duster along the gallery railing and through the spindles as they walked toward the grand staircase. "Said they were going to help Mr. Godby catch tomorrow's breakfast."

"They went alone? To the lake, at this time of the evening?" Three rascally boys and a girl. That didn't go well last time. "Where is Mrs. Tramble?"

"Attending the Women's Institute meeting in town. It's Knit for a Knight night. Ain't that a funny thing to say? Anyway, Mrs. Tramble said she'd be home by dark and that she'd bring wool back for Mrs. Lamb and m'self so we can do our part, too."

"Leaving dear old Godby to supervise the children!" She'd best go rescue him before he ended up in the drink.

"Send 'em my way when you find 'em and I'll see they're cleaned up before bed."

"Thank you, Mrs. Patten." What would she do without the woman taking on extra duties, caring for the children's quarters, supervising the two daily village girls?

Josie hurried down the stairs, out the back of the house and set off for the lake, Winnie suddenly loping past her. They didn't get more than a hundred yards down the cooling woodland path when a flurry of footfalls sounded ahead, heralding all four children, the lanky Geordie in the lead with a string of perch hanging from his outstretched arm, Winnie joining the parade.

"Looka w'at we fished outta th'lake, Miss Josie!"

"I missed you, Miss Josie!" "Me too!" "And me!"

"I missed you, too." The children swarmed around her, so pleased with themselves, rosy cheeks smeared with mud, sturdy legs green-mired in scum from the withie patches on the shoreline.

They had all arrived from Stepney with Mrs. Tramble a month before, rail-thin, pale, and terrified of everything at Nimway Hall, from the cock's morning crow to the nearly deafening silence at night, to the tall grass and burbling creeks. Geordie and Kenny suffering from head lice and ten-year-old Molly and her eight-year-old brother Robbie with clothes so threadbare that Josie had put them both to bed after their baths that evening in Mr. Broadfoot's spare night shirts, and replaced their everyday wardrobes, top to bottom, shoes included, from Nimway's attic storage the next morning.

Nimway Hall made and mended everything in their own workshops, from shoes to plowshares to parts for the tractors. And sustained everyone on the estate from its fields and farmyards and the lake. Mr. Godby kept the lake dredged and well stocked with perch and trout, which were proving to be vastly entertaining for the children, as well as a source of muck from stem to stern.

"Those are prize-winning perch you've caught there, Mr. Geordie."

"Molly stuck the worms on the hooks fer us!" Robbie made an 'eewie' face and shook the fishing rod, rattling the sinker against the reel. "They was wriggling too much for us to do it!"

"And too icky!" Lucas added with a swipe of his forearm across his forehead, bunching his wavy hair into a brown nest and spreading another swath of mud.

"You are very brave, Molly, and helpful. Thank you." The girl was blushing fiercely when she met Josie's gaze.

"Ever s'kind f'r ya to say, Miss Josie," Molly whispered, hunching her thin shoulders and dropping her chin to her chest, all the while grinning from ear to ear. So much more confident than the girl who'd arrived four weeks ago with her gaze permanently stuck to the tops of her ill-fitting, worn-through shoes.

Such a miraculous change in each of the children. "Now where'd you leave Mr. Godby? Not in the lake, I hope!"

"I'm ri' cheer, Miss Josie—" Godby came hobbling into view around the stand of birch, his ubiquitous brass ghillie stick slapping in rhythm against his hip. "I tell yer, those kids gonna run me right outta my job if they keep dragging all those fish outta the lake."

"Next they'll be trapping rabbits for you, Mr. Godby." He looked none the worse for wear, if not a tad more jolly than he'd been before the children arrived.

"Rabbits! Yayyy!" The three boys jumped up and down. "Can we catch 'em? Can we, Miss Josie?"

Godby nodded at her; with rabbits pillaging her vegetable garden and decimating crops all over the county, she knew he could use a few more hands trapping the pests and adding them to the larder.

"School starts day after tomorrow," she said, "if Mrs. Tramble reports that you all behave in class, play well together, study hard—"

"And feed the chickens! And collect the eggs." Molly said, her eyes alight.

"Yes, Molly, and if each of you do your part in the war effort without being asked, then I suspect that Mr. Godby will be glad to teach you to catch rabbits. What say you?"

"We will!"

"Now, run on up to the kitchen with your catch so Mrs. Lamb can clean them for breakfast tomorrow. Mrs. Tramble will be home from her meeting shortly. Why don't you surprise her and be washed and in your beds when she comes looking for you!"

"Surpriiiiiiise!" The children ran up the path toward the Hall until they and Winnie's wagging tail were out of sight in the twilight.

"Thanks for supervising the tribe, Godby."

"Good kids, for the most part. Keeps me young, running after them like I do. 'Specially that Lucas lad."

"Let me know if they become too much and I'll make sure Mrs. Tramble keeps a closer eye on them."

"Has Isaac talked with yer yet about his trouble, miss?"

"I haven't seen him." Nimway's lone mechanic and stable hand, the man was a treasure, sought after by every estate in the county. Too old too enlist in the military, but that didn't stop him from being the most eager man in the Home Guard.

"'Parently had an argy-bargy with that old Fordson every morning you were away, barely got the tractor running. The girls limped it back into the carriage house every evening. But if anyone can keep that tractor going, it's sure to be our Isaac."

"I'll catch him in his shop before he leaves for the Home Guard meeting tonight. What time?"

"'Leven a'clock, in the village hall. A special demonstration which I will enjoy to the fullest: How to Beat Up a Nazi Bastard with Your Bare Knuckles. If you pardon my French, Miss Josie."

She remembered the bombs raining down on the neighborhoods of London. "As long as you beat up one for me, Godby. Thanks again!"

Josie hurried back down to the range of support buildings west of the Hall, set between the lake and the escarpment. What had begun as a simple stone livery a few centuries ago had expanded into a four sided stableyard with an arch-fronted gatehouse, housing all manner of wagons and motorized vehicles on the west range, the stables and paddocks on the east, with Isaac's workshops on the ground floor of the two-story center building, his office and living quarters on the left, and a dormitory for farm hands on the right.

If it moved on four legs, rolled on wheels, was powered by a combustion engine or electricity, or had anything to do with producing food at Nimway Hall, then Isaac kept it running by virtue of his expertise and his verbal threats to dismantle the blasted thing if it didn't cooperate.

It was near dark and the windows in the stable were blacked

out by shutters and curtains. Even with all that coverage, Josie could hear Isaac's string of colorful profanity intermixed with the clang of his hammer against some piece of immovable metal. She slid open the door just far enough to let herself inside, slipped through the door curtain and watched Isaac at the vise, hammering on an iron plate, the Fordson tractor standing like a stubborn green ox in the middle of the shop, his task lit only by the shimmering gold light of an oil lantern that must have been a hundred years old.

He shifted the flat piece of metal between the jaws of the vice and gave the lever a hard yank. "Stay put, you scurvy git!" *Clang!*

"Please say you're winning this round, Isaac."

"Poxy lump of shite!" *Whack!*

"I guess not. Have the parts come in?"

Isaac looked up from his labors. "Same old story, Miss Josie: The factory's now making Spitfire parts. Said they won't be making clutch plates again until after the war. After the trouncing that bloody Hitler gave us at Dunkirk, I'm thinking that's going to be a long time. Leaving me to either scavenge one, or make it myself."

"We've plenty of old equipment for you to salvage." Two of the carriage house stalls were stacked full of unused implements from the old days.

"Couldn't Mr. Cabot forge the plate in his blacksmith shop?"

"Sure, once I'm in the queue. But he said it would be at least a week before he could get to it. Maybe I'm in the wrong business, Miss Josie." He shot her a wink. "With all that new custom I ought to take up smithing and make me some money for after the war."

"Isaac Higgins, your father and grandfather would spin beneath their tombstones if you deserted Nimway Hall when we need you the most. You are family, as they were. You were raised on these grounds, alongside my mother and my aunt; and your sons with me and my cousins. This is your home. What would I do without you and dear Mrs. Higgins who bakes our bread and tends the kitchen garden and the chickens and, frankly, keeps me sane?"

"Not to worry, Miss Josie," he said, his dark eyes glittering gold in the lamplight, "I was only jesting! Me and the missus plan to stay on at Nimway Hall as long as ye'll have us."

"Then it's forever, Isaac, and a great relief to me! Especially now."

"Leastwise our horse-flesh power hasn't let us down. I put the two Shires under harness today and they plowed a full hectare down by the north swale. Should finish the rest of the field by the end of the week and be ready to plant peas and broad beans on Monday."

"You're brilliant, Isaac! At least I've got that bit of good news to log into my accounts for the day." And that the children were thriving, her father was safe from the Blitz, the Land Girls had made real progress on plowing up the front lawn.

And she'd managed to get past the colonel's guard at her own front gate.

"I'll leave you to your delicate work, Isaac." Josie lit a shielded candle lantern from Isaac's lamp then left him to his hammering and made her way up the lane, past the rear of the Hall to the dairy barn. She inspected the milking machines in the spotless milking parlor and the milking log for the four days she'd been away and wondered at the slight decrease not only in the quantity, but the butterfat content of the milk from all ten cows.

"Coo, ladies, coo!" she called softly as she entered the cool, very dark shelter of the barn, pleased to hear Dot and Dixie's cantankerous moos echoing off the high cruck of the barrel vaulted ceiling, the gentle lowing of the others. "Did you miss me? Is that why you're keeping your butter to yourselves?"

When three formless shapes of white began moving toward her in the blackness, Josie raised her candle lantern and the blade of light it threw revealed the trio of Friesians, roaming free of their individual box stalls.

"How did you three escape? Did one of the Land Girls forget to latch your gates?" Or one of the children? Too late to ferret out the culprit tonight; the quartet of young women would be fast asleep in their rooms after a long day of plowing, or had slipped down the lane to let off steam at the Hungry Dragon in the village.

"Come, come, ladies, back into your stalls." They followed along behind her in the shambling bovine amble that both irritated and charmed Josie equally. She settled them in, checking that their water was clean and plentiful and their bedding was fresh. Jill and Jenny were in the loafing barn, just days from calving, sleeping on their sides.

She checked the other gates, then headed out of the milking barn into the near pitch-dark. The blackout regulations had darkened every window in the Hall and made the moonless night as impenetrable as a pea-soup fog. Even with the candle lantern, only the white stripes painted strategically down the outside corners of the buildings, and the blotches of stark white that marked the direction across the cobbles toward the Hall kept her from walking into gateposts, and directed her finally through the kitchen garden and up the wide steps to the covered service porch at the back of the Hall. Once inside, she hung her jacket on a hook in the utility room then continued into the old farm office that now served as the control center from which she managed the entire wartime estate. She'd set up her bed chamber in the old conservatory next door, where she was awakened most mornings by a knock before dawn to take care of something that needed her immediate attention.

Guided by the wan light of her candle lantern, Josie made sure the blackout frames were in place in the window casings, drew the blackout curtains closed, then collapsed into her desk chair and turned on the goose-necked lamp, all the while hoping the problem that had been haunting her while she was away in London had vanished.

It hadn't. The letter from the Ministry of Agriculture remained like a curse in the middle of the desk blotter. A threat to all she loved about her home. Dated two weeks ago.

Dear Miss Stirling,

It has come to the attention of the Ministry that Balesboro Wood, the ancient stand of trees on your farm at Nimway Hall, Balesborough Parish, Somerset, has been deemed by the Timber Supply Department a candidate for felling, clearing and putting the land under the plow.

It was still there: the government's threat to fell Balesboro Wood! No matter how many times she'd read the letter, the words never came fully into focus.

The arable land created by such felling would produce more than 2-tonnes of wheat per hectare, making the felled timber available for hundreds of wartime uses, including in the manufacture of our combat aircraft.

Please be informed that a team of inspectors from the Timber Supply Department of the Forestry Commission will arrive at your farm the afternoon of Tuesday, next.

Tomorrow! Good grief. She hadn't forgotten, just didn't want to remember.

At the time of the visit, you, or your representative, will conduct a tour of your fields and forest with the inspectors, answer their questions and provide information as they require, including maps, crop and timber yields, financial records, water sources and any other detail that they might request.

Following the inspection, a determination will be made in writing as to the course of action to be taken regarding Balesboro Wood.

"Course of action?" A full-out assault against Balesboro Wood! A parkland as ancient as Somerset and just as mystical. Chock full of legends. Her favorite being that her own many times great grandfather Richard Devries had gotten lost in Balesboro Wood, found his way to the Hall and right into the heart of her as many times great-grandmother, Jacqueline. If the legends were true, the men who married the guardians of Nimway Hall had each tangled with Balesboro Wood and won the hearts of their ladies.

When she was a little girl, a traveling scholar once sought shelter in the Hall on a stormy summer night and told stories of an ancient hillfort that used to sit atop Windmill Hill. An outpost used by King Arthur and his knights, so he told them. The next day, before the man left, he led Josie and her two cousins to the ruins, barely visible beneath the moss and fern and tangled roots of the hornbeam, but Josie and the two boys spent the rest of the summer bringing the stories of Arthur and Merlin to life. And there was Isobel's Bower, an enchanted grotto, where, even on the hottest days of summer, the air was cool enough for a breath to fog.

Three-quarters of the tomboy nicks and scars on her shins and knees, her elbows and hands came from Balesboro Wood. Even the jagged scar on her shoulder, just below the pale, spherical birthmark that Aunt Freddy used to whisper—in complete seriousness, was the Mark of Nimway—happened in the wood when she fell out of her favorite beech tree. Miraculously, she landed nearly unscathed on the mossy ground, because the beech had reached out to catch her—honest to God, the branch had moved, slowed her fall and saved her from a broken leg, or worse.

Balesboro Wood even had its own fragrance, different, sweeter, spicier, than anywhere in the world she'd ever traveled with her parents.

The war in Europe had been raging for a little more than a year now; it would probably rage on for more years to come; the Nazi's might even invade and attempt to conquer Britain. But if Josie Stirling had anything to say about it, Balesboro Wood would still be standing long after the war was won or lost and the armies returned home to lick their wounds. Her own granddaughter would be able to walk in these same woods, smell the same fragrance, skin her knees and play Arthur and the Round Table.

Much as she wanted to wrap a magic ward around Nimway Hall against the timber inspectors—and a certain colonel encamped in her conservatory, she didn't know how to cast a spell —didn't believe there was such a thing in the world as magic.

But saving Balesboro Wood would have to wait for the morning. More pressing and far-reaching responsibilities awaited her tonight before her meeting.

She retrieved her favorite propelling pencil out of her desk drawer where she had stashed it before leaving for London, spent a few minutes logging the day's activities and her observations into the farm journal. Made notes about tomorrow's tasks and, most importantly, created a list of demands for her meeting tonight with the colonel.

Finished, she folded the list, tucked it into the front pocket of her dungarees, then checked her wristwatch. Ten minutes until ten. Just enough time, and quiet enough in the Hall to accomplish one final task before her encounter with the man who believed that his rank and requisition letter from the War Office gave him leave to order her around her own home.

He was about to discover that the Guardians of Nimway Hall were a force to be reckoned with.

CHAPTER 3

"*A*re you sure you don't want to come with us to the pub, sir?"

"Thank you, but not tonight, Crossley." Gideon pointed to his in-basket. "I've enough paperwork to keep me busy–"

"—Until your meeting with Miss Stirling." Crossley laughed from the doorway.

"In the *library*," Easton added, slipping on his jacket.

"At *half-ten*," Durbridge said, clapping his cap on his head.

"Yes. Thank you, gentlemen." Gideon waved them on their way, then spent the next two hours sitting at his desk in the dim light provided by the single bulb of his lamp, his bad leg propped atop an overturned waste bin, preparing reports to his superiors, reading and responding to the many dispatches that seemed to arrive hourly from the War Office and the Special Operations Executive.

In addition to the deluge of paperwork and the business of siting and constructing a secret operational base, and recruiting and training the new Aux Unit, Gideon was expected to take command of the local Home Guard, undoubtedly a group of veterans from the Great War and lumbering farm lads who would resent him asserting his authority into their local company. But that was the nature of military protocol, at home or behind enemy lines. These Home Guard units needed the same training as the regular army, if they were to be effective in the event of an invasion.

The nationwide fear of invasion was as genuine as it was justified. In the few months since Gideon had been injured, he'd watched helplessly as the German army invaded Norway and Denmark, Belgium, the Netherlands, Luxembourg, France–the entire coastline of Europe in German hands, with only 26 miles of English Channel to protect her. By all accounts, the Blitz was an action meant to soften up England for a German invasion that could begin any day now.

Gideon had used his family's influence and this very real threat to national security to insert himself back into the war effort, despite not being quite recovered.

Given the code name Invictus and sworn to secrecy, he was to establish contact through a dead drop with an intelligence agent in Somerset. Together they were to initiate a secret conduit of communication to link the Transatlantic cable office in Porthcurno, at the tip of Cornwall, directly to Churchill's Cabinet War Rooms in Whitehall. Should the country's telegraph system be disrupted by aerial bombing or invasion, the Balesborough Link was to serve as the collection and distribution point for encoded messages that would save lives and help force the invading army back on its heels.

He'd learned the location of the dead drop just an hour before, when a message arrived from the SOE instructing him to approach the drop the next morning, but only if he recognized the signal indicating the drop had been made.

But that was for the morning. Tonight he was to meet with the singular Miss Josie Stirling, a confrontation he wasn't looking forward to but was eager to begin. It wasn't the outcome of their meeting that caused him concern—the requisition for billeting at

Nimway Hall from the SOE was clearly documented and unbreakable, no matter how loud the woman's objections. It was the battle itself that concerned him. Five minutes with the woman this afternoon, and she had become a fixture in his thoughts for the remainder of the day, and well into the evening.

Even now. Eyes bright and green as a new leaf, mind just as bright, as quick. The late afternoon sunlight glinting gold on her hair. Her mouth ripe and lush as a persimmon, pouting at him in her righteous anger. A woman fierce with a courage, unlike any woman of his acquaintance. A puzzle that needed solving before the night was much older.

With thirty minutes until the meeting, he locked his reports in the office safe, retrieved his cane, turned out his desk lamp then negotiated the clutter of ghostly furniture in the great hall, entering the library with every intention of unwinding with a bit of reading.

The library was almost completely dark, its deep corners shadowed, but for the fire that flickered and flared in the fireplace against the interior east wall and a reading lamp sitting on the octagonal table between the pair of tall-backed chairs facing the fire. As impressive as the library in his family's home at High Starrow, but more welcoming, a place of study and comfort.

Twenty minutes after ten. No sign of Miss Stirling. She'd said ten thirty, was the sort of woman who would walk into the library as the clock struck the time.

His fingers still cold from sitting too long at his desk in the glass and marble chill of the conservatory, he rested his cane against the drinks table near the door and went directly to the fire, extending his hands toward the marvelous heat. His palms had just begun to warm when he sensed a shift of movement behind him, then a voice—

"You must be my Josie's colonel."

Gideon made a painfully quick turn in the direction of the voice, was automatically reaching for his sidearm—which he realized too late was locked in the safe in his room, at the very same moment he located the speaker who was lounging in the chair to his right. A smiling, distinguished-looking gentleman, with a trimmed gray moustache and beard, a book open and braced on his crossed knee, a snifter of brandy and a bottle of calvados on a small silver serving tray on the table beside him.

Gideon settled his frayed nerves, gone stale and soft these many months of his recovery. "Lt. Colonel Gideon Fletcher. And you are?"

"Edward Stirling," the man said as he laid his book on the reading table. He rose from the chair in a single sweep of graceful limbs and an easy smile, coming to rest eye-to-eye with Gideon and offering a strong hand. "Late of Stirling House, London. Newly arrived father to the lady of the Hall."

"Edward Stirling? Of the theatrical family?" The connection was a surprise, but explained the daughter's unabashed spirit. "The Stirling Theatre, Stirling Pictures?"

"The celebrated actress, Kitty Stirling. And you mustn't leave out the Stirling Scandal Sheet or the arcades at Brighton and Blackpool—that would be our Stirlings. The family business. Entertaining the audiences of England, America and most of Europe since long before the time of Shakespeare. We Stirlings were mercers back in the days of the York Mystery plays, apparently took to theatricals with enterprising enthusiasm and great quantities of textiles, which costumed the new extravaganzas. This was long before my untold great-grandfather teamed up with Mr. Shakespeare and other rogues and vagabonds to form the Lord Chamberlain's Men."

Gideon found himself both in awe of the man, and relaxing considerably. "Sir, if you meant to impress me with your family tree, you have done so—"

"Edward, please." Stirling gestured to the opposite chair. "And I only meant to put you at ease after I startled you. Please sit with me. Your reflexes are quick, Colonel. Had you been armed, I fear we wouldn't be having this conversation."

"I hope that's not true." Gideon laughed for the first time in days, gripped the upholstered leather arms and lowered himself into the supremely comfortable chair, relieving the pressure on his leg and back. "I do apologize, Edward. I thought I was alone."

"And you thought you were armed, as well." Stirling canted his head in a piercing study that many a man must have shrunk from in terror. "Career military from your bearing. Either that or an aristocratic upbringing."

"Both, I'm afraid. Am I that transparent?" That out of shape, off my guard, he thought, but didn't add.

"And engaged in the secret services, if I'm not mistaken." When Gideon refused to bend to the man's silent inquisition, Stirling continued with a smile, "I only know this, Colonel, because I was there in your place during the Great War. Counter-espionage for the Secret Service Bureau; what you modern chaps call MI6."

Bloody hell! Edward Stirling, a counter-intelligence agent! Gideon hoped his surprise didn't show in his face. But the man seemed amused that Gideon wasn't offering a comment, let alone a confirmation, and continued the one-sided conversation.

"I note your surprise, Colonel. But what better training for an agent than a life spent in the theatre? I was fluent in German and French, had a bit of Russian, was well into my 30s when the war came along and was a familiar fixture on the European theatre circuits—a natural, or so 'M' said when he came to recruit me."

William Melville, himself, the founder of the Bureau. More than impressed, Gideon only nodded, enjoying the man's tale.

"You're very good at your job, Colonel. I commend you." Another smile, as though a sharp memory had lodged itself in the man's mind. "I would sit here and regale you with my adventures, but, damn me, if my long ago missions aren't still covered by the Official Secrets Act. Care to join me in a brandy while we wait on my daughter? Your secret is safe with me, by the way. She told me you were to meet her here and that I should be sure to absent myself. Which I shall, the moment she arrives."

"Yes, thank you. I'd be delighted to join you, Edward." On the advice of his family doctor Gideon hadn't had a drop of alcohol in all the months of his recovery. Until now. Now he needed one.

"I warn you, Colonel—"

"Gideon, please."

"As I was saying, Gideon, my daughter can be quite despotic when she wants something done her way." Stirling handed him the snifter of dark amber. "Comes by it honestly, from a long line of tenacious women and imperious theatre directors who delighted in making grown men cry."

"I shall keep that in mind." Gideon cupped the bowl of the glass and leaned back against the chair.

"Good man!" The clock on the mantle chimed the half hour. Half-ten. "Interesting, though—" Stirling said, with a swirl of his glass, "Josie is punctual to a fault. Claims that keeping to a schedule is the only way she can manage Nimway Hall on her own."

"An unusual role for a woman, don't you find? Managing an estate the size and complexity of Nimway Hall." He found himself curious as hell as to why and what placed her in the position.

"My Josie is an unusual woman, the mistress of an unusual estate. You'd best keep that in mind, too." Stirling relaxed against the back of the chair. "Where do you call home, Gideon."

"I'm a soldier, I live where I'm posted. But my family's home is High Starrow, near Ramsgate."

Stirling sat upright, eyes wide. "Indeed! Your father was Michael, Lord Starrow? I knew him, a thousand years ago. A Cambridge man, right? Bit of a knave?"

"My father?" A knave—not possible.

"Known far and wide as 'Flash Hot Starrow, the Lord of Misrule.' Could assemble a bacchanal with the drop of his hat."

"You're talking about Michael Tiberius Fletcher?" The most

strict and stolid man he'd ever known. "Couldn't be one and the same."

"The very one! Oh, my boy, the stories I could tell you. I understand he has passed?"

"Three years ago." Gideon whirled the brandy's sweet fumes beneath his nose, trying and failing to picture his father as the Lord of Misrule, finally slipped the calvados onto his tongue, savored its shock of apple and fire. "My older brother, Joseph, assumed the title of viscount. He tries to run High Starrow, but complains endlessly about the RAF requisitioning more and more of the estate with every passing week of the war."

"Just as your lot has requisitioned my daughter's home—"

"Perhaps." Gideon dismissed the notion out of hand. "My mother lives in the dower house. A formidable woman herself."

"Excellent! Then you'll have rehearsed dealing with a woman like my Josie. Speaking of which—" Stirling nodded toward the mantel clock "— it's ten thirty-five. Something has delayed her. She won't be happy with whatever, whomever has made her late."

As though the great Edward Stirling had delivered a cue to an actress waiting in the wings for her grand entrance, Josie Stirling appeared like a hurricane in the space between them and the fire, a wild, shapely silhouette against the dancing flames.

"Good Lord, Daughter, what's happened to you?"

Gideon found himself standing, staring at the apparition in front of him as she stepped into the glow of the table lamp. The woman was drenched and muddied from her wellies to the top of her head. A leafy twig of willow was jutting from the hair above her right ear, her cheek streaked with dirt, lips full in her furor, deep red in her passion.

Even in the dim light of the table lamp her eyes flashed with a fire brighter than his memory, more golden than the flames in the hearth. Filling him with a longing so intense, it clenched his chest, a heat so fierce it lodged in his groin. The most beautiful woman he'd ever seen. Ever.

"I fell," she said, as though the act of her falling was impossible.

"In the hallway?" Stirling stood and peered closely at his daughter, brandy still in hand, a tick of humor in the corner of his eyes.

"On my way through Balesboro Wood, thank you for asking, Father." She threaded her fingers through her hair, combed out the twig, gave it a scoffing scowl and tossed it into the hissing fire. "My own wood, which I know better than the back of my own hand."

"What the devil were you doing trekking through the woods this time of night, Josie Bear? Were you alone?"

"And without a torch." She glared at Gideon, as though he were somehow to blame, then dropped a pair of logs into the fire grate, stepping backward as billowing sparks dashed up the flue. "I do apologize for being late, Colonel Fletcher. It's never happened before. It won't happen again."

Gideon couldn't stop staring, words clamoring around inside his head. "Yes. Accepted, Miss Stirling. And understandable, given—"

"Understandable to you perhaps, Colonel, because you don't know me. At. All." As though declaring that he never would know her. "However, I see you've met my father."

"Gideon and I have been chatting about old times—"

She dashed a suspicious frown between them. "You know each other? How?"

"Not a bit, Daughter dear, until just now. Which is my cue to exit, as you've directed me." Stirling turned to Gideon with a wink. "She's lodged me up in the old nursery. Tells me she's rescuing me from the Hun and then puts me out to pasture like an old bull."

"You are an old bull, Father."

"There's my girl; quick as lightning!" Stirling whispered to Gideon in a volume that would carry to the back of the Royal Albert Hall. He then turned clearly adoring eyes on his daughter, bent and kissed her gently on her forehead and said to Gideon, "Beware, she doth teach the torches to burn bright! A pleasure, sir!"

With that, Edward Stirling exited, leaving them both staring into the shadows of the backstairs.

"You must excuse my father, Colonel," she said, the fine design of her profile lit by the golden light of the fire, lush mouth, perfect chin, high-born cheekbones, "the Stirling side of the family wouldn't know how to make an ordinary exit from a room, even if their lives depended on it."

"I would agree, Miss Stirling." He held her gaze for as long as it took for her to register the memory of her own dramatic exit from the conservatory. "And your mother's side of your family—" Gideon asked, wondering if the mother had been as beautiful as the daughter "—what did you inherit from her?"

"I inherited the guardianship of Nimway Hall, Colonel." She turned to him, her brow winged in shadow like a flight of ravens. "And now it seems I have inherited you."

Josie flushed to her toes, realizing that she had just claimed the arrogant Lt. Colonel Fletcher as her own. All six foot three of him. That broad chest, as well, the square jaw and superbly sculpted mouth. The raw fire of his gaze that seemed to snatch all thought from her brain, the maddening quirk of his dark eyebrow directed downward, right into her core.

"Of course, Colonel, I don't mean that I've inherited *you*. Yourself. Actually. After all, you're here temporarily—you and your unit." *His unit!* Dear God, she'd actually glanced down the front of his trousers. Hadn't mean to, it just happened. Her flush deepened, heating her neck, rising up to her ears. "It's—it's just that this war has created strange bedfellows—"

"*Bedfellows,* Miss Stirling?'

"Merlin's beard, did I just use that word? *Bedfellows?* And am I speaking my thoughts aloud now?"

"You are, Miss Stirling." He laughed, a deep-chested rumble that surprised her with its generosity.

"Well, good, then," she said, still blushing, furious for making herself vulnerable to him, for allowing him free access to her unguarded thoughts. "*Honesty*, sir. If we're to manage a truce for the duration of your—shall we say 'occupation' of Nimway Hall— then we must both be willing to deal in good faith with any issue that might—arise—between us." 'Arise?' Really? Oh, damn! She'd done it again, glanced down the front of his trousers like a street-corner tart. And double damn the man for the smile he was so unsuccessfully trying to hide—for noticing the double-entendres that kept tumbling out of her mouth.

"I agree completely, Miss Stirling." He took a long, deep breath, then exhaled as he set his glass down on the reading table and turned back to her. "We must encourage honest cooperation between us, whenever possible."

"Whenever possible?" The abrupt change in the man's attitude set her teeth on edge, reminded her why she was here.

"Within, of course, the dictates set by my orders from the War Office."

"And my orders as head of Nimway Hall. That said, I suggest we start by clarifying our boundaries." Hoping to separate herself from the man's unbalancing influence, Josie turned away to the wall of bookshelves that framed the huge map of Nimway Hall, its fields and farms, the woods and the village of Balesborough. "Here, Colonel. This map should help."

She flicked on the sconce lights and stepped back for the wider view of the alcove, would have collided with the man, but he caught her upper arms from behind with his powerful hands, warming her all over with the heat pouring off his chest as he held her there. An intoxicating place to be standing, with him gazing up at the map of her estate, his head above hers, his breathing strong and even, grazing her neck, lighting her nerves on fire.

"How old is this?" he asked so near her temple, his words might have been a kiss. He took a sharp breath, muttered something to himself, released her and stepped forward, drawing an electric torch from his belt and flicking it on. His beam fell so immediately on the Hall itself, she half-expected to see the light playing outside the library windows, seeking entry through the shutters and the blackout curtains. A ridiculous notion, of course, but the man had an uncanny way of spinning her thoughts into fanciful shapes.

"If you're asking the age of the house, Colonel, no one quite knows." She joined him at his side, hoping to judge what liberties he might be plotting to take against her. "The map itself was created for Nimway Hall by John Speed himself, sometime in the late 1600s."

"An original Speed? I'm impressed."

"Of course, the canvas has been added to over the decades by other artists as the estate changed and expanded. A bit fanciful in places. The Arthurian elements there in the corners, and Excalibur rising out of our Lake Myrrdin—a family legend, of course, but the map is otherwise quite accurate."

"But it's current as of today?" His beam settled on the house and its outbuildings.

"Current as of 1938." The year of her majority, when the guardianship was granted to her by dear Aunt Freddy before she and Uncle Anthony left for America with her grandparents. "Is the date important?"

"Very. I'm surprised it's still hanging in the open, with all the road names pulled down from intersection posts, and driving maps removed from the shops."

"We're not a stately home that gives tours; we don't advertise."

"Still—" His inquisitive shaft of light danced across the map, from the Hall, to the woods, then the stables, around Lake

Myrrdin, to the tenant farms on the perimeter, to the village itself, the fields and sheep folds, following roads and lanes, streams and footpaths, pausing now and then on the places she loved, before shooting off to the next location.

What had begun as a bolt of resentment at his highly invasive scrutiny of her estate was fast awakening a far more intimate sensation in her, stealing her breath, scrambling her thoughts, as though he were appraising her, his beam of heat first warming her ears, then shifting to her chin, the nape of her neck, the skin between her breasts.

"What exactly are you searching for, Colonel?" she asked, barely finding the breath to do so. "Perhaps I can point it out for you."

"Sorry, I was just—" He switched off the torch and looked down at her from his great height, as though surprised to see her standing beside him. She watched him, waiting for him to answer, realizing suddenly that he was staring at her mouth, frowning at it, really, which caused her to wonder if she had dirt on her cheek from her strange stumble through the woods tonight.

Self-conscious for the first time in years, she brushed her finger lightly across her nose, found nothing there. "Have I mud all over my face?"

He stroked his jaw, his smile almost shy. "No, Miss Stirling. I've... uh... I was just—" he glanced quickly back at the map, switched on the torch again "—just assessing the lay of the land."

"The lay of *my* land, Colonel. Isn't that the very point of our meeting tonight—to establish boundaries between us? For you to understand where the War Office's influence ends and mine begins."

He said nothing, was staring again at the map, his light roving wildly, as though mesmerized by something she couldn't see, no matter how hard she tried to figure out his intentions. The beam stopped abruptly in the middle of the northern-most field. "Are these structures occupied?"

"Not at the moment."

"Who normally uses them?"

"Sheep."

"Ah." Unfazed, he kept staring at the same spot. "Anyone else?"

"Using the sheep fold?" She laughed at the very idea. "Not that I'm aware of."

He grunted. "Abandoned, then?"

"We were forced to cull our sheep flocks last fall, by order of the Ministry of Agriculture. Seems that an acre of land planted in a food crop such as barley or wheat or sugar beets can feed many more people than can that same acre of grass, reserved as grazing land for sheep or cattle."

"Ah, yes." He turned back to her, flicked off the torch. "My second-eldest brother operates Fletcher's Packing Enterprises in Maidstone. Last I spoke with Benjamin, he was doing battle with our father's old school chum, Lord Woolton, head of the new Ministry of Food. Something about bacon processing and the diminishing supply of hogs. Frankly, I prefer soldiering to farming."

"I can't see there's a jot of difference," she said, pointedly testing the boundaries of the man's view of her world. "Between the soldier and the farmer."

He lifted a skeptical brow. "As different, Miss Stirling, as day is to night."

"Different battlefields, certainly. Different weapons, different enemies, but, farming and soldiering are equally critical to winning the war."

"A poetic sentiment, I'm sure," he said in a patronizing air that raised her hackles. "Spoken by a civilian who has never slogged through a battlefield under fire from an advancing tank. Who's never slept in a muddy trench or stalked an enemy through the woods—"

"Or slogged through the mud behind a plow until your feet bled, because the tractor has run dry of petrol, or delivered a breech calf in the middle of a blizzard, or driven the miller to the nearest hospital because the runner stone has crushed his leg— ”

"Hardly the same thing—"

"How dare you say that, sir? That my work—our work—my laborers and me, the Land Girls, my tenants, every farmer across this beloved country who work their fingers to the bone to feed your staff officers, your soldiers, the brave pilots of the RAF—that their work isn't just as critical to the waging of war as the men they support? Is that how you really feel? You implied it earlier, but I hoped it wasn't your true feelings. Because, Colonel, if so, there's no point to this meeting at all."

"How either of us feel about each other or the war is immaterial. The War Office has requisitioned Nimway Hall for military purposes and those orders require your unconditional deference to me."

"I beg to differ, Colonel. I take my orders from the Ministry of Agriculture and the Ministry of Food, who take their orders from the War Office, just as you do."

"Your point being?"

"That my duties and yours are of equal importance to the war effort. No more, no less."

"I disagree."

"I don't care if you agree with me or not, Colonel. I supervise a vast estate farm, a commercial forest, a large orchard, a cider mill, a flour mill, the village council, the local Women's Voluntary Service, the Women's Institute, the care and feeding of four evacuee children, four Land Girls, you lot, my tenant farmers and my household staff—all working toward the war effort. And, should I fail to meet the draconian requirements set down by the Ag, I might very well lose control of Nimway Hall—my family's home for centuries."

"Commendable, however—"

"What exactly do you do for the war effort, Colonel, besides hole up in my conservatory?"

He narrowed his eyes at her, his jaw hardened and working beneath the bronze skin of his cheek as he seemed to gather his temper and laid the electric torch carefully on the table in front of the map.

"Without revealing the details of my orders, Miss Stirling, I can tell you that we are to assess the work of the Defense Chain Operations Task Force. Additionally, we will be surveying and siting locations for the Taunton Stop Line."

"What are you trying to stop?" She knew exactly what a Stop Line was.

He eyed her. "A Nazi invasion."

"Must be a big chain." She added a wide-eyed blink and then tried a half-smile.

He frowned, clearly unamused. "A Stop Line is a chain of field fortifications: gun emplacements, anti-tank islands, slit-trenches, natural defenses—"

"That's why you're interested in the Speed map. The reason you and your staff were so intent on the map of the Hall when I entered the conservatory, why you were trying to hide it from me. You were looking to construct an anti-tank island in the middle of my barley field."

"There's a boundary you should not cross, Miss Stirling, should you find me or my staff wandering the estate with surveying equipment and measuring devices. We are not trespassing on your privacy, but scouting for elevated locations such as this—" he returned to studying the map, took up his infernal electric torch, shoulders straight, one hand behind his back as though about to launch into a lecture to his troops. He landed his beam of light on the top of Windmill Hill. "From this spot, we will survey the terrain across the Levels, west toward Taunton and Bridgwater to the Bristol Channel, north toward the Mendips and south along the Polden Hills."

"You're a surveyor? I thought you were a soldier."

"And an engineer. I hold dual commissions, the Royal Engineers and the Royal Marines."

"And you've been posted to rural Somerset?" She paid little attention to military matters, but there must be a story here. A fearsome soldier like Fletcher posted to the wilds of Somerset?

He left her question hanging and went on. "My staff office will also serve as a command center for a number of other DCO Task Forces who are operating in the area—"

Command center? "Just how many people do you anticipate coming and going every day?"

"Me, my staff of nine, plus or minus another ten, possibly twenty, depending on the day."

"Twenty or thirty of you, tramping through my conservatory? You bloody well better treat it with the respect it is due. That goes for the rest of Nimway. Because if I find any damage, anywhere, I will blame you personally and raise holy hell with Mr. Churchill, himself. A man who has been entertained in that very conservatory on countless occasions."

"We are not barbarians, Miss Stirling."

"Some of your lot have proved otherwise! I've heard horror stories from family friends who live just a few miles south of here. Bannington Manor, their once stately country home, has suffered a collapsed ceiling in the entry hall, broken furniture, not to mention the damage to the grounds, turned to mud by the reservists and volunteers being trained and billeted there. Lady Bryce is beside herself with the extent of the destruction."

"Ah, yes, I know the case in question." He had civility enough to look contrite. "I assure you that the officer commanding that particular unit has been disciplined and demoted as a warning to others. Myself included."

She wanted to believe the man, for no other reason than the earnest expression on his handsome face, so deeply planed in the shadows of the library. But this was no time to falter in defense of her home. The sooner she plowed and planted every inch of arable land for the war effort, the safer Nimway Hall would be from additional requisitioning by the military, or from her practices being found in default by the Ministry of Agriculture and losing possession of the estate.

"Now that you've shared the nature of your operations with me, Colonel, it's time for you to listen to my list of concerns and demands."

The lout crossed his arms and leaned against the bookcase. "I am agog."

"You are not."

He shrugged. "I'm listening, then. Will that do?"

Best to ignore the man and the flickering quirk of his smile. His wry sense of humor humanized the hell out of him. Not a good sign.

She grabbed his electric torch and focused the beam on the map, landing squarely on the entrance to Nimway. "First and foremost, Colonel, I require full access to my own front gate and my own front door. If I'm to keep the estate running in top form, I must be able to freely come and go as I normally would. That goes for deliveries, hay wagons, tractors and everyone in my employ."

"I have no quarrel with that. Through the main gate, with my guard posted day and night. Anyone who shows the proper papers and identity cards is free to come and go."

"You mean to have me stopped at my gate every time I—"

"Every time, Miss Stirling. Strict orders from the War Office to keep the enemy from sneaking into our operations."

"Sapper Mullins knows full well who I am. We met today, as I told you. Met my father, as well, a man with an unforgettable face."

"I'm certain that Mullins well remembers you and your father, however, that's not the point—"

"And I don't see the need for a guard at the front door of the Hall. Post a guard at the door to your office, but having one at the front door is a waste of manpower."

"Seems reasonable."

"I also have five tenant farmers, their families and a variety of farm hands that work on the holdings, depending on the season. If any of them walk or ride across the fields as they usually do when they come to the Hall for business, what then?"

"Do your tenants carry identification papers?"

"Yes, they do. And gas masks."

"Then we'll take care of those situations as they arise. Nimway Hall has a vast uncontrolled perimeter that can be monitored only if everyone on the estate is on guard for strangers or unusual activity, and reports to me anything suspicious. The main gate will guard against overt enemies and unsecured vehicles."

"Enemies of Nimway Hall?" The blasted man was beginning to make a certain amount of sense and she didn't quite know what to do about it, what to say. "If only you could stop the Timber Supply Department at the gate and refuse them entrance."

"Who is this?"

"They arrive tomorrow morning to lay waste to Balesboro Wood, Nimway's ancient forest."

"A timber operation? No one cleared that with me."

"They won't start tomorrow. I can guarantee it. In fact, Colonel, they will start felling my trees over my dead body."

He blinked, scowled. "Explain please."

"Two inspectors from the Timber Supply Department will be here tomorrow to assess the suitability of Balesboro Wood as a source of timber for the war effort. Our wood has been here since time immemorial, and it will survive the war, but only if I protect it with my last breath."

"You sound very like my family's forester. He would lay himself in front of the timber van before he would allow our woods to be abused."

"Your family has a forest?" Another surprising detail about the man who was asserting dominion over her home.

"Starrow Wood. My favorite place to ride."

And yet another surprise. "You ride, as well?" He surely didn't seem the type.

"Not often since my long-ago college years. I do miss it though. The quiet of moving through the morning woods on my bay."

"We've two hunters in our stables," she heard herself say, as though the man were a guest, not an invader. "You're welcome to ride our woods when they're not needed for the farm."

He tilted his head, lifted a brow, the corner of his mouth where his smile seemed to lurk. "Thank you, Miss Stirling. I may take you up on your generosity. Now, is there anything else?" As though the disruptions caused by the man's very presence had been smoothed over by her allowing him a horse to ride in the wood.

"Yes. Since you and your men are taking all your meals here at the Hall, you must surrender your ration books to me immediately. Mrs. Lamb will be shopping tomorrow and needs to register you and your staff at the butcher and the grocer."

"I will fetch our ration books when we're finished here. What else is on this list of yours?"

Josie had shoved her list into the pocket of her dungarees, now retrieved it because she couldn't recall the remaining items until she consulted the smeared pencil markings. "The children. You must remember that we are host to four evacuee children who have the run of the estate. They are curious and inventive and fearless in their play. They get into everything. Their health and safety is my prime concern and should be yours as well. You must not leave dangerous items where they can find them, because they will."

He frowned deeply, seemed to be considering this carefully. "Define dangerous."

"Guns, ammunition, hammers, saws, vehicles, construction material for your anti-tank islands. Come, Colonel, you were a boy once. You must have put yourself in danger more times than your mother would care to have known."

His wry smile was answer enough, before he added, "Thankfully, she still doesn't know."

"You just think she doesn't."

"Point made, Miss Stirling. Next item on your list."

Distracted again, she straightened the damp and crumpled list. "Chickens? Ah, yes! Please make it clear to your staff and visitors that Nimway is home to a wide variety of living things that need as much care as the people. Dairy cows, new calves, horses, free ranging chickens, active beehives located at the margins of fields, hedgerows that provide homes to badgers, rabbits, birds, voles, hedgehogs—"

"What are you saying? Are we to feed them? Milk them?"

"No. Just don't run them over with your vehicles or poison them with your—"

"With what? Our mustard gas?"

"Dear God, you're storing mustard gas? Here at Nimway Hall?"

"Are you mad, woman? This is a farm, not a military reservation. And why the bloody hell would you think we'd be in possession of chemical weapons? They were banned by international law twenty years ago."

"Of course I don't think that. I was just—just mind the welfare of the animals and the children. They don't understand the danger they're in."

"Miss Stirling," he said, leaning close and whispering as though a secret, "I know just how they feel."

Josie's pulse set off like a rabbit, her heart racing alongside. He smelled so good, of wood smoke and leather. "How do you mean, Colonel? Are we in danger after all?"

He made a soft sound in his throat then straightened. "Not if we keep careful watch, Miss Stirling. Agreed?"

"Agreed," she said, not entirely sure what she was agreeing to.

"And to that end, I have a proposal."

"A proposal?" The bloody man had dashed her logic to pieces, was now walking toward the library door.

He stopped at the drinks table, picked up something as he turned back to her. "May I suggest that you and I meet every night—"

"Where?" She felt suddenly bereft of his circle of warmth, a chilly reminder that her clothes were damp through.

"Here, in the library. Say ten o'clock?"

Another night like this one? Sparring, speaking their minds, warming their hands by the fire? Well, now there was a danger! "Why, Colonel?"

"To compare our schedules for the following day and, as you say, to avoid conflicts as best we can." The lamplight from the reading table could barely reach him from that distance. Yet, its glow planed his face, broadened his shoulders, rendering her without words. "While you think on it, Miss Stirling, I'll fetch our ration books. Where shall I deliver them?"

"I'll wait for you here. And yes, Colonel, a nightly meeting with you would be lov—" good grief, she'd been about to say a meeting with him would be lovely "—logical. Quite logical. Though I insist on half-ten."

"Half-ten it is."

The library door clicked behind him and she was left shivering in the cold.

CHAPTER 4

osie turned off the pair of sconce lights above the map, and the library went dark as a cave, the fire in the hearth reduced to the red glow of embers. She turned her back to gather its remaining warmth as she waited for Fletcher to return with the ration books and looked out into the darkness that shadowed the rest of the library.

She loved it here in her fairytale forest, a magical place where all the characters danced and played when the lights were out and the Hall was asleep, like tonight, with the world locked away behind the tall shutters and thick blackout curtains.

Except for an odd glow coming from the turret corner where her father had placed his boxes from Stirling House. A pale, ethereal shimmer rising like a mist in the darkest reaches of the room. A will-o'the-wisp that had slipped through the shutters and into the library.

More likely a very real shaft of moonlight that had thwarted her every effort to mask the light. Which would mean that any light from the library, including the fire could be seen from without by their nearly fanatical local Air Raid Protection Warden. Which could mean a court appearance and a hefty fine.

Despite the darkness, Josie easily dodged the familiar clusters of chairs and tables and book carrels, the dictionary stand with the large bust of Samuel Johnson as the base, feeling her way past the map table and the pair of Chesterfield sofas toward the odd glow in the corner.

She went directly to the window opposite the light, pulled aside the curtain and searched the edges of the shutters where they met in the center. Finding no spill of light, she opened one of the panels and peered outside, assuming she would find the full moon bathing the landscape. The night was dark as ink beyond the glass pane. Because, of course, the moon was in its first quarter, fully hidden inside the earth's shadow.

Then where was the damn light coming from? She closed up and fastened the shutters, pulled the curtain and turned back to the room, hoping the glow had vanished.

But it hadn't. The light seemed to be tucked into the jumbled pile of her father's belongings on the round table in the turret nook. The source could be most anything. The Stirling family had owned that same house since the time of Shakespeare, as Tudorish today as it had been when it was built of crucked beams, wattle and daub, with a roof of lichen-gray slate. The place was an endless warren of twisting hallways connecting cozy rooms with low ceilings and uneven floors. Generations of theatrical keepsakes filled every nook and cranny—and there were hundreds of nooks and crannies, from cellar to attic.

Father must have left an electric torch burning inside one of the boxes when they closed it up. Rather than letting the batteries drain — and curious as to how it had managed to remain burning all these hours since packing the box last night in London, she homed in on the glow and began moving the boxes and cases out of the way. But the more she moved the more deeply the glow settled into the pile.

Until one box at the very back of the table seemed to tip over on its own and spill out into the narrow slot between adjacent boxes. The contents shimmered as she parted the boxes and reached into the cascade of items from her father's life at Stirling House, felt the fringe of a wool lap robe, then the cool brass of a bowl, a small picture frame, a wooden cigar box, other odds and ends she remembered hastily packing the night before, the blue-white glow of the electric torch still stubbornly buried somewhere within.

"Come here, you!" Frustrated, she finally reached deeply into the pile with both hands, and pulled the entangled mess toward her, grateful when the glow at last came forward. The torch had managed to ball itself up inside a lap blanket, its light source radiating through the rose and green plaid of the weave.

No, it couldn't be an electric torch. The shape inside the blanket was all wrong: oblong instead of tubular, cool instead of warm, weighted in the palm of her hand like a large stone.

She peeled away the final fold of wool and found herself holding in her bare palm, not an electric torch, but a perfectly oval stone, silky cool, and silvery white, reflecting its pale glow from inside the fierce golden claw of an eagle, or a dragon, or some other mythical beast.

"What the devil—?" She smoothed her other hand across the surface, peering into its flickering depths, wondering how a stone could capture the rays of the moon and reflect them outward into a completely dark room. Making her feel... a bit breathless, warm and, and almost 'swoony.' Making her conjure the face of—"

"Is that a moonstone?"

Josie startled at the voice that came from above and behind her shoulder. His voice!

"I brought the ration books, as promised." He reached around her and set the stack of books on the table in front of her. "What have you got there?"

"It's a— Oh, damn!" The warm scent of his aftershave caught her off guard, made her fumble crazily with the orb and caused her to lurch sideways into his shoulder to keep from dropping the bloody thing. But it seemed to wrench itself out of her grasp an instant later, landed on the hardwood floor and bounced once before it began rolling toward the settee.

"Sorry, I'll get it!" Fletcher was only a fast-moving shadow against the soft glow of the orb.

"Let me!" Josie dove after it, had it in her hand for an instant, but must have struck it because it went shooting out from under the table, rolling between Fletcher's boots as he was squatting to pick it up from the opposite side. Josie caught the briefest glimpse of his face as the orb rolled wildly past him, was struck dumb by his strong, chiseled jaw, the straight bridge of his nose.

"Isn't that the damnedest thing?" she heard him say as they watched it skitter under the sofa, the gold of its embracing claw glittering madly as it wobbled along in its progress, the only light in the room.

"I'll stop it from this direction." Feeling as though she had somehow released a demon into their midst, Josie crawled out from under the atlas table, glad of her dungarees, wet as they were, stood and felt her way around the back of the Chesterfield, only to watch the streak of blue-white keep rolling across the room through the darkness and actually launch itself up onto the Aubusson carpet, leaving a trail of moonlight in its wake.

"The floor must be badly slanted, Miss Stirling," Fletcher said from the shadows.

"It isn't at all, Colonel, I assure you." But the orb and its claw just kept rolling about, bouncing off the base of the Chinese vase with a clang, ricocheting off the wheel of the tea cart before finally coming to rest under the long, library table as though it had grown tired, or was waiting for them to catch up.

Not trusting that the errant thing was finished with its feints, Josie scurried toward the pulsing glow, dropped to her knees, ducked her shoulders and head underneath the tall legged table and reached for the orb just as Fletcher did the same from the opposite side. His large, hot hand covered hers, shaping her palm against the smooth stone, sending a thrill up her arm to the center of her chest. She was breathless and felt as though she were falling headlong toward him.

"I've got it!" They both said at the same time, lifting the orb between them, its radiance lighting the chiseled lines of Fletcher's face, revealing that his eyes were the azure of ice and indigo, his lashes thick, his dark hair now mussed and rumpled from their tussle with the bizarre object that seemed to pulse in their shared grasp.

Those piercing blue eyes warmed as he looked at her, his mouth canting into a smile. "Hiding a secret weapon in your library, Miss Stirling?"

"No! I— I've never seen it before. I have no idea where it—" Josie gazed deeply into the stone for the first time, felt a throb of heat deep inside her chest— oh, no! The sudden shock of recognition struck her breathless. She drew back quickly, bumped her head on the underside edge of the table— "Ouch!" —leaving the orb to fend for itself in Fletcher's hands. "No, Colonel! I have no idea what it is."

A lie. Because she did know! At least, she suspected! But no! It couldn't be! Not Aunt Freddy's fanciful Orb of True Love! Couldn't be!

Her head aching, she scrambled backward from under the table like a crab, stood up and closed her eyes against the stinging stars, rubbing her head where she'd whacked it. Hoping she was wrong.

"Are you all right, Miss Stirling?" That voice again, tender now, his breath breaking against the nape of her neck, his hand replacing her own on the back of her head. "You'll have a bump here for a few days. But there's no blood."

"Thank you, Doctor." Embarrassed to the marrow and shaken to the core at the idea of standing so near this man in the presence of the orb, Josie pulled away from his gentle tending and snatched the orb out of his other hand. The bloody thing continued to glow brighter than before, so bright that she used its light to march it back to the box on the table where she'd discovered it. "My father must have brought this with him from London. Probably one of his theatrical effects."

"If so, the War Office needs to talk with the Stirling's effects master," he said from the darkness at the center of the library.

"That's absurd, Colonel." If it was truly Auntie's orb, it was so much more powerful, more significant than the War Office could ever understand.

"I'm an engineer, Miss Stirling. I know the laws of physics, and that, that thing—what ever mechanism causes it to glow like that —shouldn't be able to do what it was and is still doing. Not on its own."

"I agree completely, Colonel!" It surely should not be doing what it was doing! Glowing at the two of them like an oracle, a gypsy fortune teller! Their fates sealed together. Pointing its white hot finger at their mutual hearts, probing where it oughtn't be allowed.

She finally located the lap robe on the table and wrapped the orb tightly inside, righted the box that had tipped itself, stuffed the lot back inside, and stacked another box on top. The glow was gone, leaving a chill that settled across her shoulders.

"There," she said, with a sigh of relief as she turned to the darkness at the center of the library, "whatever the glow was, Colonel, it's burned itself out. Forever. Thank goodness."

Silence. Darkness.

"Colonel?" She listened for the rustle of his presence, the leather of his belt, the stalking of his boot heels, even the closing of the door. "Hello?" But nothing.

"Valiant try, oh Orb of True Love. You've met your match in the Colonel and Josie Stirling. We'll not fall to your assault on our hearts, no matter how hard you batter us. Might as well give up now and keep your bloody glow to yourself."

Dismissing the entire incident as a shared madness, she

grabbed the stack of ration books Fletcher had left on the table, banked the fire in the hearth then headed off to her office where she locked the books in the safe for the night.

She dropped into her desk chair and went to work on tomorrow's list of chores, projects, meetings and responsibilities, and finalized her strategy for defeating the timber inspectors. It was nearly mid-night when she fell into bed, exhausted, expecting sleep to overtake her immediately.

But try as she might to banish the incident between her and Fletcher and the bloody moonstone orb, its moments danced in her head, his blue eyes reflecting the moon, the heat of his touch, his breath against her neck, the white glow leaving traces like starlight.

Plagued by a niggling sense that the orb was still glowing in the corner of the library, waiting to be discovered by some innocent—Mrs. Lamb or one of the curious housemaids, Josie finally jumped out of bed, stuck her arms through the sleeves of her dressing gown as she ran through her office, hurried down the hallway and burst into the dark library.

She'd been right to worry. The box was glowing away in the corner like a searchlight! Damnation! She hurried through the darkness, fully expecting to carry the pesky box back to her office and store it in the wardrobe until she could sort out the problem in the morning. But the orb wasn't in the box where she'd left it, wasn't even wrapped in the lap robe. It was resting at the edge of the table, the golden claw clutching the radiant moonstone as though it was waiting on the roadside, thumb extended, for her to stop and pick it up.

This bloody figment of her imagination that was glowing like a delirious beacon, a poison-tipped arrow pointing right at her future. She rolled the orb inside the blanket, hid the bundle in the folds of her dressing gown and ran for her office, feeling safe only when she'd at last locked it in her desk drawer and stuffed the key inside her pillow case.

The last thing she needed was to plunge head-long into a romance with a soldier. Especially this soldier, a man who set her teeth on edge and her heart to racing.

"Sir, are you sure you don't want me to drive to the village post office instead of you?" Sapper Mullins was squinting at Gideon through the open driver's window of the idling Austin staff car. "Not much for me to do during the day, with Miss Stirling ordering me to stand down this morning."

"You will absolutely not stand down entirely, Mullins." The young man's eyes brightened, his shoulders straightened. "Use your judgment, go easy. If you recognize someone trying to gain entrance during daylight hours, go ahead and nod them through the gate. You'll make more allies using honey—"

"—than vinegar, as my mother says. You mean 'easy' like this, sir?" Mullins leaned back against the stone gatepost, in an overly casual at-ease pose, the butt of his rifle resting on the ground, his hand gripping the muzzle.

"Brilliant, Mullins! Carry on, soldier!" Gideon put the Austin in gear and motored down the quarter-mile drive toward his clandestine business in the village, pleased that no one dared ask him the reason he was driving into the village on his own, instead of walking.

Nimway Hall itself was less than a half-mile from the outskirts of the village as the crow flies, an easy stroll on a lovely morning like this, but nearly twice that by car on the narrow hedged lanes. With petrol rationing in full swing, even for the military, every journey by vehicle, railway, cycle or horse was scrutinized for its necessity and logged into daily reports.

Fortunately he had the perfect cover this morning: that of introducing himself to the postmaster and delivering an important package to be registered and mailed. More importantly, according to the map of Balesborough village drawn up for him by MI4, his route would take him past the location of the dead drop signal site—a chalk mark on the drystone wall abutting the right side of the lych gate of St. Æthelgar's Church. If all went to plan, the mark would signal that the first drop had been made by Agent Arcturus and was ready for him to safely collect at the secret, previously agreed upon spot in the churchyard.

But so much for sneaking into the village unremarked by the locals. Every person he passed on the street paused and watched the Austin drive by, some gave a wave. With most of the young men of the village enlisted in the services, the population of Balesborough seemed limited to children, women of all ages, older men and the few young men employed in reserved occupations.

The village itself was tidy and well-cared for—both the shops and the dwellings. The market square at its heart held pride of place with a restored butter cross and the date of 1483 carved into the limestone plinth holding up the roof. The architecture of the individual buildings spanned the ages, from the imposing old medieval tithe barn and its service range opposite the butter cross, to the local Georgian-era council house, with a few dozen shops of various vintages, and a modern petrol station with an attached motor mechanic shop.

All the trades were represented in the thriving little village, the butcher with a line of shoppers out the doorway, a bakery and sweet shop, a bicycle and car repair shop, the grocer, the goods merchant, a doctor and small infirmary, a cobbler, a feed and coal seller, a printer, a bookstore, the telephone exchange and a very busy blacksmith. Everything expected of a Somerset village, including the church and its clock atop the silent belltower, the local primary school, the cricket pitch behind the village hall, a substantial inn and at least three pubs of varying custom.

Gideon drove slowly through the narrow high street and finally parked the Austin in front of the bookstore, next door to the newsagent's shop, which also served as the post office and tobacconist. He waited while two noisy tractors and an empty hay wagon lumbered past him, then opened the car door and stepped gingerly out of the vehicle onto his good leg before pivoting his bad leg into position and bracing his boot against the pavement then settling his weight against the anticipated pain as he stood.

Not too bad, considering that he and Miss Stirling had scrabbled around on the floor of the library on all fours the night before and that the resulting ache in his knee had awakened him before dawn with its throbbing fire. The memory of the chase, that oddly glowing ball, and the fiery triumph in Miss Stirling's eyes every time she thought she'd trapped it, had kept him awake until he finally decided to rise and meet the day full on.

Damned strange object. Needed investigating. He'd take a closer look at it tonight when they met again. A surprisingly pleasant appointment to look forward to, in the way that one looked forward to participating in a rugby match.

He left his cane on the front seat and retrieved the heavy box from the boot, managing to carry it inside the post office to the window counter.

"Good morning, sir!" A middle-aged woman greeted him in front of the neat rack of newspapers with an eager grin, iron-gray hair pinned to the top of her head in a dramatic swirl of curls that resembled the style worn the Hollywood actress on the movie poster in the display window of the bookstore next door.

"Good morning, ma'am."

"Billeted up at the Hall, are you? With the other soldiers? All those Land Girls and the evacuee children! Oh, and I heard that Miss Josie has rescued that handsome father of hers from those Nazi bombs, so he's living there, too."

Newsagent, mistress of the post, tobacconist, gossip and supervisor of the telegraph office that he could hear clacketing from the other side of the door behind the postal cage. A woman who knew every secret in the village and for miles around, in wartime and in peace.

"Yes, ma'am, I'm posted up at the Hall. Lt. Colonel Fletcher, of the Royal Engineers."

"Welcome to Balesborough, Colonel. I'm Mrs. Peak, Vice-President of our Women's Institute. My husband's the Chair of the Parish Council, and the Commander of our Home Guard. He's spoken highly of you, has my Mr. Peak." She let herself into the postal cubical as she talked, swung open the window grate and pulled the package through the opening. "What have you got in here—rocks?"

A rather good guess—soil samples of the area, gathered the day they arrived. But instead of answering immediately, Gideon offered a secret-seeming smile and began filling out the postal forms that would direct the package to SOE Headquarters, Baker Street, London.

"Official Secrets, ma'am."

Mrs. Peak leaned her elbows against the counter. "There's nothing I like better than keeping secrets, Colonel."

"Good, then, Mrs. Peak. We're of a single mind on the subject of King and Country. I'll inform Mr. Churchill of your loyalty next time I see him." He slid the form and pencil toward her.

"Mr. Churchill—how lovely, Colonel Fletcher." Dropping the Prime Minister's name seemed to quell further questions about the package and made the woman a fellow conspirator. "Will you and the other soldiers be coming to the village Spitfire Fund Fete at the end of the month?"

He couldn't imagine what the woman was referring to. "Probably not," was his answer, the one with the least amount of risk to his standing in the village as a representative of His Majesty's military.

"No probably about it, Colonel, if you're staying up at the Hall. Miss Josie will likely make the lot of you attend, no excuses. After all, she's the one came up with the idea that the village should buy a Spitfire for the RAF."

"The village is going to what—buy a Spitfire?" What a cockle-brained notion that was. "A whole fighter plane? And give it to the RAF?"

"Where've you been keeping yourself, Colonel? Haven't you heard of the Spitfire Fund? Lord Beaverbrook's idea—everyone doing their bit. Last month we had a whip-around at the cricket match and raised enough to buy a propeller blade." Mrs. Peak pointed to a poster with the outline of a Spitfire, the propeller and the entire tail section shaded over in red crayon. "See there, sir, already raised £857—enough for both ends of our own Balesborough fighter plane to send into the war."

Beaverbrook—that explained the ballyhoo—the Baron of Fleet Street. "That's a commendable feat, Mrs. Peak. How much does an entire Spitfire cost?"

"£5,000 according to the price list. Quite a lot of money." Tears glistened suddenly in the woman's eyes. "But wouldn't we do anything for our boys in harm's way? We brought 'em back home from Dunkirk, didn't we? If we're to send them into battle again, then the least we can do is to fit out Britain's finest with the finest fighters possible."

"Indeed. Have you a son in the service, Mrs. Peak?"

"We had two sons; lost our eldest at the Mole during the evacuation. But our Robbie's with the Western Desert Force, last we heard from him." She dabbed at her eyes with a handkerchief, offered a wan smile, the ache in her heart so visible his own chest ached. "Promoted to staff sergeant. Very proud—of them both, you know."

"As you should be." Gideon wondered suddenly how his own mother must have taken the news that he was missing in action. She'd told him that she knew he wasn't dead, that he would return to her. But she couldn't have known, really. Took care of him day and night when he was convalescing at High Starrow. Had been his greatest champion as he recovered and drilled him through his physical therapy course. He loved his mother dearly, but she had been unexpected source of strength and hope.

"Thank you, Mrs. Peak." He finished his transaction at the postal counter, bought yesterday's copy of The Times, took his leave of Mrs. Peak and returned to the Austin. Having no reason to be found strolling the streets of Balesborough at this hour of a weekday morning, he slipped into the driver's seat, checked the street for tractors and speeding military vehicles before pulling away from the curb and making his way very slowly toward the lych gate in the church wall where he hoped the dead drop signal would be clearly marked near the top of the wall cap.

And it was. Clear as the blue morning sky to anyone who might be looking for the sign: a single, short slash of chalk drawn randomly across the face of the uppermost gray stone abutting the timbered gatepost, just inches from the latch.

Good. Whatever message Agent Arcturus had hidden in the dead drop was ready for him to collect sometime tonight after the Hall was quiet and the inquiring Miss Stirling was safely contained.

He continued down the High Street, past the church and a scattering of dwellings, noting the lay of the landscape that skirted the vast perimeter of the Nimway estate, until he could turn the car around in a farmer's gateway. As he started back through the village, he saw Mrs. Lamb leaving the grocer's shop, pushing a small wheel barrow heaped with groceries that the woman obviously intended to wheel up the hill, all the way back to the Hall.

Knowing he would feel guilty as hell if he didn't offer a lift, Gideon hailed the woman, and, after five minutes of convincing her that she wouldn't be putting him out, loaded the wooden barrow and the groceries into the Austin. He started back with the talkative cook sitting beside him in the passenger's seat, learning that Miss Stirling was unattached, but was the catch of the county. That Edward Stirling had been the best friend of Miss Stirling's mother's sister's husband—whoever he was. That Mrs. Lamb's daughter was in the WAAFs working at the airbase in Yeovilton, and that her own signature dessert—a blancmange—was a favorite of Churchill's, though she hadn't been able to make since rationing began.

Having not found a space to wedge in a response to Mrs. Lamb's narrative, Gideon drove silently through the gates of Nimway Hall, returning Sapper Mullins' ostentatious salute, and noticed an unfamiliar saloon car pulled up in the forecourt.

"Must be those wicked timber people Miss Josie was expecting," Mrs. Lamb said with an enigmatic chuckle. "Like to see them try to get the best of her inside that wood. Said to have a mind of its own, does Balesboro Wood. Wouldn't catch me setting a toe inside the place if my life depended on it."

Gideon swung the car around to the kitchen block at the back of the house and pulled the brake. "Are you saying the woods are dangerous, Mrs. Lamb?"

"Not dangerous, per se, Colonel. And not to worry." She smiled and patted his hand as she opened the passenger door to her two young helpers who had bounded toward them from the kitchen. "Miss Josie won't let nothing happen to the men while they're in there with her. Thank you kindly for the lift, sir. Come on, girls, let's you bring in the groceries and I'll get lunch started. "

Gideon lifted the wheelbarrow out of the boot then drove the Austin to the carriage house and pulled it into the garage.

Not that he held any stock in Mrs. Lamb's tale of Miss Stirling and the mystical power of her Balesboro Wood, but he couldn't help wondering if the lady of the Hall would approve of him locating the secret Operational Base inside her beloved woods.

If she ever discovered it. Which he could not allow to happen, no matter where he sited the OB.

Secrecy was the order of the hour. Best to scout the wilds of Balesboro Wood on his own. On a horse. If Miss Stirling happened upon him with her "wicked timber people" he could easily explain his presence, that he'd had decided to take her up on her offer to ride.

After consulting with Isaac about saddling a mount, he dressed in clothes more appropriate for riding and was heading out on one of the hunters a half-hour later. Prepared to face Balesboro Wood and Miss Stirling together, should they cross paths during his search.

CHAPTER 5

"Just a few more yards to go, gentlemen," Josie called from the ledge of the rocky cleeve, "and our tour will be finished—" As would be the two hopelessly out-of-shape inspectors from the bloody Timber Supply Department, once they finally made it to the top of the trail where she was waiting in the cool, dappled shadows beneath the canopy of alder.

She'd purposely tramped the blighters through the roughest territory possible. Around the muckiest part of the lake, up the north side of Windmill Hill into the thick understory of brambles and blackthorn, across the wide hilltop of beech, then down the eastern slope of broadleafs, across muddy streams, uphill and downhill again, through a gauntlet of face-slapping branches. Exactly what they both deserved-exhaustion and a head full of confusion.

"Nearly—" the older Mr. Rufus dropped to his knees at the top of the trail, braced his hands against the rocky ground, his wool trousers bristling with weeds and thistledown, his rucksack sagging off his shoulder "–there."

"Thir-sty," the younger Darby said in a croak as he stepped over Rufus, dropped his satchel and himself onto the ground beside a thicket of brambles and berries. He swabbed the sweat from his eyes with his sleeve, blinking blindly out over the countryside that overlooked the lake, the paddocks and the Hall in the far distance.

The dearest view in all the world.

"Well, gentlemen, now that you've seen the extent of Balesboro Wood, have you any more questions regarding Nimway's timber yields and harvest schedules?"

The men remained unmoving, silent but for their panting, the guide maps she'd provided for the tour folded away and hopefully forgotten. She waited for one of the men to respond, content for the moment to be wreathed in the downy soft hum of bees among the honeysuckle overgrowing a nearby hazel.

Still they didn't speak; she hadn't allowed them enough time between dashing sprints to catch their breath.

"I hope I've shown Balesboro Wood in the best possible light. That it thrives because we've always taken care to know every tree and sapling, every frog and bower, every patch of monkshood and bluebell. For untold generations, we harvest the single oak in its time, and let the stand mature."

"Never seen the like, Miss Stirling," Darby said, finally sitting upright, pulling a damp and grimy kerchief from his trouser pocket. "Thorough as a dose of salts. You've a dab hand at forestry —for a woman."

And you're a chuckle-headed arsehole, Josie yearned to say. "Balesboro Wood is in my blood, Mr. Darby, as sure as its timber is woven into the fabric of Somerset, its barns and houses, churches, village halls, Wells Cathedral and Nimway Hall itself."

Rufus wobbled to his knees, joining Darby in his unfocused gazing. "You've given us much to report—" he drew in a deep breath "—to our superiors, Miss Stirling."

"Per the Timber Supply Department's request, Mr. Rufus, I've compiled a full accounting of every tract and stand. There's a copy waiting for you in my office."

"We are impressed, as I said. However—"

However, *nothing!* "Assure your department, Mr. Darby, that should they require telegraph poles or pit props for coal mines, or wooden fairings for Spitfire wings, Nimway Hall will fell and deliver our timber goods, per their exact specifications, on schedule and under-cost."

"We do understand your concern, Miss Stirling—" Rufus was finally on his feet, had mostly recovered his breath and was pulling his note pad and pencil from the breast pocket of his jacket. "But as a farmer, you must realize that an acre of grazing land for cattle and sheep feeds only 1.2 people. That same acre planted in wheat will feed twenty."

"Yes, and it will feed forty if planted in potatoes. But you can't plant potatoes on land as steep as Balesboro Wood. Or beets or barley! The very idea is not only absurd, but—"

"My dear Miss Stirling, for the duration of the war—" Rufus brushed at the air about his ears, "—these decisions are not yours...to make." Another swipe at the air with his right hand, then the left. He spun and fluttered his arms over his head.

"What Rufus means, Miss Stirling, is that—" Darby stood up and flicked his kerchief into the leafy thicket, looked down and stomped his foot "—the Timber Supply Department receives its orders from the War Office, and we—"

"Ouch! Damn! The wicked little bugger bit me—" Rufus began dancing around, swatting at his arm "—right through my jacket."

"Ow, my ear!" Darby slapped at his head, his trouser legs then his torso. "Careful, Rufus, there's one on your neck!"

Slap! "Owwww!" Rufus swatted his neck twice more and started digging into his collar. "Get off!"

It was that time of year, when the bees and wasps were easily riled as the summer's plenty began to disappear. "If you'll just stand still, gentlemen and the bees should—"

"The hell I will!" Darby took off down the slope toward the lake below, with Rufus on his heels, both men bellowing at the top of their lungs as they wheeled and wobbled down the rocky path.

"Ask Mrs. Lamb for a poultice!" Josie shouted after the fleeing inspectors, trying not to laugh out loud—not at their pain, but at her momentary reprieve. "I'll bring your satchels!"

Josie stood for a long moment, watching, chiding herself for not feeling bad for the pair.

"You're a heartless woman, Josie Stirling."

Josie whirled at the voice, knowing it was Fletcher before she found him standing at the edge of the dark woods. He was smiling like a cat who'd been spying on his dinner, just about to pounce.

"How long have you been watching, Colonel?" And why hadn't she heard him approach? She usually heard everything that went on in the woods within a hundred feet around her, could sort the rilling of a stream from the rustle of a vole through leafy clutter.

"Long enough to feel sorry for those two." He stepped out into a patch of sunlight. Standing there in the full glare of the sun, the man looked every inch the well-trained soldier. His shoulders broader than she remembered from the shadows of the night before, his muscles sharply defined beneath the lighter weight of his khaki cotton shirt, his forearms thickly corded where he had rolled up the sleeves. "Seems Mrs. Lamb was right to worry about those two."

"Mrs. Lamb exaggerates. About everything." Was forever trying to fix her up with a husband. "What did she say about the inspectors?"

"The 'wicked timber people'? Quite a bit, actually, mostly nonsense about Balesboro Wood. And that I shouldn't worry, because you wouldn't let anything happen to them."

"She doesn't like the woods, believes the local legends."

"So I gathered. I gave her a lift from the village. Couldn't let her wheel that barrow of food up to the Hall while I drove past in the Austin."

"Mrs. Lamb knows that she's perfectly welcome to drive Bess

into the village on market day to pick up the week's groceries. But thank you, Colonel. She's not as spry as she was when she first came on as a kitchen maid forty years ago. And how did you fare in Balesboro Wood?" He looked none the worse for wear; it must approve of the man. "Did you find a suitable site for your survey?"

"Site?" He frowned sharply as though he'd forgotten last night's conversation, then nodded and scrubbed his fingers through his dark hair. "Ah, yes—I did. A perfect location, can see all the way across the Levels to the Bristol Channel."

"Care to show me, Colonel?" There were only a few places that offered such a sweeping view. Best to know which and where so she could keep track of him. "Or is it an official secret?"

"What about your inspectors? Shouldn't you at least check on them? They can't be happy with their treatment in your woods."

"Mrs. Lamb will dose them with feverfew, poultice their wounds and fill them up with one of her farmhouse lunches; they'll sleep for two hours and awaken without a welt. At which point, I'll return their satchels, hand them a copy of my harvest records, load them into their car and send them happily on their way."

He raised a skeptical brow, as though she were spinning a tale just for him. "You're serious?"

"It's the way we take care of people who get in our way here at Nimway Hall."

"Should I consider that a threat?"

"A simple fact, Colonel. Do with it what you will."

Fletcher opened his mouth as though to speak, paused to shrug before he spoke. "All right then, Miss Stirling, I'll show you the siting location and you can tell me if you know of a better place."

"Anything to aid in the war effort." She picked up the rucksack and satchel, slung them over one shoulder and started toward the woods.

But she'd misjudged the weight of the rucksack and it swung

her off balance, knocking into the back of her knees. She would have fallen like a sack of turnips if Fletcher hadn't caught her on the way down, countered all that momentum and pulled her against the hard length of him. His arms, his chest, his hips, his—

"Colonel!" His mouth was inches from hers, alive with that enigmatic humor of his.

"Perhaps these woods are magical, Miss Stirling." His eyes were dancing as he held her, bright and blue as the sky.

The woods and the orb and this very intrusive man! Magical nonsense!

"I'll thank you to restore me to my feet, Colonel."

"If you think you can walk on your own without crashing to the ground?" He straightened with her, held out the rucksack.

"I'll do my best." Her cheeks ablaze with embarrassment and her pulse drumming against her ears, Josie retrieved the rucksack and ducked into the cool shadows of the understory. A dozen steps further she heard the nicker of a horse, saw familiar movement in a stand of trees. "You rode Cassie up here?"

"Isaac assured me that you wouldn't mind."

"I don't mind at all." She truly didn't. She smoothed her hands along Cassie's cool neck, let the mare's warm tongue lave the palm of her hand for its salt. "In fact, I appreciate you giving her an airing. I've been too busy since the war began for pleasure riding and my girl does love these woods."

"She did seem to know her way around the trails and tracks."

"We often log up here with our Shire horses." She looped the straps of the rucksack and the satchel over the pommel. "Cassie tags along, doesn't like to be left behind any more than Winnie does. Or me."

"Where is Winnie today?"

"With the children. Their last day of freedom before school starts tomorrow."

"Then come see the survey site if you insist, Miss Stirling," he said, gathering Cassie's reins beneath her bit. "I could use your opinion."

"I've plenty of those, Colonel, on a variety of subjects. Lead on."

∽

While Gideon was still thrumming with the scent of her, the lady of Nimway Hall seemed to have quickly forgotten their brief encounter as she led him along the ridge of trees.

"I thought this might be where you meant, Colonel." She cast her smile back at him then stepped lightly through a patch of brambles and ivy in her wellies. "We cleared this place for a skid two years ago, last time we thinned the Overlook. You can still see along here where we staged the logs after felling—" she stepped toward the drop-off and peered over the edge. "The gouges in the stone from the skid track are still there where we lowered the logs down the slope to the road level."

Pleased that he'd scouted a suitable survey site for his cover story, Gideon looped Cassie's reins over a branch and followed the woman, realizing that for all his hiking about for the past two hours, the expected ache in his knee hadn't materialized. In its place was a persistent curiosity about the intriguing Josie Stirling.

He'd caught sight of her a half-hour ago, marching the hapless inspectors through the understory as though they had been enchanted by a sorceress, the Pied Piper leading the innocents into the mountain where they'd likely never have been seen again if the woman had had her wishes. He'd remained silent in his cover on the trail above, amused by her determination to save her woods from the ministerial marauders, grateful that Cassie hadn't given them away.

Dressed in dungarees, a white cotton thermal top, a blue and green plaid shirt over that, a wide-brimmed hat topping her golden hair, and a pair of aviator sunglasses perched on her perfectly shaped nose, Josie Stirling was every inch the formidable castellan of Nimway Hall. The inspectors ought to have been forewarned, as he had been.

"We're less than two-hundred feet in elevation here, Colonel, but you've chosen the perfect view across the Levels for your survey site." She slid her glasses into the pocket of her dungarees and waited for him to work his way through the brambles, then pointed to the north with the efficiency of a Prussian tour guide. "That odd-shaped hill is Glastonbury Tor, *Ynys yr Afalon* in Old English—" the words rolled off her tongue like a fairy language "—the Isle of Avalon. Very Arthurian."

"The Tor, yes, I've marked it here on my map, though I didn't know its name." He unfolded the nearly featureless sheet from his pocket, oriented it toward the hill and filled in the name. "But what's that structure on the top? Is it recent?"

"Thoroughly medieval. A solitary stone tower; all that remains of the monastery of St. Michael's after the Dissolution. But the legends surrounding the Tor itself are older than time. Have you heard of the Red Dragon and the White doing battle beneath the Tor?"

She tipped the hat off her head, letting it hang at her back and turned the startling green of her gaze on him. Fringes of curling gold had escaped the bundled hair at her neck and now framed her face. While the soft spray of golden freckles across the bridge of her nose branded her as a farm girl, the fineness of her features spoke of an ancient, aristocratic lineage blended with the artful boldness of her father's Stirling line.

"*Red dragon*," Gideon heard himself say, wondering why those words, because he'd completely forgotten the subject they were discussing. "You said something about dragons?"

"Fanciful folklore of course, Colonel. But I'm afraid I know far too much about the mystical madness of all things Arthurian, especially when it comes to Glastonbury and Somerset. Even the name Nimway Hall has all to do with the legend of Nimue and Merlin."

"King Arthur's wizard? That Merlin?"

"The very same, the whole Matter of Britain affair. Nimue was the Lady of the Lake, ruler of Avalon, bestower of Excalibur upon Arthur after his battle sword broke, and, according to family gossips—Merlin's lover."

"His lover?"

"Apparently Merlin made Nimue so angry at some point in their relationship, she trapped him inside a tree. Or a stone, or a cave, depending on what you believe, or don't. Nimway Hall itself is supposedly sitting atop the site of Nimue's cave. Very mystical."

Like everything about the woman. Last night's incident with the oddly glowing orb popped into his thoughts, the iridescence of her face as she chased the object through the library. He brushed the memory aside and returned to his map.

"This long, low ridge below the Tor—"

"Wearyall Hill, location of the Holy Thorn where Joseph of Arimathea landed his boat and stuck his hawthorn staff into the ground, where from it grew a tree that blooms every Christmas."

"Joseph of Arimathea. You mean the uncle of Jesus?" Gideon couldn't help his chuckle. "He came to Glastonbury?"

"Founded the first monastery. And, according to Blake, might have brought the boy Jesus along with him."

"'And did those feet in ancient time / Walk upon England's mountains green–' Blake was referring to Glastonbury?"

"Quite plainly, according to scholars and true believers." She grinned as though teasing him, smoothed back her hair and replaced her hat. "But to continue your two-penny tour, Colonel, the Levels used to flood from here to the sea, before the monks of Glastonbury began channeling the water into the Brue."

"A hell of an engineering project: excavating by hand, all the way to the sea."

"But just imagine before that—the people of the Iron Age,

standing on this same hill, on a moonless night, looking out as far as they could see onto a lake as still as glass, its black surface mirroring every star in the sky."

The woman's imagination was a palpable thing, filled his head with a glittering dark night and the sense that he and she had stood together here long ago, on this ancient hill, buffeted by the same breeze. "A carpet of constellations," he said, surprising himself.

She swung her gaze around to him and smiled. "A lovely turn of phrase, Colonel."

Gideon, he wanted to say, to invite her to use his given name so that she might allow him the same liberty in moments like these. But the wind had cooled and was buffeting him off balance. "Yes, well, you paint a vivid picture, Miss Stirling."

"*Josie*. Please call me Josie, Colonel Fletcher. If we're to work together."

Bloody hell, does the woman read minds?

"And may I call you Gideon?"

Damnation! "Well, I—"

"I understand if you'd rather not, Colonel. But, for the sake of efficiency, in our private dealings, and as a gesture of good will between us, I thought—"

"*Gideon*." Hell, yes. "Of course. We needn't stand on formalities." He felt caught out in his every thought about her. Exposed, when he'd rather have taken the upper hand in this relationship. He and she were not equals. Not in the eyes of the War Office. And not by his lights. She was a woman. A farmer. Her grasp of the complexity of war was limited to what she could see from atop the hilltop she loved so fiercely. She might be a crack forester and run her estate like a field marshal, but when it came to her 'war effort', as she so proudly referred to her activities, she was a civilian and would only get in his way if he allowed her to distract him from his orders.

He cleared his throat, hoping to clear his mind. "Yes, well,

Josie, if you will be so kind as to confirm the name of this town—"
he tapped the map which he'd been issued as a completely, utterly
frustrating blank outline of Somerset county "–here, to the west
of Wearyall Hill–"

"That would be Glastonbury, with the ruins of the Abbey,
quite marvelous also quite mystical."

He made a crosshatch to indicate the location of the town,
then ran his finger along his own penciled-in squiggle. "This
range of hills to the south–are they the Poldens?"

"Yes, and behind them farther west is the town of Taunton,
which I suppose you already know."

He made another cross-hatching for Taunton. "Not well
enough."

"Closer in to us, along that avenue of trees, is our village of
Balesborough. That's the roof of the council offices, the village
hall and the church tower of St. Æthelgar in the nearer distance."

The site of the dead drop. He wouldn't chance a look today, in
broad daylight; the cover of darkness would have to suffice.

"We're very proud of Æthelgar's baptismal font; it dates from
Saxon times. If you should find yourself nearby, take a look inside
the sanctuary, if you've an interest in ecclesiastical architecture."

Hard to best a direct invitation by the lady herself, as an excuse
to be discovered wandering about the churchyard. "I might just
do that."

Her eyes brightened suddenly. "I hear a Spitfire." She pointed
directly at the glint of a low-flying airplane coming toward them
across the Levels. "Looks to be heading out of Bristol."

"You know your plane spotting," he said, as the aircraft
reduced its speed and slid past them just above eye level, through
the airspace between them and the Poldens.

"Home Guard training."

He laughed. Couldn't help it. "You can't be a member of the
Home Guard. You're a woman."

She narrowed her eyes at him. "Most of the parish still belongs to my family, Colonel—I mean Gideon—" her eyes flashed again "—I can do most anything I want. Such as insisting that the Home Guard conduct monthly classes on a subject that everyone in the village can attend. Including school children, old men, those in reserved occupations, and, yes, women."

"Instructions on what? Knitting?"

"The first was plane spotting, very popular. Then blackout hints. How to make a Molotov cocktail. Hand-to-hand combat using farm tools and kitchen implements."

He wanted dearly to laugh at her bravado. "And people actually attend these classes? Men and women?"

"Standing room only. I suggest you mind your manners around the housewives of Balesborough, Gideon, and accept their invitation to the Spitfire Fund Fete, or you might find yourself with a flatiron-shaped dent in the back of your head."

"Wielded by Mrs. Peak, I assume?" He could well imagine. "She told me all about the fete this morning. And that the lady of Nimway Hall would demand I attend, since the fete was her idea."

"It was my idea, but I would never presume—"

"You bloody well would. You presume more than any woman in my experience."

"Then you must be a man of very little experience with women." Her eyes grew large; the innuendo obviously unintended. "By which I mean—"

"That the women in my life are suppressed by me? Persecuted? Tyrannized?"

"Why? Have you many women in your life?" Her cheeks pinkened, setting off her pale freckles.

"Plenty."

"A wife?" More blushing, her eyebrows raised.

"A mother, three younger sisters, two sisters-in-law and a few nieces. And I can assure you that each of them would laugh at the idea. Would never allow me to suppress them or their opinions."

"But you have most certainly tried."

"What do you mean?"

"Would you ever dare try to suppress the opinions of your brothers?"

"My brothers are significantly older than I and—" theirs had been childhoods based on fierce and unrelenting competition fomented by their father.

"And, no, of course you've never questioned their opinions or their actions—they're men and anything they do or say has value."

"That's not what I—"

"So, will you attend the fete? The entire parish of Balesborough will be there because the point of it all is not only to raise funds to buy a Spitfire, but also to raise our collective spirits, to give us all something to believe in. To rise up together and help save England in her hour of greatest need. Just like King Arthur promised to do."

"That's a tall order."

"Just you watch and wait, Gideon. Once we've bought the Spitfire, we're planning to start saving for a tank for our boys in the Western Desert Force."

A tank. A ridiculous notion on its face. A dark disappointment when they failed. But a sharp lesson in the harsh realities of war: that battles were fought on the field, not in the village square. Certainly not by women. "I wish you well."

She stared at him for a long, challenging moment then jammed her aviator glasses onto her nose. "I hear Winnie." She stalked back through the patch of brambles. "This way, Gideon."

"Where?" He hadn't heard a thing except his pulse and the wind, and then a yelping bark that blew up from below.

"One last marvel. I want to show you Maximo—"

"Maximo?" A large rock?

"Our Pendunculate oak." The woman plunged into the shadows, and, damn, if she and Winnie weren't soon leading him and Cassie down the hill on a trail toward the abandoned ice house he'd settled on for the Auxiliary Unit's Operational Base. He'd chosen the site because of it's obscure location, hidden from prying eyes and curious lads on the southern most edge of the forest, just off the old logging track that ran along the base of the hill.

But she thumped along the wooded path in her determined stride, right over the earthen top of the abandoned ice house without a remark, crashing through the bracken and out into a clearing of golden meadow grass where she came to a stop at the margins. At its center stood an enormous common oak tree, with a broad and spreading canopy that surely measured a hundred feet across.

"I kept the inspectors far away from here." She stood gazing up at the crown, fists balled against her hips. "I feared they'd find a reason to cut it down."

"I understand the reason it's called Maximo." He followed with Cassie as she began walking toward the monumentally tall tree. The breeze came up, shaking the brightest colored leaves loose and fluttering them to the ground.

"Thirty-two feet at its girth, nearly hollow inside and thought to be more than a thousand years old. Winnie's favorite place on a hot summer day—go girl!— and my favorite place to hide when I was a little girl." The dog barked and bounded toward the oak, disappearing into a dark split in its thick trunk.

"Who were you hiding from?"

"My two cousins. Both boys. Tony, a year older and Frederick, two years. The closest I have to siblings. Balesboro Wood was our magical kingdom. I was the queen and they were my knights. Still are."

"Where are your cousins now?"

Her eyes misted over. "Tony's in the Royal Marines and Fred's just entered the Naval College at Greenwich."

"I can quite easily see you playing here. Plotting with, and against, your cousins."

"I learned from the best."

"Remind me not to cross you, Josie."

"What do you mean?"

"If your mystical powers are as potent as your family legends claim, then I fear you might one day trap me inside a tree for the duration."

"Just as Nimue did to Merlin?" Her smile grew devilish. "If you knew Balesboro Wood as I do, Gideon, you'd best heed your own warning!"

Not at all certain how to read the woman, he nodded. "I'll keep that in mind."

"Now, if you'll excuse me, I really ought to be getting back to the Hall. I have a busy afternoon and the inspectors will have calmed down by now and are tucking in to Mrs. Lamb's delicious Eve's pudding. With Nimway's own Somerset apples topped with warm custard. Irresistible, my dear colonel." She licked her fingertip as though it tasted of cream and cinnamon, then hoisted the rucksack and satchel off Cassie's pommel. "I'll leave you to finish your survey. By the way, if you get thirsty, the village is through that break in the stand of alders; I can recommend Nimway's scrumpy at the Hungry Dragon. When you get to the churchyard wall keep to the right and you'll find yourself back on the High Street. Safer than trying to find your way home the way we came."

"Tonight, in the library?"

"Wouldn't miss it." She challenged him with a provocative smile and a lift of her eyebrow, hitched the two bags over her shoulder— "Come, Winnie!" —then strode away through the tall golden grass until she and her black dog vanished into the shadows of the woods, leaving Gideon to stare after her, his pulse racing, his head tangled with her yarns.

Cassie nickered and nudged him in the middle of his back, as though urging him to follow her.

"Not a good idea, Cassie," he said, wondering that his leg

hadn't given him a pinch of trouble since he'd arrived in the woods.

He easily swung up into Cassie's saddle and rode back to the site of the abandoned ice house to more completely examine the site for its suitability. The three other possible locations had points against them.

Judging by the overgrown track, the ice house must have been abandoned nearly thirty years before. The entrance had once been a half-barrel shaped vestibule made of red brick, most of which had collapse backward against, what he could only assume as he reached through the curtain of trailing ivy and pulled a few bricks from the jumble, was a thick oak door. All to the good.

The blocked entrance would serve as perfect camouflage for the trapdoor entrance he hoped his sappers could dig through the limestone from the low wooded ledge a dozen feet above. He wasn't sure what was on the other side of the blockage—a natural cave or a brick-lined room—but either case put the ice house at the top of his list of options for the Operational Base.

He took a dozen quick measurements, sketching out the site on a notepad, included the approaches and current placement of the surrounding trees and understory which would need to be protected from any disturbance made by the construction.

The sun was nearly setting when he finished and realized that the debriefing meeting wasn't for another hour. He decided to chance being seen on his casual approach to the churchyard. After all, hadn't the lady of Nimway Hall invited him to have a look?

Ten minutes later he had secured Cassie to a branch just inside the woods and was standing at the low stone wall, looking out at what seemed to be an ancient section of the churchyard. Tall stalks of nearly spent wildflowers waved between moss-covered tombstones that tipped every which way, some leaning against each other, some fallen, a few propped in a line against the wall itself. The gray stone of the old Norman belltower was barely visible through the weedy trees. Not a soul to be seen anywhere.

And there it was: the yew tree, a dozen yards further on, exactly as described in last night's message, its trunk embedded in the dry stone wall itself, hundreds of cloth clooties hanging from its branches, waving in the breeze. He hoisted himself over the wall and made his way through waist-high weeds and canted stone grave markers.

The yew tree was much smaller than Maximo, but doubtless much, much older, older than the church itself. Its heartwood was long gone, leaving only a massive pair of trunks rising from the base and intertwining in an upward spiral to represent what had once formed the perimeter of the original trunk. The canopy of deep green needles branched upward and outward in a series of arcs that sheltered and shaded the tombstones gathered under its spreading branches.

Secluded, singular, yet unremarkable. He couldn't have chosen a better drop site himself. He glanced around the churchyard, saw nobody, no movement at all but the breeze buffeting the tall weeds and the festoons of clooties hanging above his head. And among them, the deep red strip of linen looped three times around a lower branch. The correct tree and his first contact with Arcturus.

He stooped beside the irregular-shaped base on the right side of the trunk, near the wall. He reached through the narrow cavity between the tangle of roots and felt around for the metallic object placed somewhere inside by his contact. Found handfuls of leaf litter and a store of last year's acorns from a forgetful squirrel. He positioned himself closer, bent onto one elbow and reached more deeply into the hollow. Nothing in the lower section, but when he felt around the upper recesses, his knuckles struck the object, tucked neatly into a niche at the upper back of the hollow.

He retrieved the small metal capsule, a little larger and longer than a cigarette, and knelt low as he twisted off the cap and opened it. He removed the curled piece of paper with its coded lettering and flattened it before buttoning the message into his shirt pocket. He would decrypt and read it tonight.

He retrieved the red clootie from the tree, rolled it around the encrypted message he'd prepared in advance, then shoved the roll into the case. Now that the red clootie was no longer hanging from the yew, Agent Arcturus would know that a message was waiting in the dead drop.

These first messages were only a test of the system, a chance to assess the dead drop and the signals, before transmitting real information. Gideon had paraphrased and encrypted Churchill's recent speech to Parliament:

> *Let us therefore brace ourselves to our duties, and so bear ourselves, that if the British Empire last for a thousand years, men will still say, this was their finest hour.*

A pithy and fitting phrase to launch this liaison with his counterpart at the SOE, Churchill's redoubtable Agent Arcturus.

CHAPTER 6

*J*osie kept catching herself smiling like a loon as she hurried back to the kitchen, whistling even. Tried hard to settle the fluttering in her stomach and the racing of her heart each time the colonel–Gideon–found his way into her thoughts.

She discovered the timber inspectors exactly where she'd expected to find them, resting in the servant's hall under Mrs. Lamb's capable care, Rufus slumped against the back of an arm chair, Darby lying face up on a bench, eyes shut tightly.

"How are the wicked timber people?" Josie asked in a whisper, peering at the welt on the back of Darby's hand.

"Much better, if a bit tipsy after two doses each of my tincture of stinging nettle."

"Thank you, Mrs. Lamb. I do need to finish up with them before we send them home."

She roused the men with copious amounts of sympathy then settled them into the farm office where she coached them through their reports on the state of Nimway's forest reserves, and finally sent them on their way with pots of Mrs. Lamb's bee-sting poultice, a basket of cheese, jam and bread, and a half-dozen bottles of Nimway Scrumpy.

After all, with the fate of her beloved Balesboro Wood still firmly in the remorseless hands of the Timber Supply Department, she wasn't above a bit of bribery.

"All in for the war effort, right, Winnie, my girl?"

Winnie agreed with an enthusiastic wag and a woof and a toothy smile, cocking her head to the side, ears flopped like a pair of wavy black flags.

"Good, then. Let's go find out how the new schoolroom is coming along! Children, Winnie!" Josie's highly anticipated gesture sent the dog chasing out of the farm office and barking up the gravel lane toward the make-do school, perched on the upper edge of the newly turned field of winter wheat.

She couldn't have been more pleased when she finally caught sight of the building, gleaming in the sunshine. Winnie went chasing past, her delighted bark bouncing though the valley as she went in search of the children.

Mrs. Tramble and Mr. Broadfoot were standing under the eave of the shed roof, examining one of the windows.

"You've done a spectacular job of it, Mr. Broadfoot!" Josie said as she approached. "Don't you think so, Mrs. Tramble?"

From the outside the structure still resembled the old stone-built loafing shed, but Mr. Broadfoot had repaired the slate roof, added a timbered floor, a fourth wall with a door and two awning windows, plus a small pot-belly stove.

"Indeed, he has, Miss Josie! I'm thoroughly delighted! Better even than our school in Stepney. The children think so too. Never in my life had students so excited about starting their first day of school!" A cloud of squeals and laughter rose up from the apple orchard, as though to put a point on the children's approval. "We thank you so much!"

Freedom and fresh air—a clean classroom and the great

outdoors; how could they not thrive after the squalor and neglect of their lives in London?

"Class time should be right comfortable in here in the school-house for the next few months, Miss Josie—" Broadfoot gazed up into the eaves. "Until the weather turns bitter and we get our first snow storm."

"Of course." She hadn't had time to think that far. "Let's plan to relocate the class to the east parlor after Christmas. Unless the SOE requisitions another wing of the Hall." Not entirely impossible. "Anything else come to mind?"

"I just been tellin' Mrs. Tramble here, that I'll be pluggin' up these soffits with reeds from the lake to reduce the draftin' on those windy days ahead."

"You're always thinking well ahead of me, Mr. Broadfoot." The man and his family had been a vital part of Nimway Hall since long before Josie herself was born; he knew the ebb and flow of the seasons, how they effected every field and tree, the livestock and everyone on the estate. "Then I'll leave you both to your work. And thank you. This war is bringing out the best in everyone."

Almost everyone, she thought as she strode back toward the farm office to face the two hours she needed to spend typing and assembling the heap of reports she owed the Ministry of Ag. Gideon and his staff of officers were doubtless doing their best, but damn the man for not recognizing the same effort in the people around him. Perhaps their time together in the woods today had served to soften his opinions somewhat. The test would come at half-ten. She doubted he would pass.

Still, she'd been hoping to see the man at dinner, became increasingly annoyed at herself for repeatedly glancing up from her plate of Lord Woolton's ghastly vegetable pie and the Ministry of Ag's weekly circular every time someone new entered the dining room, chiding herself for being disappointed when it was one of the Land Girls or Mrs. Lamb and not him. Gideon. Quite a fine name.

"Dreamy, ain't he, Miss Josie?"

"What's that, Trina? Who?" Josie glanced down the length of the table toward the young woman sitting at the opposite end with the other Land Girls, felt a telling blush that threatened to unmask her guilt.

Damn if she wasn't being called out for staring at the door to the butler's pantry, her mind wandering to the conservatory just beyond, actually listening for the sound of Gideon's deep baritone that would let her know he'd returned safely from the wood.

"The colonel, of course," Trina said, looking toward the same door, elbows propped on either side of her bowl, her sharp chin resting on the back of her clasped hands. "Haven't you noticed, Miss Josie? He's so, well...manly."

"And virile." Francie sighed, flicked her dark hair over her shoulder, and took the same pose as Trina. "Like Clark Gable in Gone With the Wind."

"Brawny, is the colonel—like a Scot!" Maureen said, broadening her brogue and sharing a blushing giggle with her compatriots.

Josie did her best to ignore their girlish gossip, trying to read the Ag's hideously boring new circular on current theories of planting, cultivating and harvesting sugar beets, but failing each time his name was mentioned.

"Sure, the colonel's unholy handsome," Patsy said, "but don't you ever wonder how a big strapping soldier like him got himself wounded? I surely do."

Wounded? Josie set down her fork and stared at the door again, as though she could see him through it. Gideon, wounded?

"I mean," Patsy said with a catch in her voice, "I can't help wondering at the colonel's wound, because my husband's in the 1st Royal Tank Division in North Africa, fighting the Italians, and I haven't heard from him since early August—goin' on two months, now." The girl's pale brows came together in a worried frown. "I think about soldiers getting wounded all the time. Worse than just wounded, actually."

"Now, now, mustn't worry yourself, Patsy." Trina rubbed Patsy's forearm. "Your Bert probably falls right asleep every night after driving his tank across the burning sand all day. That's why he hasn't written."

"That's probably true, Patsy," Josie said, still confused by the mention of Gideon's wound and ashamed at how little she knew about the young women living under her roof, "the general mail from the front is unreliable at best. But I'm sure you would have heard if he had been badly wounded."

"Miss Josie's right," Maureen said, touching Patsy's hand. "My own brother, Dougal, was shot in the shoulder during the evacuation and my mum didn't know it until he showed up on her doorstep in Clydebank with his arm in a sling."

"But ladies, back to the colonel's having been wounded–how do you know this?" And why wouldn't he have mentioned something to her?

The four young women looked directly at Josie, actually stared. Trina canted her head to the side. "You must have noticed, Miss Josie. That limp of his, on his left side. A dead give-away there's something wrong with his leg."

"Cane's another give-away." Francie gestured at her own leg with a piece of buttered bread.

Gideon has a limp? Walks with a cane? Since when? She'd spent nearly an hour with him in the woods today, crawled around on the library floor with him last night. Surely she would have noticed.

"Was it an accident?" Josie asked, feeling horribly unsettled, but certain it must have been that afternoon, after she left him. Otherwise, how could she have missed him limping through the wood? "When did it happen?"

"Didn't ask," Maureen said, spreading blackberry jam across a slice of bread, "and soldiers don't like to talk about that sort of thing. But I've been imagining he must have been wounded in hand-to-hand combat with a Nazi stormtrooper."

Trina let out a low whistle. "I certainly wouldn't mind a bit of hand-to-hand combat with the colonel." She laughed and nestled back against her chair, closed her arms around her chest in an embrace. "Those smoky blue eyes—"

"That square chin!" Francie said.

"Those luscious lips! Ooo, I just want to bite them!"

"Maureen!" the three young women said in a single voice, before they all fell to laughing.

Still dumbfounded at their claim that Gideon had been limping around with a cane, Josie could only look on and listen in stunned amazement as the young women kept up their wild fantasies about him.

"You'd best take care, Maureen," Patsy said with a wag of her finger. "Don't let your Lieutenant Crossley hear you say such things about another man, especially not his Commanding Officer, else you'll be buying your own beer tonight at the Hungry Dragon."

"That is if the lot of them are back in time for a tipple in the village." Trina giggled along with Francie.

"If?" Maureen sat upright, her eyes wide. "I hadn't thought of that!"

Josie couldn't help but ask, "Where have the colonel and his staff gone, Patsy?"

"Dunno any more than that, Miss Josie. Mrs. Lamb told us she served them an early dinner in their headquarters, while they were working behind closed doors."

Francie dropped her fork into the center of her empty bowl and pushed it away. "I saw them leave through the French doors as Trina and I were driving the Fordson into the stableyard. Must have been near seven o'clock."

"Francie, did you see which direction they took?" Josie heard herself ask again, too quickly, too openly, wondering why she cared where the man was or what he was doing. Let alone whether or not he had been injured, or that he walked with a limp, or carried a cane. Or still planned to meet her tonight in the library.

"I think I did," Patsy said as she piled up the empty soup bowls onto her own. "I was pulling carrots in the garden for Mrs. Higgins when I saw them heading around the paddocks toward the woods. The colonel, his staff and three of those sapper fellows."

"Ah." That made sense, then. Gideon would be showing his men the survey site he'd settled on that afternoon. "I just wanted to know where they were, for a head count, in case of an air raid." Though not a single siren had sounded in Balesborough since that week of practice drills the day after war had been declared, and in the first week of the London bombings.

"I pray there's no air raid, tonight, Miss Josie!" Patsy said as she added Josie's bowl to the stack. "It's my turn for a bath. I plan to wash my hair in the sink then soak for at least ten minutes in my five inches of warm water. After that, I'll write to my husband again—"

"—then you'll sneak down to the kitchen for a hot milk and a slab of honey bread," Trina said, "as usual."

"And find you there before me, Trina!"

"Well, thank you ladies," Josie said as she stood with her empty plate, "for another hard day's work in the fields. Nimway Hall couldn't possibly survive the war without you!"

"Thank you, Miss Josie!" Francie said. "You're a right good egg, you know. The four of us hooked the brass ring when the Women's Land Army assigned us to Nimway Hall."

Josie stopped at the butler's pantry door. "Why would you say that, Francie?"

"Oh, miss, the stories we've heard from the other girls. Slighted rations, dangerous farm equipment, sleepin' stacked like cord wood in tiny rooms, or on moldy mattresses alongside the bats in the attic, treated like slaves—"

"We're only two to a room at Nimway, Miss Josie, not in the barn but in the main house," Patsy added. "Our beds are soft and warm, plenty of food, you let us play the gramophone in the parlor for as long as we like, you trust us like the grown women we are—"

"And we bless you for your kindness every day."

Josie couldn't help her broad smile or the catch in her throat. "Well, thank you. We're each doing our best to bring Patsy's Bert, and all the others who are in harm's way, safely home. Enjoy the rest of your evening, ladies. If anyone should ask for me tonight —" like a certain injured colonel "—I'll be at a meeting of the WVS in the village hall and should be back by ten o'clock." In time for her meeting with the injured, or perfectly healthy, Gideon Fletcher.

Josie left the young women still gossiping about Gideon and his staff of eligible officers. She found Mrs. Lamb and Mrs. Tramble eating a late supper with the evacuee children in the servant's hall dining room, their animated conversation turned to the badger sett they had discovered in a copse of alder near the apple orchard—a capital event that had kept them out until near dark.

"Sleep well, children," she said, "work hard at your new school tomorrow and listen to everything Mrs. Tramble tells you."

They wished her a chorus of good nights and caught the kisses she blew back to them.

Josie donned a farm jacket, grabbed a shielded torch and took the shortcut to the WVS meeting, through the new fields south of the Hall, all the while trying to think back on her hike through the forest with Gideon. Tried to recall him limping, or stumbling. Propping his gait with a make-do walking stick, or relying on a tree to steady his balance. He'd led Cassie as they ambled over the trails, keeping up with her pace, seemed to pick his way along the pathways as steadily as she.

Had easily caught her up in his arms when she knocked herself off balance; she would have fallen to the ground had he not been quicker than gravity.

And oh, those arms that held her. Powerful and steady. She had lain back in his embrace for longer than she ought, had stared up into those sparkling blue eyes, focused on his mouth, wanting him to kiss her. Maureen had it right. Lips to nibble on, and oh, to be nibbled upon, by those strong, straight white teeth.

Oh, stop! And stop wondering about the sudden appearance of Aunt Freddy's Orb of True Love. What balderdash! Better to believe in fairies and Father Christmas than in her auntie's tales of love fulfilled.

The nearly moonless night had fallen hard and the village was shrouded in wartime darkness as she approach from the churchyard, with every household window blacked out, shop and pub doorways closed and draped against light leaks that would guarantee a hefty fine from the Air Raid Protection Warden.

Nothing to warn her of the next hazard but the pale amber beam of her shielded torch. Hearing a motor engine rumble toward her round the corner, Josie stopped on the grassy verge near the lych gate outside the church and waited as two army lorries lumbered slowly past, their shuttered head lamps barely illuminating the road surface ahead.

She crossed the roadway to the pavement, negotiated her way along the familiar row of shop fronts, around the corner at the butter cross and finally made it into the darkened vestibule of the village hall without grazing a knee or falling over Mrs. Lister's bicycle as she'd done last week.

"There's Miss Josie, now!" she heard above the din of female voices as she ducked through the blackout curtains into the comparatively harsh brightness of the old village hall, its fat oaken cruck beams still holding up the roof after a few hundred years. "Let her decide who must take the older boys this time!"

"Sorry I'm late, ladies," Josie said, ignoring the opening salvo as she shrugged off her jacket and hung it with her hat on the communal rail of hooks along the wall. "I see we have a full house tonight, thank you all for coming."

"The County Evacuation Officer is sending us fifteen more evacuees, Miss Josie," Mrs. Hartley said from her seat at the long table in the center of the room. "Ten of them are teenage boys from Bristol. I'm a woman alone, as you know—I'll not be safe a moment if I take in one of them— "

"That was your excuse about the young ones that come here last month. Eight-year-olds!"

"Vera's right, Edith Hartley! You've an extra room in your house; it's time for you to—"

"How dare you, Myrna Sykes!" Mrs. Hartley stood, knocking her chair over backward with a crash. "That room belongs to my own boy—"

"He's twenty-four years old, and in the RAF, Edith, he's got a perfectly good bed in his barracks at—at, wherever he's stationed."

"Roy needs his room when he comes home on leave—"

"Ladies, please!" Josie said as she took the seat at the end of the table, seeing a too-familiar fear in Mrs. Hartley's eyes, hearing it in her voice. Her only child, her son, flying nightly against a ruthless enemy. "We're here tonight hoping to find a fair and kindly way to house these new evacuees, the children especially—for their benefit, not our own."

Myrna Sykes stood, thumped the table and got everyone's attention. "All I can say, Miss Josie, is that we ought to be thankful the reception officers no longer line up the poor dears against a wall at the train station and allow the billeting families to choose on their own."

"Agreed, Mrs. Sykes," Josie said as the chattering began to die down and she leafed through the evacuee log book. "We've seen fewer broken hearts since we began matching the incoming children with the proper family situation."

Lots of nodding and peaceable agreement around the table.

"And, Mrs. Hartley," Josie continued quickly, before anyone could interrupt, "I see here on the list that we'll be taking in a middle-aged blind woman, a retired school teacher who lost her sight in the first wave of bombings. Perhaps, you'd consider sharing your home with her."

Mrs. Hartley scanned the intent faces of the women now sitting around the table and seemed to relax some. "Well, perhaps."

"Good then. Shall we get started?"

A simple question that launched another hail of opinions that took the better part of a quarter-hour, three pots of blackberry leaf tea and a plate of carrot biscuits to finally bring the subject back to ground.

And an additional two hours to match fifteen names to fifteen beds. The blind woman to Mrs. Hartley. Four children to Nimway Hall, two little girls and two of the older boys who she could only hope would be kept well in hand by the mere presence of Colonel Fletcher and his men.

"You were exactly right to choose this spot for the Operational Base, Colonel," Crossley said from the near utter darkness on the rise above the tumbled entrance to the ice house. "There's certain to be a passage into a cave just below here; the hills of Somerset are riddled with them." Crossley washed the shuttered beam of his torch across the ground, the light flickering through the underbrush like a wild fire. "The roof can't be more than four feet thick up here, the same limestone as the surrounding hillside."

"How long will it take to get through to the chamber?" Gideon asked from his position in front of the entrance below.

"Six hours, seven at most, sir, depending on the composition of the strata, and the power of the charges we can set without making too much noise–"

"And causing too much interest from the locals," Gideon said, remembering Josie's warning, "including the evacuee children, who seem to be as inquisitive as a tree full of squirrels."

"Best to do the work in the dead of night, Colonel," Easton said, "when the little imps are abed."

"And camouflage the works by day. Good idea, Easton. Let's finish surveying the site tonight. Estimates will suffice until we know what's behind the rubble and the old door behind that."

"And if we can get through the roof," Durbridge said, his boots appearing in Crossley's beam of light on the ridge above.

"Indeed." All things being as they appeared, his staff would verify the specifications in the next day or two, then draw up construction plans, arrange for the delivery of supplies from the air field at Yeovilton and, with the help of his crew of sappers, be finished by the middle of next month.

Finished and moving on with his unit to the next assignment. He hadn't spent a moment considering the timetable of his mission. The Operational Base, training the Aux Units, securing the Taunton Stop Line and, most critically, establishing a relationship with Agent Arcturus that would guarantee a permanent communication hub here in Balesborough.

A lot to accomplish for a man reduced to relying a cane. Yet, each accomplishment would bring him closer to the moment when he could return to special intelligence work on the front lines, where war was waged and a soldier belonged.

It was nearly half-nine by the time they returned to the Hall. Most of the men cleaned up and eagerly headed off to the Hungry Dragon to blow off steam in the village.

"Comin' with us, sir?" Sapper Mullins asked, running a comb through his hair as he came out of the bath he shared with the other sappers.

"Thank you, Mullins. But I've reports to finish in my office before tomorrow." Besides that, his knee ached like fire and made him feel like an old codger in the company of his men when they weren't on duty.

And there was the meeting with Josie.

"No rest for the man in the commander's chair, eh?" The young man tucked his comb into his back pocket and flashed a smile.

"Something like that." Gideon watched Mullins hurtle toward the stairs, relieved when the crash he expected to hear from the floor below didn't come.

He was on his way to clean up in his private bathroom when he noticed a light on in Stirling's sitting room in the opposite wing of the Hall from his own, the faint sound of music and humming coming through the open doorway. It had been on his mind all day to share an idea with the man, but the father had been as elusive as his daughter.

Gideon found Edward reaching into a large wooden crate and rapped on the open door. "Have you a moment, Edward?"

Stirling looked up and smiled broadly. "Gideon, hello!" He waved Gideon into the room. "Do come in, have a seat."

"Can't just now," he said, clasping Edward's proffered hand, surprised at the earnest strength. "My clothes are a mess."

"Nevertheless, you're welcome any time to my *ad hoc* gentleman's club." Edward swept his arm in a grand gesture to include the paneled sitting room with its desk and pair of upholstered chairs. "Not the Garrick, but I prefer the old nursery to being bombed to oblivion. Don't tell my daughter—she'll gloat."

"Official secrets."

Edward raised a dusty bottle from the divided box. "Join me in a Cognac? Rescued a crate of my finest from my cellar. Must make the lot last till the end of this bloody war. Those bloody Ruperts at the War Office have any idea how long that will be?" The twinkle seemed to never leave the man's eyes.

"If only they did. But, on the subject of prosecuting the war, I may have a job for you. If you're interested."

"Of course, I'm interested, man. This bull is already bored of the pasture. What sort of job?"

"Right up your alley, I think." Gideon stepped inside the room and closed the door. "I'm quietly recruiting a group of men to join Churchill's secret, stay-behind army."

"Ah, yes, I believe I've heard of Winston's secret army."

"You have? How?"

"My dear man, the Garrick is not only a venerated gentleman's club made up of actors, artists, writers and men of letters, it's also a hot-bed of military intrigue. Not a few of us are veterans of the Secret Service Bureau in the last war. We've old connections, as you can imagine, buried deep in the halls of government. Also, my Anne and Churchill's Clemmie were in school together, remained dear friends until Anne's death. The two families go way back."

So there was the lady of Nimway's link to Churchill, a name she had casually strewn across his path like caltrops.

"Then, Edward, I could certainly use a man of your experience in the Auxiliary Unit," he said, wondering—but not caring in the least—what the man's daughter would think of him recruiting her father. "And as you're already covered under the Official Secrets Act, you'll not mention our conversation to anyone."

"Especially not my Josie Bear, eh?"

Stirling's smile was damn near as contagious as his daughter's. "Especially not her. Thank you, sir. We'll talk later."

Just now he had to clean up for his meeting with the lady in question.

He stood naked in the bath, scrubbed and hosed off, letting the cold water sluice over the incision that ran from above his knee half-way down his calf. He dried off, determined not to spend more than a moment patching up the angry-looking wound, before dressing in clean brown trousers and a white shirt.

Ten-fifteen, not enough time to decrypt the message from

Arcturus before his meeting with Josie. There would be time enough to do it later.

He left his cane in his room and took the backstairs, and timed his arrival in the library to exactly half-ten, expecting Josie to be waiting for him with a quip about proving how punctual she was. He was ready with a witty comeback, hoping to ignite the emerald green of her eyes when she laughed.

But Josie wasn't in the library. Wasn't lounging out of sight in one of the wingback chairs in front of the flames dancing in the hearth. Both chairs were empty.

So he switched on the reading lamp between the chairs, added a few logs to the fire then sat down and began idly thumbing through a copy of *"Country Life"* magazine, hoping to look as though he had been waiting hours for her.

More than fifteen minutes and a dog-eared article on cultivating edible ornamentals later, his "always punctual" hostess still hadn't shown herself. Had begun to make him wonder if she had forgotten—

Slam! And another slam! The Hall had been so quiet that the sounds echoing in the service corridor behind the hearth brought him to his feet, would have sent him searching for the source, but in the next breath the library door swung open and Josie burst into the room.

"I'm late. I know. Sorry, Gideon. Couldn't be helped." She was drenched to her knees in mud, though the skies had been clear for the past two days. Her jacket and hair were strewn with twigs and leaves, which she was trying to tug free. "I'm afraid I've given you the wrong impression of me."

"Hardly that, Josie." She was breathing hard, eyes flashing in frustration with herself and whatever mischief she'd been making since their idyll in Balesboro Wood. "No need to apologize. We live in disorderly times. I was late myself. And you should stand over here, closer to the fire."

She slipped in front of the hearth and sighed. "But at least you're presentable."

He'd been as bedraggled as she an hour before, but she didn't need to know that detail of his work. "You look more than presentable, Josie, but if you'd like to adjourn until tomorrow night at half-ten—"

"I'll stay. And I'll be here tomorrow night on time, I promise." She threw off her coat and turned her back to the fire. "Because I won't have spent the last two hours leading the WVS meeting in the village. Seventeen women, and as many opinions about what to do with the new group of evacuee children we've been told to expect at the end of next week. Like herding badgers."

"The children?"

"No. The women, not the children. So far the evacuees have been generally delightful, once they adjust to life in the country." She combed her fingers through her hair, the image of an untamed creature from the forest. "That said, I'm deeply proud of each member of our group, for their willingness to sacrifice their time and treasure to help win this horrid war. Hitler and his commanders discount their contributions at great peril." She shot him a challenge. "That goes double for our side as well, Gideon. 'The WVS never says No', as you've probably heard."

"Countless times, from my own mother." And his three sisters. A rallying cry that accompanied their rationale for taking on wartime roles that only a man should be assigned.

"Is your mother a member of her local WVS?"

"President."

"I thought as much. Has she taken in evacuees?"

"No children, but the last I heard from my sister, Mother had turned the Dower House into a way-station for older women displaced by the bombing in Maidstone."

"Your mother and I have a lot in common, Gideon."

Wise, iron-willed, compassionate to a fault; yes, more in common than he cared to admit. "Plainly."

"Yes, plainly," said as though she were holding back a question that she was too shy to ask–this woman without a shy bone in her body. "Well, then, Gideon, what are your plans for tomorrow? Anything I should be warned about in advance of your men setting off explosions in the paddock?"

Bloody hell, had the woman been spying on them at the ice house? "Explosions?"

She laughed and caught back her hair in a bundle. "Only that school starts tomorrow morning for the children and I prefer they not be distracted by military maneuvers in the middle of the lake."

Josie Stirling was a crack shot at hitting the truth. "I've no plans to blow up anything in particular. And you?"

"Just more of the same. Winning the war against tyranny." She picked up her jacket by the collar and grinned.

The air was warm now, the fire crackling. She was standing not two feet from him, mouth damp, cheeks pink, her eyes raised to his and glistening. Every ounce of blood in his body raced toward his groin, urging him to finish the embrace they had begun that afternoon in the woods.

Oh, but that wouldn't be a very good idea, old boy. Not in the long run. "Well, then," Gideon said, to his great regret, "shall we meet again here tomorrow night?"

She sighed then nodded, smiled wanly. "Yes, of course. Half-ten, on the dot."

Then she was gone, taking the brightly charged air with her, leaving an empty space inside him that he'd never known needed to be filled.

Tomorrow night, half-ten, was the only thought remaining in his head.

Having plenty of work to do before tonight's assignment was finished, Gideon banked the fire, turned out the light and made his way upstairs to his sitting room with its very yellow decor.

Finally he would have a moment to decrypt the message from

Arcturus. He removed the rolled-up piece of paper from the floor safe then, out of habit, positioned himself in his desk chair so he was facing the door should anyone enter as he was decrypting the message. As arranged by the SOE, they were using a simple poem code in these initial messages, simply checking that the drops and signals between them were working.

And Arthur and his knighthood for a space
Were all one will, and through that strength the King
Drew in the petty princedoms under him,
Fought, and in twelve great battles overcame
The heathen hordes, and made a realm and reigned.

Tennyson. Poetic and patriotic. Not the sort of message he had expected from an SOE agent, especially one as highly thought of as Arcturus. Even for a test message. But the finely wrought sentiment spoke to the character of the agent he'd yet to meet but couldn't help admiring. A man of unwavering honor, stalwart, brave, willing to sacrifice his life for his comrades, his country, to willingly face down the fiercest enemy.

Arcturus could be any man who regularly passed through the area: a lorryman or a local officer at the air station, a farmer, a regular soldier posted to the base in Shepton Mallet; anyone at all with a set route along the A37 and an easy exit into Balesborough, a stop that wouldn't seem out of the ordinary to a local or the casual observer.

Not that the identity of Arcturus mattered to him or his mission at the moment.

Once the dead drop communication line was secured and trusted, he and Arcturus would meet in a planned live drop and would then set about establishing a vital link between a half-dozen strategic centers that would go into action in the event of a German invasion.

His knee and back beginning to ache and stiffen from the day's exertions, Gideon stood and stretched as he read through the message from Arcturus one final time, absorbing its words and meter, stowing away his speculation about the identity of the man on the other end of the message before he finally struck a match to its corner and watched it burn to ashes on his teacup saucer.

He read reports until he could no longer hold his eyes open, then spent a restless night on a feather counterpane on the floor instead of in the great buttercup yellow tester bed, in solidarity with his men whose mattresses had yet to be delivered.

Try as he might to shift his thoughts to Arcturus and the work ahead of them, he finally relented and drifted off to sleep with Josie on his mind, slipping lithely through in his dreams.

CHAPTER 7

*T*he next day began for Josie as so many others had since the war began, and seemed to go on forever. Awake before dawn, followed by a dozen tasks that needed her immediate attention, never quite catching up with herself–seeing Gideon only from afar as she and the children were helping Mrs. Higgins chase the chickens into the secure yard for the night.

She shared dinner with Mrs. Tramble and learned all about the first day of school, the many successes (recess and lunch) and where the patient woman could use additional help. Especially if Nimway was adding four more school-aged evacuees.

A few hours later, Josie and Winnie were on their way back to the Hall from the dairy barn with time to spare and plans to prepare for her meeting with Gideon–more than prepare.

A quick bath and time to change into a soft blouse and wool flannel trousers, perhaps to dash on a bit of foundation powder to cover her freckles. Certainly to comb and style her hair into something less like a bird's nest and more like a young woman who appreciated being noticed by a man. Even this particular man, who aggravated and attracted her like both poles of a magnet.

They had nearly reached the kitchen garden when she noticed a pale light shining through the trees, coming from the direction of the schoolhouse in the upper field.

With all the excitement and confusion of the first day of school, Mrs. Tramble must have left a light on and the blackout curtains open. Not wanting to suffer an encounter with the ARP Warden, Josie whistled for Winnie and the dog went loping up the path ahead. By the time Josie arrived, Winnie had bounded inside, the door was gaping open and a blue-white glow was spilling out onto the gravel stoop.

Even before she entered, she knew the light wasn't going to be the golden glow of an incandescent bulb, it was coming from Aunt Freddy's orb.

Oh, damn! Wanting no part of the devilish thing, Josie snatched it off of Mrs. Tramble's desk, wrapped it inside the folds of her jacket and slammed the door behind her and Winnie.

"Let's find a place to hide the thing, girl!"

Winnie took off down the dark slope toward the lake and Josie followed, slipping and sliding all the way to the bankside.

"As good a place as any, for now." Certain she hadn't seen the last of it, Josie gave the orb a wild toss through the darkness, hopefully toward the water, heard a great splash just as she felt her boots slipping out from under her. She wheeled her arms, tried to gain her balance only to have her legs slip out from under her and land on her backside into a cold, mucky patch of reeds.

"Oh, damn, damn, damn!" Mud from head-to-toe and late again for her meeting with Gideon! Still, with any luck, the orb would take the hint and stay put for a while.

Fifteen minutes later, Josie stomped into the library, dripping mud, teeth chattering, startling Gideon, who was lounging in the wingback chair in front of the brightly flickering fire.

"I'm late again. Sorry. Couldn't be helped."

Double damn the man for standing, as though she were a princess and he her subject, for that charming smile and those understanding eyes. "Somehow I was thinking you might need this tonight."

He slipped her jacket off her shoulders and wrapped her in the blanket that had been warming on a footstool in front of the fire.

"How could you possibly know I would fall into the water?" Was he suddenly in league with the orb?

"Was that it?" He laughed, tugged the blanket closer around her shoulders and moved her closer to the fire. "It was raining earlier. I thought you might be cold when you arrived."

"Well. Thank you." She couldn't help snuggling into his warmth, savoring his breath on her cheek as he looked down at her. "How does your tomorrow look?"

He smiled again, took a step back from her. "Certainly less interesting than tonight. And yours?"

"Apart from the usual, your mattresses. They're arriving in the afternoon. Someone will need to sign for the delivery and move them into the upstairs rooms."

"Consider it done. My men and I will be grateful beyond words. Your carpet is soft, but I'm a man of flesh and bone and I'm beginning to creak."

Of course! Gideon had been sleeping on the hard floor. No wonder the girls had seen him limping! She'd be limping too if she couldn't fall into her own comfortable bed every night and sink into an exhausted sleep.

"Ah, then, good!" she said, gathering her jacket from the floor and the blanket more tightly around her shoulders. "Shall we try this again tomorrow night."

"Half-ten?"

"Absolutely."

∾

With the plans for the Operational Base complete and the construction materials in process, Gideon was able to spend the next evening working on his training notes for the Auxiliary Units and composing another reply to Arcturus' most recent communique, the second exchange. A test of their codes, public news of the war in Africa, equipment requirements for the Aux Units. Soon he would request the roster of names so he could start building the unit.

He'd seen Josie only twice today, in the morning, hurrying toward the dairy barn and later with Isaac in the garage with the Fordson. Both distant encounters, but just the sight of her had made him glad all day that he would be seeing her again that night.

He'd arrived a few minutes early, was sitting in the library, absorbed in a book, certain that Josie would be late again.

But as the mantel clock chimed half-ten exactly, the door to the service corridor swung open and Josie ran into the library, her dungarees covered in straw and mud.

"I'm not late this time, Gideon. But I can't stay. Jill is giving birth–"

"Good God, who is Jill? And why aren't you with her!"

"Jill is a lovely young Guernsey and she's about to calve. Let's try to have our meeting again tomorrow night."

"All right. Go."

She reached the door, returned and touched his arm. "Would you care to lend a hand? Since the war has called up every man and woman, I'm always short on help in the loafing shed. Especially at this hour."

It wouldn't be his first calving, only the first spent in the company of the remarkable Josie Stirling.

"Let's not keep the lady waiting."

"Thank you, Gideon!" She grinned broadly, grabbed his hand and ran with him through the darkness all the way to the barn.

～

Gideon was still dazzled by the adventure two days later, still exhausted, still in thrall to a woman who had entered his days and his dreams like a whirlwind.

Her scent of mint one day and fresh lavender the next, her laughter, her bright eyes, her gentle encouragement to the calf and its mother at the birthing, the flush of elation on her cheeks as the cycle of life was made new again. He'd caught himself tearing up and turned away while he composed himself, and cheered along with her when the calf stood and began nursing like a champ.

The days went by quickly in the planning of the OB, and the nights as well. He was sleeping much better now, on the mattress with his knee propped on a pillow, the wound healed enough in his judgement to abandon the dressing altogether.

Their meetings in the library now started on time, but always seemed too short. Tonight he was going to suggest they play a game of cards, or something. Anything to keep her from dashing off to her office and leaving him alone.

Ten-fifteen. He switched off the lamp at his desk, plunging the room into darkness that would have been complete, had it not been for a throbbing glow around the margins of the blackout shades and shutters against the northwest windows.

When he opened the interior shutter and pulled aside the blackout curtain, a helpless dread ran through him. Bristol was aflame on the distant horizon. The pulsating orange glow was doubtless the docks again, the German offensive against English shipping went on nightly. There had been no local air raid siren warning of the action in Bristol, but crews from all over Somerset would be on their way to fight the fires and rescue people from the destruction.

He was about to close the curtain when another glow caught his attention. Much closer by, in the darkened garden that stretched beneath his window to the far hedge. A blueish glow moving like a ghost along the gravel paths. Not the faint amber of a shuttered torch lighting someone's way, more like a ball of moonlight carried through the darkness by a fantastical creature.

Quite fantastical, he realized, as Josie stepped out from under the cover of an arch of lime trees and hurried along the pale gray pathway toward the back of the Hall.

As he watched, the brightness abruptly vanished, seemed to be absorbed by the woman as she tucked it beneath the folds of her coat. The very same device she had dismissed and tried to hide from him that first night in the library.

He'd thought of it often since then. The strong, white ball of pulsing light, embedded inside a milky oval of opalescent glass, encased inside a metal bracket of some sort, with a slightly pointed base that had caused it to roll and wobble across the floor like an American-style football.

It was the base that intrigued him most, the source of the power. An astonishingly new sort of accumulator, obviously developed by the military. But developed where? By whom?

If that was the case, what the devil was Josie doing in possession of such a powerful device?

Rather than waiting for Josie to meet him in the library, he went down the backstairs to the darkened utility room just outside the farm office, where he paused in front of the closed door. He raised his fist to knock at the very moment Josie yanked the door open.

"Gideon, hello!" she said, stepping back and smiling in surprise, the device glowing from somewhere behind her. "Am I late for our meeting? I was hoping to surprise you and be five minutes early!"

"Actually, I'm early." Hopefully, just in time.

"Good, then. Shall we have our meeting here tonight instead of in the library? Then we're both on time."

"Agreed." He followed her into the office, unsure what to expect. Certainly not to find the device sitting openly in a basket of onions on the worktable.

"Can I get you anything? Tea? A sherry?"

"No thank you, Josie," he said, trying to sound nonchalant as he continued, "Oh! I see you found the device from the other night. Where has it been hiding?"

"I don't know—" she shrugged out of her jacket and hung it on a hook by the exterior office door. "Around, I guess."

"Do you mind if I examine it?" Do you mind if I kiss you, was his other thought, his most pressing desire.

She nodded. "Go right ahead, Gideon. Take the damn thing with you if you'd like."

A bold offer, or a feint? No. Not his Josie. "You don't mind?"

"It's not up to me. Here, it's yours." She lifted the device from the basket with both hands, her face lit as though by the brightest moonlight. Its rays streamed through her hair, spilled across the floor onto his own trousers, his shirt, into the center of his chest, nearly blinding him to everything in the room except the woman who was now holding out the orb toward him. "Here you are, Gideon. Take it, please."

His thoughts jumbled by the sight of her and suspecting the power source would somehow extinguish itself should he touch it, he took a wool scarf from the bar of coathooks and bunched it onto the desk blotter. "Could you please set it here?"

"Of course."

He felt her gaze follow him as he bent closely to examine the thing under the tungsten incandescence of the desk lamp. The design surprised him, intricate and obviously crafted by an artisan of rare skill. The milky glass object was held in the fierce grip of a golden eagle's claw, its base made of gold.

"How did you acquire the device, Josie?"

"I didn't 'acquire' it." She sat on her desk chair and dropped one of her wellies onto the floor. "It acquired me."

"What do you mean?" He wanted dearly to look at her, to share this electrifying moment. But danger lurked there in her eyes, hidden and all-consuming.

"It's been in my family for ages—" she dropped the other wellie "–but I'd never seen it myself before that first night in the library. With you."

Another fantastical Nimway myth that had no basis in science, though the memory caused his pulse to race, his senses to rise. The device was exhibiting energy properties completely unfamiliar to him. He was an engineer, deeply familiar with current military technology. A portable power source such as this could only have been created in a secret lab and must be returned immediately.

"Where did you say you found this?"

"In the yew hedge on my way back from checking on the new calf–who is doing very well, by the way."

"Yes. Good." Her smile was soft and lit her eyes, nearly distracting him from the track of his question. "You found this— this object lying in the hedge, where anyone could find it?"

"Not just anyone, Gideon. Me. Or possibly you."

"Me? What are you saying? Who gave this to you?" He pulled her to her feet by her upper arms, brought her close, suddenly terrified by the implication. "Josie, did anyone—a stranger, perhaps—approach you about hiding the device until it could be collected by someone else."

She narrowed her eyes at him. "What do you mean?"

"Josie, there are German agents all over England, looking for people just like you–"

"Like me?"

"Innocent citizens who might inadvertently serve as a conduit for our country's greatest secrets, stolen by our greatest enemies, and used against us."

"Are you calling me an enemy spy, Gideon?"

"God, no." Please no! "Just—"

"Just what? Stupid?" She flattened her hand against the middle of his chest and shoved him away. "A traitor?"

This wasn't going well. "I didn't mean to imply–"

"No. You meant to call me either a traitor or a useful idiot. I am neither. Here." She picked up the device and the scarf and dropped it into his hands. "It's yours, Gideon, take it wherever you like."

"I will. Whatever its story, it cannot remain here." The less she knew, the better for them both. He wound the scarf tightly around the device. "Just know that I am officially taking possession of the device and will deliver it to the proper authorities at first light."

Her smile didn't reach her eyes. "Then good luck with your mission, Gideon."

"It's not a matter of luck, Josie," he said, wanting desperately to believe that she was uninvolved with the device.

"I'm just warning you not be disappointed if you can't find the orb come morning."

He'd reached the door, his hand already on the latch, when he turned back, his heart sinking with dread. "Is that a threat, Josie?"

She sighed, herself again. "On the contrary, Gideon. A simple fact, is all. I can only warn you that the orb is part of the fabric of Nimway Hall. It won't let you remove it from the property—"

He laughed, certain she was taunting him now. "Won't let me?"

She smiled as she stood in the center of the room. "Good night, Gideon. Sleep well."

The woman was as mad as she was beautiful. But that was for another time. Another day.

"Good night, Josie."

∾

"What a beastly little orb! And such a misguided man." Josie could only watch helplessly as Gideon charged out of her office, the tell-tale orb tucked under his arm as though he were disposing of a ticking time bomb.

He was correct about one thing: The orb was powerful, all right, more powerful than any weapon of war. If what she understood about it was to be believed, it was fueled by the most powerful force in the universe. Love. Whether the two parties wanted it or not. Which she didn't. Not now. Not this way.

But she and Gideon seemed to be a captive audience for the pesky thing. It had performed its magic tricks with a playfulness Aunt Freddy had never mentioned. Showing off with all the shameless melodrama of a primadonna. Appearing and disappearing at will, tantalizing them, making her laugh, him growl in frustration.

All she had ever known about the arbitrary thing was what Aunt Freddy had said with a nod and a smile, "your time will come, my sweet girl. You'll understand then."

Now she understood only too well. As she switched off the light beside the bed and burrowed beneath the bedclothes, she remembered her own father's amusement over tales of the orb. He'd never said why he thought it so amusing, only that he seemed quite proud that her mother had found him without having to resort to the "mad orb business." Might be good to ask him about it in the morning, maybe even let him know that the dreadful thing had begun targeting her and Gideon.

As she dropped off to sleep, Josie knew with the certainty of a psychic that she would be awakened at first light by angry knocking on her bedroom door. And the accusing glare of Gideon Fletcher when he discovered she had been right after all.

⁓

Josie's alarm clanked her awake at five o'clock, well before first light, with no Gideon in sight. She dressed in her dungarees and cardigan and hurried up the backstairs to help Mrs. Tramble rouse the children for their morning lessons, then herded them down the stairs to the kitchen.

"Mr. Tramble and I were never blessed with children of our

own," the older woman was saying as she cut thick slices from a loaf of Mrs. Lamb's bread.

"You certainly have your fill of children at the moment," Josie said, putting a pot of brambleberry jam on the work table, "with four more on the way."

"Quadruplets!" Mrs. Tramble laughed and her gray hair came loose of the paisley scarf she'd begun wearing after arriving at the Hall. She leaned toward Josie and whispered, "Don't tell the children, but I'm rather enjoying taking care of them at night as well as during the school day. I've learned so much about each of them, more that I ever did when I just saw them in class."

As Josie helped with breakfast in the kitchen, she watched the back court window for signs of first light and the kitchen doorway for sign of a very angry Colonel Fletcher.

He arrived on schedule, just after dawn, as the children were stuffing themselves with thick slices of bread laden with globs of farmer's cheese and dolloped with jam.

Mrs. Tramble tapped her plate with her knife and trilled to her brood hunkered around the table, "Say good morning to Colonel Fletcher, children."

"Gooood morrrrning, Colonel Fletcher." Their voices rose as each child tried to out shout the other.

He didn't notice. Clearly Gideon was seething, his gaze hot and fixed solely on Josie herself as she poured Geordie a cup of milk.

"Can I help you, sir?"

"I will speak with you, Miss Stirling. Now."

"About—" she asked as she returned the pitcher to the large refrigerator built into the wall.

"Please, Miss Stirling." Gideon looked very like the enormous grizzly she remembered encountering on the camping trek she'd taken with her parents through the Canadian wilderness. The beast had stalked through their campsite early one morning as they lay quietly in their tent praying they wouldn't become breakfast.

"The man wants you, Miss Josie," Mrs. Tramble said, with a wry smile, her plump cheeks bunched beneath her gold-wire spectacles.

"And I know the reason why," Josie said under her breath, untying her apron and wiping her hands on it as she tried to think of the best place to contain the conversation that was sure to follow. "Shall we step into the east parlor, Colonel Fletcher?"

"No, Miss Stirling, you'll come with me."

Gideon led her up the backstairs, through the common area shared by his men and motioned her into his sitting room. She entered like a prisoner to the dock, about to testify against her own best interests, and stood in the center of the yellow floral rug.

"Where is it, Josie, the power device?"

You obviously didn't take my warning about the orb to heart, was what she wanted to say, but it wasn't wise to taunt the beast, though he deserved so much worse for calling her a traitor. As though she were stupid or vain or would intentionally commit treason and betray her country to anyone. What would he think if he knew that the very opposite was true? Given his low opinion of a woman's value to the war effort, not much at all.

She said none of this, only asked, "Where did you last see it?" As though he were a boy who'd misplaced his favorite cricket bat.

"I think you know." He was close enough for her to marvel over the muscle that flexed in his cheek, his skin bronze and clean-shaven this dawn to within an inch of his life, the scent of bay rum wreathing her senses.

"Why don't you remind me, Gideon."

"It was in my safe, issued to me by the SOE, requiring my private combination to unlock it. How did you manage to sneak into my room, without waking me, and open my safe?"

"I didn't."

"Someone did. You or your confederate—"

"–or a phantom enemy agent, Gideon? I have no confederate. But I can guess why the orb left your safe after you locked it in."

"You can guess?" He stepped to the window, dragged his fingers though his hair, then turned back to her. "Damn it, Josie, do you understand what you're risking?"

Most assuredly, Gideon: Embarrassment. Disbelief. Rejection. The truth would hardly set either of them free. It would surely bind them forever–whether they agreed or not.

The man would scoff at the idea of a mystical matchmaker that glowed in the presence of true love's potential. And that the diabolical object seemed to have identified a romantic coupling between them.

If Gideon believed her at all about the Orb of True Love, he'd laugh and run as far from her as he could. Which would make her heart ache more than a little, but…that might be the best thing in the end.

"Whatever you think of me, Gideon, you've got the wrong end of the stick."

"I've got evidence, Josie!" He pointed at the small floor safe tucked between his desk and a file drawer as though it meant something to her. He leaned down and blocked her view of him working the combination, finally standing and throwing a glare at her as he swung the door open. "Do you see what I mean?"

"Oh!" Admittedly she was surprised to see the orb sitting inside the safe, plain as day, glowing from beneath the same scarf as before. It seemed to have spent the night just where Fletcher put it. Was that a good omen or a bad?

"I do see the orb, Gideon, just where you say you left it. But I don't know what you want me to say about it."

He blinked at her, frowned more deeply than she'd ever seen, looked at the safe, then back at her. "Bloody hell, how did you do that? One of your father's theatrical effects?"

"His what?"

He stared at the safe, checked behind it, gave the side a knock with his boot then frowned at her again. "Dammit all, Josie, the bloody device wasn't here this morning when I went to fetch it."

Of course, it wasn't. She'd warned him. "Perhaps you overlooked it." She bent down and peered inside. "It's rather dark back there, beyond the glow."

"I didn't miss it. It wasn't there when I opened the safe. I don't know why. I don't know how you managed to snatch it from inside this SOE-issued combination safe. But I don't have time to investigate." He grabbed the orb out of the safe, shut the door and spun the lock.

"Where are you taking it?" she asked as he wrapped the orb more securely in the scarf, then settled it into a metal utility box and latched the lid down tightly.

"I've already been in contact with the new air station at Yeovilton. Didn't mention the device, of course; something as critical as this is to the war effort shouldn't be spoken of over an unsecured telephone line. But the commander there is a colleague of mine and is expecting me this morning. Whether you approve or not."

He stared at her, seemed to be waiting for her response. "I have no opinion in the matter. You do as you please. And so will the orb. But remember, I've warned you, Gideon."

Another frown and a sharp exhale that sounded of misery. "Bloody hell, Josie, it pains me to the quick to think of the trouble you may have brought upon yourself and Nimway Hall."

"Don't worry about me, Gideon. Just be safe in your journey. And hurry back in time for our meeting."

"Yes, well, thank you." He straightened his shoulders, tucked the box under one arm and his hat under the other. "Now, if you'll excuse me, I'm already late for my appointment."

Josie followed Gideon out of his sitting room and watched him hurry down the main stairs into the great hall with a firm step that bore no hint of a limp. He carried no cane, was too busy with his hat and the box. Indeed, Gideon seemed fit and able-bodied, quite the finest specimen of a man she'd seen lately. Ever, really.

Yet, as stubborn and obtuse as they came. Quite certain the orb wouldn't allow him to take it off the grounds, Josie followed him down the stairs, through the marble entry and out onto the porch. She watched him drive away in the Austin, caught his scowl as he turned down the drive, wondering when 'it' would happen. When Auntie's Orb of True Love would decide it was time to return to Nimway Hall.

She was just as certain that when he discovered it missing, he wouldn't be pleased. But maybe then he'd finally be ready to hear the truth.

Question was: Would she be ready for him—this very bewitching man—to hear it?

CHAPTER 8

"*M*orning Colonel. Will you be away long?" Sapper Mullins peered into the Austin, curiosity and an indelible memory among the young man's most valuable assets.

"I'm not sure, Sapper." Gideon glanced down at the metal box in the seat beside him, suspicion making him finger the latch to confirm that it was fastened tightly. "I should be back by supper. I'll send word if I'm staying overnight. Carry on, Mullins."

Gideon returned the young man's eager salute and sped off down the drive, wondering how the devil he would explain to Todd how and where he acquired the device. And possibly from whom, if the worst happened.

He could hear his old school chum now: "You're mad, Gideon."

Because this old school chum was Colonel Todd Nichols, the SOE liaison officer at the Royal Naval Air Station at Yeovilton, recipient of an OBE at the ripe old age of thirty-one for his essential contribution to the Royal Signals, brilliant engineer, holder of a dozen top-secret military patents, a man who had never spent a moment in combat, but who'd risen in the ranks because of his legendary intellect.

Remember, I've warned you, Gideon.

Josie's confounding warning circled around inside Gideon's head like a tune he couldn't shake. A tune that stopped him at the bottom of the drive, just before entering the lane that would send him toward Yeovilton.

Just in case," he heard himself say as he unlatched and opened the lid of the box, satisfied to see the shape of the device still wrapped inside the scarf. Just to be sure, he cupped his hand around the object, felt the now-familiar warmth, the sensual roundness that fit his palm as he had imagined Josie's breast would fit. Perfectly, though this 'orb' was firm and unyielding and she would surely be soft and pliable and sweet—

"Oh, bloody hell!" He slammed and latched the lid, shoved the Austin into gear and swung into the lane, then onto Balesborough's High Street.

He slowed long enough as he passed St. Æthelgar's church to notice that Arcturus had left another chalked signal mark on the lych gate. Their drop system was working perfectly. But no time to retrieve it now, tonight would be soon and safe enough, after his top-secret errand. By then, he'd know better what he must do about Josie and her suspicious involvement with the device, a fear for her that flipped his stomach and made him question his own loyalty to King and Country.

He bounced along the rugged lanes toward the main roadway, slowing down to pass three horse-drawn wagons and wait for a tractor to sputter across the road into a field. The traffic along the A37 was far more busy as the sky began to lighten, with delivery vans in both directions and military and construction vehicles restricting his progress as he approached the security gate into the air station.

Even with his name noted on the list, one of the guards called ahead to confirm his appointment while the other stared across him to the box on the seat beside him. Had Gideon not been sporting the pips of a Lt. Colonel on his shoulder tabs, the sergeant would undoubtedly have insisted that he open it.

"You're through then, sir." The guard cradled the receiver and stepped toward the Austin, handing him a slip of paper with a time, a date and a location. "Colonel Nichols is expecting you. Building C is just beyond—"

"Thank you, gentlemen." Gideon returned their salutes then drove past a long row of administration bungalows that looked brand new, as did every structure he passed.

A year ago the air station had been a series of badly-drained fields. Now it was a hive of activity. A single working runway, with more under construction, a half-dozen hangars, support buildings, as many civilian workers as uniformed military personnel.

He found Todd waiting for him on the steps of Bungalow C, a round-topped corrugated metal Nissen hut sitting on a wooden platform.

"Welcome, Gideon!" He hurried down the steps and met Gideon as he emerged from the Austin, offered a forearm hand-shake, then pulled him into a backslapping embrace before setting him at arm's length. "Been too long!"

"Nearly two years, Todd. That bachelor's party for Carson at the In and Out Club." Gideon grinned at the memory. Old friends. Then remembered: two gone now, sacrificed to the war.

"I had a headache for a week."

"Lots of water under the bridge since then."

"Is that why you look like hell, old man? Not sleeping? A woman's to blame, I'll wager."

"Not quite. But I'll let you be the judge after you see what I've brought you." Gideon reached into the car and retrieved the metal box from the passenger seat, relieved and not a little surprised that it was as hefty now, as it had been when he'd set it beside him ""

"Well, now there's a mystery! You sounded like a spy on the phone last night. Bring it inside, we'll take a look."

Todd hurried up the stairs and Gideon followed too quickly,

took a wrong step in the gravel and twisted his knee hard enough to sting his nose. Damn it all! In his rush to leave Nimway Hall he'd forgotten his cane. But he carried on after Todd, more slowly, favoring his leg, limping slightly.

"Bad luck, that leg, Gid," Todd said as he held the door open. "Still, it's not the end of the world. You're a crack engineer, best in my experience. SOE's got you right where they want you, safely behind enemy lines where you can do the most good."

Gideon flushed beneath his collar and hid his embarrassment behind a laugh as he entered. "You know me, Todd, I much prefer muddy ditches and bullets flying over my head than being stuck behind a desk, or, God-help me, training old men in the art of trade craft."

The last of his words stuck suddenly, firmly in his throat. Bunged up by long forgotten knowledge that Colonel Todd Nichols had never been on a battlefield, not out of choice, but because he wasn't able to hold a gun properly. A childhood accident that had broken his arm and partially paralyzed the thumb and index finger of his right hand. And yet the man out ranked him. Out honored him, ten-fold.

"You'll be back in the hedgerows dodging bullets and catching Nazi spies with your bare hands in no time, Gid. For now, we're both rowing the same boat, doing our duty behind the front lines. Come, show me what you've got there. I'm all agog!"

Todd led him toward the rear of the large hut, to a windowless room across the back, flicked on the harsh overhead lamps, then rapped on the metal wall with a knuckle. "Welcome to my office and workshop. Hotter than Hades in the summer and I'm thinking I'll be freezing my balls off come winter. Frankly, not much different from my quarters in the officers' barracks. Where are you billeted?"

"Posted to Nimway Hall about ten miles north, and quartered there. The estate is vast, the Hall is a bit smaller than High Starrow, but every inch as well-appointed." Gideon laughed at himself as he set the box on the worktable. "I hate to admit it, but I've a suite of my own in the west wing and my headquarters is in the apparently legendary conservatory."

"Tough quarters. But then we all eat from the same rations, don't we? Side by side, the high and the low. It's a funny old war, makes for strange bedfellows."

"The exact words of my hostess."

"You're *bedfellows*, are you? Good work, old man! She's a looker then?"

"Not bedfellows." But more beautiful than Todd could possibly imagine. "Let's just say that the woman presents a constant challenge. Speaking of beautiful, how is your wife? I haven't seen Corrine since your wedding."

"Still in Oxford for the time being." Todd poured hot water from a kettle into a teapot. "Our wee Clark is two now and we've another on the way, none of which kept my brave girl from jumping feet first into the Women's Volunteer Service the moment the war began. I miss her madly. Would love to have my family living nearby, but there's nothing more scarce in the English countryside these days than lodging."

"I can testify to that. But that's not the reason I'm here."

"Yes, yes! Your mystery box." Todd joined him at the table. "Some sort of map case? A stash of cigars, maybe? I do miss our college smokers, Gid. A half-dozen great young minds gathered round the fire of an evening, discussing science, philosophy—"

"—and women, mostly, if I remember right. And there you were, Todd, at the same time, developing your inventor's skill. I've followed your successes with immense pride and admiration. Which is the reason I came to you."

"With your box." Todd leaned on his elbows and peered at the utility box as though it were a Christmas pudding. "Don't keep me waiting! Open it!"

"First, a bit of background. Uhm—" Gideon stared at the box, unable to decide where to begin. "I was posted to Nimway with a staff of four officers and five sappers. My orders are to site and build an OB and then recruit and train the Auxiliary Units who will man them—"

"In case of a German invasion. I've done the same with a Base here in Yeovilton."

"Simple enough work. Proceeding on time. And then—" no need yet to bring Josie into it "—this device appeared."

"Appeared from where?"

"I don't know exactly. It showed up twice, a week ago and then again last night."

"Showed up? Where was it between times?"

"Good question."

"You keep using the term 'it', Gid. Don't you know what it is?"

"It's a power device, I think."

"What sort of power device?"

"That's what I hope you can tell me. It's a light source of some sort, nothing like I've ever seen before. Glows the color of the moon, pulses on its own with no sign of an accumulator or power storage. Whatever it is, I believe it has vast military possibilities as a weapon of war."

"Good God, Gideon!" Todd laughed, then sobered. "You're serious. How does it work?"

"No idea. But if it's as powerful as I think it is, I'm certain it was stolen from a secret military research lab. Ours or theirs, I'm not certain which."

"Damn you say!"

"And if anyone can tell me what it is, where it came from, and how to return it to the right place, it's you."

"You've caught me, Gid." Todd moved in beside him. "Let's see this marvel of modern warfare."

"Don't let its outward design throw you. For whatever reason, to disguise its purpose or perhaps to provide insulation, the inventor chose to house the light inside a—" he was going to sound as mad as a March hare "—a solid gold eagle's talon."

"He what?" Todd laughed.

"See for yourself." Gideon carefully lifted the toggle latch, then the lid, and let it fall back against its hinges.

Gone. Bloody hell! Nothing left but the scarf he'd wrapped it in, lying neatly folded at the bottom.

"Is it under this?" Todd lifted the scarf out of the box, leaving them both staring into a completely empty, army-green utility box.

"Hell and damnation."

Todd cast him a wry smile. "Did you run off and forget to bring your infernal device?"

Remember, I've warned you, Gideon.

He'd damn well left Nimway Hall with it. And unless he'd been waylaid by Nazi spies and administered a memory erasing drug, he'd had the box in his sight the entire journey, from his own floor safe into Todd's office.

You do as you please. And so will the orb.

"Apologies, Todd. Seems I've been bamboozled." Or enchanted. Or gone stark raving round the bend.

"You, Gideon? You were always the sharpest knife in the drawer when it came exposing plots and conspiracies, designing stratagems and infernal devices. No one can get past you."

No one but Josie Stirling. "Except that I did drive all the way here with an empty box and an implausible story to tell you about an invisible apparatus that I thought might save the world."

Todd nodded, clapped Gideon on the shoulder. "If you say this thing exists, this power device, then I believe you. And I trust that you'll track down the culprit and straighten out the matter when you return to your lady at Nimway Hall."

"She's not my lady." Could never be, for more reasons than he dared count.

"So you say, my friend. But I say we ought to head over to the officers' dining hall and catch up over a plate of eggs and toast. I'll bring along a pot of brambleberry jam made by the ladies of my Corrine's WI and we can make short work of it."

"Why not, Todd? I'm starving." Chagrined. Staggered. And he damn well wasn't looking forward to returning to the Hall, to confronting Josie about...about *what*, exactly? After all, she'd warned him that the device—the orb—would do exactly as it pleased. And it did. What the devil would he say to her? What could he, after accusing her of being a traitor? Good God, what a bloody pile he'd made of it. But at least he'd kept her name out of the matter.

He spent a surprisingly pleasant hour with his old friend, relaxing for the first time in years, laughing over their shared past and care-free college days, old friends, catching up with the present and even imagining what they each might contribute to ending the war sooner rather than later.

"Point of fact, Gideon," Todd said through the open window of the Austin, "We could use a man with an artful mind and engineering skills like yours here at Yeovilton. You know yourself that there's more to the SOE than foreign agents and digging holes for the bulldog's secret army to hide in. Think on it. Seriously."

Gideon did just that, thought about many things on his way back to Nimway Hall. Dismissed the notion of spending his days in a research lab when he was determined to return to combat as soon as he was able.

Thought about the nature of the peculiar device that had entranced him with its illusions and sent him on a fool's errand.

But he thought longest and hardest about what he was going to say to Josie. And how to apologize without sounding as though he could ever possibly imagine she was anything but a woman to be admired for her intelligence, her strength of character and her devotion to the same cause that had driven him to be a soldier.

～

Josie had watched Gideon speed down the drive in the Austin until it was out of sight, then spent what would have been a thoroughly ordinary day, doing the same work as every other day since the war began.

The only difference was that today she found herself listening for his return, no matter where she was on the estate, or what she was doing. While walking the field furrows with the Land Girls, sitting in on the children's reading lesson in the schoolhouse, helping Isaac grind a set of disk harrow blades, even while eating lunch in the kitchen with the household staff.

Not that she was keeping track, but by mid-afternoon, Gideon had been gone nearly six hours. He'd only gone to the air station in Yeovilton, barely ten miles distant. What could he have been doing all this time?

He was a proud and accomplished man, quite determined in his love of country to deliver the orb to the 'proper authorities.' Hopefully he hadn't taken a plane to London without first opening the box. How embarrassing he'd be to discover the orb missing, in front of his superiors. At least, she assumed that it hadn't traveled with him. The annoying thing was probably in the Hall somewhere, waiting to pounce on them the next time they were together in the same room. Which she hoped would be sometime today.

She was just walking back up the escarpment from the cider mill at mid-afternoon when she heard the children calling her name then saw them running toward her from the lake.

"Miss Josie! Look what we found!" Streaming out behind Molly was a large white cloud of fabric and strings. The boys flanked her, their legs wheeling as fast as hers.

"What have you got there?" She knew the answer even as she caught them in her arms before they could plummet down the slope and the billow of silk enfolded them all.

"A parachute!" They all shouted at once from inside their

cocoon. Excited little faces and wide smiles, busy, berry-stained hands batting at the silk.

"I see it's a parachute," she said from inside the tent that had settled over them. "Where'd you find it?"

"Can we keep it?" Lucas asked, making a hood of the silk.

"Let's make a fort with it!" Robbie shouted and jumped as he always did when the least bit excited.

"Let's first find out where it came from," Josie said, making a grab for the fluid fabric and the strings and plucking it off the children, finally gathering the bundle against her chest and pulling the silk off her own head. Her hair crackled and snapped with static electricity, wrapping her head in a web of curling strands that clung to her face.

"Helloooo, Mr. Colonel, sir!" the children bellowed as they gathered around her.

Oh, damn. Josie swept the hair out of her eyes and found Gideon standing not ten feet away, watching, his eyes bright with humor and some other emotion she couldn't name.

"Good afternoon, Colonel Fletcher," she said as she dropped the parachute on the ground in front of her and raked her fingers through her hair, attempting to tame it while the man stood silently watching. "We didn't hear you come up."

"Look what we found, Mr. Colonel!" Geordie said, gathering the bundle of silk that was nearly bigger than he and stumbling toward the man.

"A parachute," Gideon said, a worried frown gathering on his brow as he knelt and caught the boy before he could fall. "Where'd you get this, Geordie?"

The children converged on Gideon with their stories: "Up there! Molly found it! It was caught in a tree!"

Gideon took up a fistful of the silk, looked closely then raised his eyes to Josie, as he asked the girl, "Which tree was that, Molly?"

"Up by the fort!" The girl looked pleased with herself beyond containment.

"Windmill Hill," Josie said to Gideon, suddenly concerned by his serious study of the lines and the sturdy metal hardware.

"One set of suspension lines ending in a payload ring," he said. "Rigged for equipment, not personnel. If I'm not mistaken—" he stood, closed the distance to Josie and whispered softly against her ear "—a gift from our foes across the Channel."

"German?" she whispered back, "What's a German parachute doing on Nimway property?"

"Indeed." He turned to the children, standing close enough to Josie for her to feel his heat, to notice the muscle working in his jaw. "Did you find anything else near the 'chute, Molly?"

"We didn't look. I pulled it off the tree branch and then the boys took off running down here with it. I followed and then we brought it to Miss Josie."

"That was probably for the best, Molly," Gideon said, as he tucked the bundled parachute under the skirt of a sapling yew tree. "Can you lead us back to where you found it?"

"Oh, yes!" The children started running up the escarpment.

"Stay with us, please!" Gideon shouted after them. "We don't want to get separated." To Josie he said, "That 'chute had a payload of some kind."

"Pre-invasion supplies, do you think? Radios and maps, contact names, pound coins."

He cast her a look of approval—or suspicion, she couldn't tell which—as they caught up with the children on the hillside. "A pre-invasion drop. Yes, I do think that, Josie. Hopefully nothing more worrisome than that."

Dear God. Explosives. Booby traps.

"Then we can't allow the children to reach the site before we do." Suddenly terrified, she ran ahead and caught them back as they entered the wood. "Come, children, we'll pretend we're scouting for enemy agents. Behind me, please, single-file, like soldiers. That's it. Quiet now."

She glanced back at Gideon as he fell into line behind them.

He tipped her a smiling salute with a finger to his forehead and her heart swelled like a foolish girl's at her first dance.

Something was definitely wrong with him. Or right with him. He was so...not angry, when she was certain he would have been raging when he returned. After all, he couldn't have gotten very far down the road with the orb. Must have been livid to discover it was gone. Just as she had warned.

But why was he so calm, so amicable? So broad shouldered and handsome, so...bloody attractive as he scooped little Geordie off the trail when the boy stumbled, then set him back on his feet with a quiet word that made the boy giggle and catch up with Lucas.

Good thing she knew Balesboro Wood blindfolded or she'd have been stumbling up the trail and running into trees for all the attention she was paying to anything but the man bringing up the rear of their little squad.

"There it is! " Robbie shouted, would have run ahead, if Josie hadn't caught him around the waist.

"Wait, Robbie!" Josie stopped the rest of the group as they neared the ruined foundations of the old windmill. "Is this the place, Molly?"

"The parachute was hanging on that tree," Molly said, pointing to a single birch standing free on the margins of a small clearing. "On a branch I had to break so I could get it down."

"All right. Everyone stay here with me." She met Gideon's gaze and nodded. "Colonel Fletcher is going to go see if he can find anything else."

The children clung to Josie as they all watched Gideon search the area in such a methodical way that she knew he'd done it many times before. Perhaps he wasn't just a Royal Engineer. Of course he must have had some training and experience in the Royal Marines.

"All clear," he said finally, standing over something in the thick understory, just a few yards from the base of the tree. "Come see what I found."

The children dove into the thicket with him.

"It's a suitcase, Miss Josie!" Molly said with a squeal, "a metal suitcase!"

Gideon caught Josie's attention as she ducked through the bank of ferns, nodded at the object. "Just as we assumed," he said quietly, "a pre-invasion kit. I'll send a team of sappers to pick it up here and see that it gets to my contacts in London."

"It feels just like an invasion in itself, Gideon," she said, tears welling in her eyes as she dropped to her knees and opened the lid to the carefully packed and secured contents. A radio transmitter, a very old Baedeker map of Somerset, English pound coins, a notebook and pencil—everything an invader might need for comfort when he arrived. "Sobering, really. And makes me angry. That our enemy could be so certain of their victory over our fair land that they send their luggage ahead."

"Can we keep the parachute, Miss Josie?" Lucas asked. "We can play paratroopers and jump out of the trees!"

Gideon laughed. "We'll find out first if the Army wants it, Lucas—"

"—but there'll be no jumping out of trees," Josie said, "ever."

"However, Miss Josie and I are quite proud of all of you for leading us to this very important piece of equipment."

"Important, how, sir?" Geordie asked.

"Can you all keep a secret?" he asked. They nodded, whispering already as they surrounded him as though he were Father Christmas. "Good then, listen up and I will muster you into my secret force of loyal cadets."

"Oh, good," Geordie said, "I like mustard!"

"Then you will like the duty I am assigning to each of you. Very secret and very important." He looked quite animated as began to enthrall the children with his plan. Though where he was going with it, she couldn't imagine. "When you're in the forest or the fields, or anywhere, you must be on the look out for just the sort of enemy drop that you found here. But next time, and every time afterward, I want you to mark where you found it with a kerchief—you carry kerchiefs, don't you?"

"We don't!" Wide-eyed, they all agreed.

"Then I'll issue each of my loyal cadets an official white kerchief that you're to carry always. So that when you find another parachute, a suitcase, or anything at all made of metal, anything that doesn't belong where you found it, you're not to touch it. You're to tie a kerchief to the nearest tree, and all come running to find me. Or Miss Josie. Do you understand?"

Josie did. He was warning the children against UXBs. Nimway was on the Luftwaffe's flight path to Bristol. Their pilots thought nothing of off-loading any bombs they hadn't dropped during their raids, before returning to their bases in Germany. Most exploded upon impact and the damage was immediate. But the unexploded bombs lay in wait for innocent children playing in the forest.

She joined Gideon. "Children, you must swear a sacred oath to Colonel Fletcher that you will do exactly as he orders, just like good soldiers of the King's Army. Do you swear?"

"We do!" Their little faces might be smudged from their play, but their raised hands and their eager nods gave her hope that they understood the gravity of Gideon's warning.

"This is for you, Molly," Josie said, drawing a clean pink floral kerchief from the pocket of her dungarees and handing it to Molly. "We'll start with your brilliant discovery today. Molly, will you please tie this to a tree branch and then let's head down to tea. You all deserve extra jam for your hard work today."

Molly chose a branch and tied the kerchief to the end, grinning from ear to ear when she turned back to them. "Like that, Miss Josie?"

"Just like that!" Josie said, relieved beyond measure that the children would be safer when they were playing. "I think Colonel

Fletcher's men will have no trouble at all finding the metal kit and bringing it back to their headquarters for examination."

"Then it's tea time, sir?" Robbie asked of Gideon, on pins and needles.

"Dismissed!" Gideon said with a sharp salute. "Now, to your tea, troops."

Off they sped, out of sight among the trees in a moment.

Josie closed her eyes, suddenly weary with old responsibilities and a brand new worry. Nimway Hall had always been a given, then came the war with its demands on the farm. Now the children. Until this moment they were just lodgers — dear and sweet and funny, but somehow outside her worry. Now she wondered how the devil she'd be able to let them run free when danger lurked in the very wood she loved and trusted with her life.

"You surprised me, Josie."

She laughed and scrubbed her fingers through her hair. "That I carry a kerchief?"

"That you are not only a trained plane spotter and a civil defense warden, but you just now rattled off the contents of a pre-invasion enemy drop."

"Air Raid Protection printed circulars for every eventuality. All required of me as head of a large estate like Nimway." Better than elaborating on the true extent of her training—he wouldn't approve. "And you, sir, did very well with your new recruits. I confess, I'm surprised." A sudden thought came bursting out of her, "Are you married, Gideon? Do you have children of your own?" A question he'd never really answered.

"Not married—" the faintest dimple appeared at the corner of his mouth when he smiled "—no children. But I'm an uncle, many, many times over. Four nephews and five nieces ranging in age from three months to fifteen years."

"Good grief!" And how odd to be so relieved that he wasn't married. He seemed a solitary man to have such a large family waiting for him at home. "So our houseful here isn't so very unusual for you?"

"Not at all. Nimway Hall and High Starrow are of pair, even in the time of war. You should see the place at Christmas."

The statement landed hard between them, an invitation that would never be offered, let alone accepted. So Josie walked beside and behind and ahead of him in shared silence as they negotiated a large stand of birch before rejoining the main pathway that dropped down toward the lake.

Where she finally found the courage to ask: "Your visit today to the air station—how did it go?" She felt suddenly, oddly shy, her stomach flipping at the intimacy between them, the secret knowledge they shared.

He took a long, long time to say, "We'll talk about that later."

Later? After all his steaming about, raging over the orb. His warning that she was in danger of treason, of stealing military secrets and abetting the enemy. Later! What an enigma Gideon was turning out to be!

"Just now I'd best return to work before my staff thinks I've gone on holiday." He cast her a sideways glance, then gestured for her to take the lead and they continued down the trail toward the Hall.

'Later' turned out to be more days than Josie had imagined. Days filled with chores and responsibilities, nights when Gideon would beg off their meetings that she'd come to adore, then disappear with his staff until long after she had gone to bed.

Three whole days, in fact, without learning what had happened between the colonel and Aunt Freddy's Orb of True Love.

With the coming of autumn, daylight hours were beginning to diminish, the plowing schedules lengthening into the night. Meals at Nimway came and went in a rush, Jenny decided to have her calf during an air raid, and the children were gleefully antici- pating four new evacuees—new friends, they said—making plans to invite them into their company.

Which was the reason that three nights after Gideon had returned from Yeovilton, Josie found herself dashing between the Spitfire Fund Fete committee in the parlor, the Knit for a Knight ladies in the library, and the Christmas Box Committee in the dining room, their donated goods spread out across the table in piles of wool scarves, boxes of sweets, small tins of tea, all to be packed and sent to soldiers posted in far away places.

And no sign of Gideon. The last time she'd seen him was late that afternoon; he and his staff officers were heading down the drive in a canvas-covered military lorry. The third such trip in the past two days. He must have found a site for one of his anti-tank islands.

To top off Josie's responsibilities for the evening, the Balesbor- ough Home Guard was training in the old threshing barn and she'd promised Mr. Peak she would deliver him a supply of pencils and a leather bound notebook for each member.

She finally excused herself to each committee, explaining that she'd be back in a quarter hour, then set out to the barn with the supplies, lighting her way with the shielded electric torch Gideon had given her.

It's dangerous out there at night with your candle lantern, Josie, he'd explained in a note she'd discovered yesterday morning in the middle of her desk. The first time she remembered seeing his handwriting, bold, block letters with a precision that surprised her.

The humpbacked roof of the old barn loomed ahead in the utter darkness, its few, high windows painted black for the dura- tion. The only sign of life was the sound of voices from within. One voice in particular reaching out before she opened the door and let herself through the blackout curtain.

"It's vital to remember, gentlemen—" Gideon was standing in front of a group of men seated on benches at the far end of the barn. He was lit by a single overhead lamp, holding a branch of yew over his face "—that carelessness in the use of camouflage, such as tracks in the earth or even the most subtle movement—" he lowered the branch "—may give away a well concealed position to the enemy. Now, let's all have a go at not being seen."

The men broke into spirited chatter and nods of agreement, a few stood. Mr. Peak, the company captain. Isaac, Mr. Broadfoot, the blacksmith, the vicar. Familiar profiles and silhouettes. One profile in particular. Quite familiar, quite famous in his day, for being the toast of London and the sensation of Europe.

"Father! What are you doing here?" In the middle of a Home Guard training session, she was tempted to add.

"Josie, Bear!" He turned his famous grin on her, waved a hand, his cheeks and forehead smudged with finger-streaks of soot and grime, laurel branches sticking every which way from his brown uniform shirt. "Glad you're here."

"Can you see me here in my twigs, Miss Josie?" the elderly Mr. Short waggled his arms at her.

"I can, Mr. Short, but not very well." Every man in the room looked as though they'd just walked off the stage of a pagan play in the role of the Green Man, equally smudged, equally bristling with greenery.

And at the center of the madness was Lt. Colonel Gideon Fletcher, looking quite pleased with himself, doing a wicked bad job of hiding that know-it-all smile of his.

"Welcome to our camouflage training meeting, Miss Stirling," he said, "I didn't realize you were coming."

"Neither did I."

"You'll be glad to hear that the Balesborough Parish Home Guard, under the command of Mr. Peak here, are a crack bunch of fighters."

"I know that, Colonel," Josie said, trying to keep her outrage tucked under her hat. "May I speak with you? Alone."

"Of course. Gentlemen, continue your camouflage exercise. I'll return in a moment and we'll practice fitting out your puggarees with lichen and moss." He caught Josie by the elbow and led her back to the door. "Now, Josie, how can I help you?"

She grabbed the knot of his tie and brought him close enough to whisper, "You can tell me why you recruited my father for the Home Guard!"

He wrapped his hand around hers and leaned in even closer. "I asked and he agreed, quite readily, I might add."

"Of course, Father agreed to this madness! What man wouldn't love marching around all day with a loaded rifle, playing soldier?"

"Protecting his country, feeling useful. Is that what you think of the Home Guard? That these men are playing at war?"

A swift blow to her argument, her own words stinging like nettles. "My father is a man of arts and refinement—" she caught sight of him tucking another branch under his lapel and groaned in disgust and terror. "He knows nothing at all about guns or warfare."

Gideon straightened, still holding her hand against his chest. "Are you so sure of that?"

"He's my father; he wouldn't know a bullet from a cuff-link. I'll not have you putting him in harm's way—"

"Edward Stirling joined the Home Guard, Josie, not the Expeditionary Forces. He wants to serve."

"Then I'll appoint him to the Parish Invasion Committee."

"You'll appoint me to what, Daughter?" Her father came to stand between her and Gideon, a frown creasing the smear on his brow.

"Father, you can't honestly mean that you want to serve with the Home Guard. "

"Why the devil not?"

"Frankly, Father, this is hard for me to say but—you're too old."

"Ha! I thank you not very much for that, my dear girl. But what nonsense! Just look around. Half the men in this barn are older than I. And, as I've informed the colonel here—" he lifted one of his patented eyebrows toward Gideon "—far, far less experienced at military matters. You'll have to do better than that if you want to keep me in the upstairs nursery." He turned on his heel and made a dramatic retreat, returning to his comrades. "Gentlemen, let me demonstrate for you a trick I remember from the Great War."

"What does he mean by that?" Josie stared after her father, blinked up at Gideon. "What have you been saying to him?"

Again, Gideon smiled away his bloody secrets, his face half in shadow. "Now, Miss Josie, if you've nothing more to add to our meeting then I need to get back to—"

The air raid siren in Balesborough began to wail. A shrill, harrowing sound that chilled her to the marrow, even as it set her heart to racing.

"You know what to do, company," Mr. Peak shouted from their midst, a commander once more, "to your posts."

"Good work tonight, gentlemen," Gideon called over the tumult, pulling Josie backward, out of the stream of men in camouflage who were spilling into the darkness, to the distant but unmistakable rumble of airplane engines.

She caught her father's arm before he could follow. "Where are you off to in this? Tell me, so I can worry."

He cupped her chin in his warm hand, eyes glittering with a passion that she hadn't seen in years. "To guard the bridge on the Brue, Josie Bear. Let's catch up at breakfast, shall we?" With a kiss on her cheek, he was gone into the howling night.

"Do you plan to find shelter, Josie, or take your chances inside this medieval tinderbox?"

"It's Jacobean, and no," she said, dropping the notebooks and bundle of pencils on the table by the door. "I'm warden for the Hall and at this moment I have three minutes to shepherd nearly fifty people into the air raid shelter before the bombers arrive. You're welcome to join the party."

"Wouldn't miss it for the world."

CHAPTER 9

$\mathcal{G}$ideon followed the pale, narrow-beamed bounce of Josie's electric torch as she led him quickly toward the cluster of older outbuildings, through ankle-high grass, along a deer path.

"Two air raids in three days, Gideon," she said, calling back to him as he kept up with her, wincing with every step. "Not Bristol, this time. Too far south."

"Plymouth, from the flight path," Gideon said as Josie swung open the wooden kissing gate and passed through ahead of him.

"Or Exeter. I hope not." She paused long enough in her progress to cover his hand with hers as he swung the gate open, her eyes damp and glinting as she looked up at him. "Isaac lost a brother in the first bombing there, back in early August. A niece and two nephews as well."

"The Luftwaffe's program of terror: randomness designed to provoke fear and panic in the civilian population." He could only hope that the war would end before Britain and the RAF were forced to carry out similar programs.

As they neared the dairy barn, the sound of an approaching

aircraft sent them running. She grabbed hold of Gideon's sleeve and ducked with him under the eave of the loafing shed.

"A Junkers 88," she said, out of breath, flicking off her electric torch and looking up into the coal dark sky. "Listen!"

He was listening, all right, to the thrum of her in his veins, the thump of his heart against his chest. Josie Stirling was becoming the bright spot of his days, the longing of his nights.

"How the devil do you know a Junkers from a Heinkel?" And the mystery of his every waking moment. He'd missed her these last three days. Owed her an explanation.

Her eyes glinted in the darkness as the aircraft passed on to the southwest. "ARP training. Other reasons. But now I need to get to the Hall. Are you coming inside, Gideon?"

"Lead on." Why not? His staff was occupied for the night at the OB, working inside the ice house, turning its natural cave into a remarkably dry and livable headquarters for the Auxiliary Unit.

He dodged along behind the woman in the blinding dark, followed her through the cobbled yard, around to the front of the hall, where she took the steps two at a time before bursting through the front door into the great hall like a fearless champion come to the rescue.

Just in time to find the redoubtable Mrs. Patten standing on the main staircase, shouting into the chaos below her like a stationmaster at rush hour. "Down the backstairs, everyone! The backstairs!"

The children came pouring down the staircase in their bedclothes, carrying their gas mask boxes as they eddied past Mrs. Patten like a school of trout coursing round a stump, Mrs. Tramble in their wake— "Slow down, children, else you'll fall!"

"Follow me, please!" Josie shouted from the doorway in her most imperial voice. "This way! Hurry, but watch for the person in front of you!"

She led the surging group through the library, down the backstairs, and into the cellar. Once the passage was clear, Gideon followed after, then watched from the safety of the landing as Josie moved among the others like a balm.

The expansive cellar was a dimly lighted forest of thick stone pillars and vaulted ceilings that supported all the floors above and now sheltered a small city of people who seemed content to settle into their various constituencies.

Mrs. Tramble shepherded the sleepy children toward the camp beds and blankets tucked away in the farthest corner. The knitters rounded up chairs into an alcove and kept knitting and chatting. The household staff went to work ensuring everyone was comfortable. The Spitfire Fete Committee descended upon a long table and continued charting their program—which was to happen at the end of the week.

Until last night's message at the dead drop, the fete had meant little more to him than an event he hoped to attend with the lady of Nimway Hall. Now the live drop would happen there, at the crowded fete. Arcturus would hand off to him the list of names for the Aux Unit and he could begin recruiting the patrol.

But that was days from now and as easily done as any other live drop.

Tonight he ached to be with Josie, but had lost track of her in the orderly bedlam. He'd avoided her like a coward since his trip to the air station because he'd been trying to formulate an explanation for his unforgivable behavior toward her. Which required him understanding the nature of the orb—which still eluded him.

No excuse. Josie deserved better than—

"Ah, here you are, Gideon." He felt the sudden warmth of her hand as she slipped it into the crook of his arm, the heat of her palm like a brand. "Come with me."

"Gladly." He let her lead him away from the others, down a dark-paneled corridor that took a left turn and eventually opened into an stone-built, dimly lighted alcove with a great, arching oak door set into the longest wall and fitted out with thick iron hinges, and latched with a massive brass lock.

"Where have you brought me, Josie? To your secret lair?"

"You found me out!" She unlocked the latch with a shiny brass skeleton key, pushed the thick door open and gestured into the cool darkness beyond.

The aroma was familiar and pleasant. "A wine cellar."

"Designed by my great-grandfather, Richard, for this unused section of the undercroft." She slipped into the darkness and he hesitated to follow, implausibly suspecting a trap, feeling she might lock them both inside for some nefarious purpose. Not a bad fate.

"Do come join me inside, Gideon." She turned a switch and the room suddenly filled with golden light from the iron chandelier hanging from the timbered rafters. "Or are you afraid?"

"Terrified." And he meant it, felt the world shifting beneath his feet, a charge in the air between them, heady and exquisite. But he stepped inside anyway, felt the room embrace him.

The barrel-vaulted ceiling was made of very old stone and braced with thick timbers. Brick alcoves on either side, each fitted with cross-hatched shelves, laden with wines of all types and vintages. The enormous old cabinet that filled the back wall, its shelves studded with bottles of rare spirits, its drawers and stoneware crocks and glass jars of dried herbs giving it the air of an apothecary.

"This part of the undercroft is very old, Gideon." She switched on a table lamp beside a wooden settle.

"I see that." Fine wines, expensive and rare, as carefully curated as his brother's cellar at High Starrow.

"We're actually not under the Hall at this point. We're beyond the foundation, inside a passage that extends into the hillside, walled off long ago."

Thump! With that, the door slammed shut. Josie had slipped past his notice into the shadows behind him while he'd been listening to her tale and was now standing with her back against the great door, arms crossed, chin jutting, her mouth as pouting and enticing as a plum.

"Welcome to Nimue's Cave."

Trapped like Merlin—what a lucky man he was. "If you're planning to seduce me, Josie, you should know in advance that I'll offer no resistance."

"Neither would I, Gideon, but I'll not have you changing the subject again."

"The subject being what?" All he could think of was her bold declaration that she would offer no resistance to his seduction.

"The subject is the orb. You're not leaving here until you tell me the truth about what happened to the orb. I've not seen it since you absconded with it three days ago. Where is it?"

"No idea. But most concerning to me, Josie is that I don't know *what* it is. Do you?"

She nodded emphatically. "I absolutely do."

"You do?" How could she know for certain, when its physical properties were a confounding mystery to him? "Do you intend to tell me?"

"Only if you're in a proper frame of mind to know the truth. Are you?"

"I'm a soldier, Josie, and an engineer; facts, figures, proof. My stock in trade is the truth. I am nothing without it. I've already made a great fool of myself because I hadn't taken the time to understand how the bloody device works, so I'd appreciate you enlightening me."

"All right, then, Gideon. I'll tell you everything I know about the orb—" she looked up at him with brightly shining eyes, cheeks flushed, her mouth damp and lovely "—the good, the bad and the... unbelievable."

"I've had my fill of unbelievable." Her assertion that the device had been in her family forever. That it operated independently, came and went at will. "I'd be content with the bad."

"Then I think you'd best sit down first, and hear the good." She gestured to a pair of leather-upholstered wooden chairs that faced each other.

The good? Deciding he had no choice, Gideon sat and so did Josie, leaning forward, her elbows propped on her knees.

"You see, Gideon, I first learned of the orb from Aunt Freddy."

"Aunt Freddy?" What a perfect code name for a dangerous foreign agent. If Josie were a part of some espionage ring—which she couldn't possibly be. That sort of deception wasn't in her character.

"My mother's younger sister. Frederika, actually, mother to my cousins. I lived here with her and my Uncle Anthony after my mother died."

"Freddy, is your actual aunt? Where is she?"

"In America. Hollywood, actually, and New York, with my uncle and grandparents, but that's of no moment. As I was telling you, I first learned about the Orb of True Love from my Aunt Freddy—"

"Wait, wait, wait just a minute, Josie. Say that again. The Orb of *What?*"

"I know, I know, Gideon! The Orb of True Love." She shook her head and fell backward into the chair. "It's a stupid name to call such an irritating thing."

"Irritating?" It was far more than that. Whatever its physical properties, it was astonishing on its face. "What did you call the damn thing again?"

"Not me. My Aunt Freddy." She sat forward again. "She called it the Orb of True Love. But, since it's decided to plague you and me, I've renamed it the Stone of Certain Doom."

"Doom?" He leaned forward, his nose just inches from hers. "It's dangerous, you mean?"

"To the unsuspecting. But, I swear, Gideon, that I had no idea the orb was real until that first night when the bloody thing found us in the library."

"Found us?"

"Aunt Freddy use to enthrall me with stories, fairytales, I thought, of how she and Uncle Anthony had encountered the orb in the most inappropriate and embarrassing situations. How it had caused them to fall madly in love with each other when they had rather not."

"Are they happy now?" The question popped out of his mouth on its own, seemed to startle her.

"Why?"

No idea. He shrugged, hoping to hide his own confusion. "Just wondered."

"Well, yes, my aunt and uncle seem more in love than ever—rather unseemly at times considering their advanced ages."

"Is this the 'good?'"

"The what?"

"You said I needed to hear the 'good' before the 'bad,' Josie. So far, we've gotten no further than the 'unbelievable.'"

"Because you keep interrupting my story. Do you remember the night you took the orb back to your room?"

"Distinctly." And every damnable moment that came after. He sat back in the arm chair. "I saw you with it in the garden. That's the reason I came to your office. To catch you with it."

"I assumed as much when I saw you at my door. The orb had been waiting for you to be watching me before it showed itself in the hedge. Knew I would pick it up, knew you were watching me."

"What?" Impossible to follow, let alone believe. "Why would it do that?"

"Because—" she closed her eyes and took a deep breath, held it so long he finally had to ask—

"Because why, Josie?" He could hardly believe that he was falling headlong into her story, falling madly for everything about her.

She opened those lovely, honest green eyes. "Because, according to Aunt Freddy, the orb thinks you and I are supposed to be—" she took another breath, released it in a rush "—together."

"Together, how?"

"Good grief, Gideon. You're a handsome, red-blooded male. Have you no imagination? The orb thinks you and I ought to be romantically involved. With each other." All he could do was stare at the woman, dumbfounded by her madness. "I've no idea how it works, how it chooses its targets. Nor do I care, but for some reason my aunt's Orb of True Love has decided that we should be a couple."

"A couple." He leaned closer, compelled by her scent, the amber lamplight riding the strands of her hair, said softly, "that's absurd, you know."

"Well, of course it's absurd, Gideon. My entire family history is absurd—both sides, if you knew the truth–but especially when it comes to that bloody orb. I was horrified when I saw it in the library and realized what it was. How it had caused the two of us to chase after it 'together' as it rolled around on the floor. Because I knew immediately what it wanted, why it revealed itself. What it's now trying to do to us."

"*To* us?"

"To you and me, Gideon. You see, it has a mind of its own. It's pushy and rude and thinks it knows best—"

"It thinks? Josie, are you mad?" One of them was. Probably himself, because she seemed altogether cool and in control. He, on the other hand, was aroused and aching to take her into his arms. "How do you mean it 'thinks?'"

"It just does. Not like we 'think,' of course. But remember that first day in Balesboro Wood, I told you that Nimue and Merlin were lovers?"

"How could I forget?" The sunlight on her cheeks, the breeze catching strands of her hair.

"What I didn't tell you at the time—because, why would you ever believe it—was that their grand passion was a brilliant, living thing and Nimue cast a spell that embedded their love in the moonstone atop Merlin's staff."

"Nimue cast a love spell?"

"And so, to secure the spell after foiling Lancelot's theft of the staff and his attempt to ensorcel Guinevere—"

"King Arthur's Guinevere?"

"Arthur's wife, of course."

"Of course." Now, he was actually listening to wholesale magical nonsense, watching her lush mouth as she spun her tale for him.

"Merlin then cast a spell of protection so the orb would act only when it sensed a deep and honest need for true love."

A deep and honest need for love. For her. For Josie, who was fingering the buttons on his shirt cuffs, gazing up at him with those enticing green eyes. "Is there more to your story?"

"Only to assure you that none of this is your fault."

"My fault?"

"If anything it's mine. Because Merlin made certain the orb only works when a female descendant of his and Nimue's finds herself in need of, of—" her luminous eyes found his.

"Of true love?"

"Yes."

"And are you?"

"A descendant, yes. According to my family's madness. I've even have the legendary birthmark, a pale oval on my left shoulder."

"But are you in need of true love, Josie?" He was desperately in need of her, the feel of her skin beneath his lips as he searched for this legendary oval.

She blushed and cleared her throat, straightened in her chair. "Not that I've ever noticed. I'm quite happily managing the estate alone. Too busy at the moment for such frivolities as true love, what with the war, and all. Besides, I'm fairly sure that the orb changed its mind about us."

"Why do you say that?" And why did her pronouncement feel like a stab to his heart?

"Because it's disappeared. You've been back from Yeovilton these three days and I haven't seen hide nor tail of the orb in all that time. Not a glow in sight. Not that I care in the least, mind you. Have you seen it since?"

"No, but then I've been very busy."

"I've noticed." She sniffed and crossed her arms over her chest. "Too busy to let me know what happened on your trip to the air station. Did the orb stick with you?"

"No."

"I gave you fair warning—"

"You did, Josie. I even stopped at the bottom of the drive and checked again. It was there in the box, wrapped in the scarf, just as before. So I drove with it to the office of my good friend and colleague—a highly-regarded inventor, where I built up the importance of the device until he was as convinced as I that it would turn the course of the war. Only to open the lid and find nothing but the scarf."

"What did he say?"

"That he believed me." He could laugh now at the memory. "What else would he say to an old friend who'd gone barmy? I drove away embarrassed, empty-handed and at a loss."

"I am sorry, Gideon. I really am. I'm not gloating or boasting that 'I told you so,' because—who in their right mind would ever believe in such a thing as an Orb of True Love that comes and goes at will and only shows itself to Nimway guardians it thinks are in need of—"

"Does the orb ever make a mistake when it chooses a target? Does it ever give up?"

"I don't know. But that's brilliant, Gideon!" She stood, grabbed his hands and tugged him to his feet. "What if we try to stop the orb in its matchmaking tracks by proving to it once and for all that you and I are not in the least compatible? You know it, and I know it, but the orb is hard-headed."

"It is a rock, after all, Josie." She laughed as brightly as he'd ever heard her laugh and it set his pulse afire. "What is your plan?"

"We kiss."

"Sounds simple enough." Dangerous as hell. The deepest yearning of his heart.

"We kiss—" she caught her lower lip with her teeth in a shy smile "—and then, when it turns out that we feel absolutely nothing romantic toward each other—"

"Which we won't—" A question, not a conclusion.

"Then the orb senses our disinterest—"

"And leaves us alone after that?" Another kind of madness, if she could imagine that happening.

"Yes, and returns to Nimue's Cave or wherever it lives when it's not pestering innocent people like us." She caught the front of his shirt, drew him close and whispered, "Do you think it's possible?"

The entire conversation with the enchanting woman had been impossible, from the moment she invited him into the wine cellar to this very moment, from the afternoon she'd first entered his life.

"That's all, Josie? You think a simple kiss will be convincing enough?"

"Gideon Fletcher!" A blush bloomed on her cheeks, a quirky slant to her smile. "Are you suggesting we go further? Because—"

"No, Josie." Not yet. Though his pulse had risen like a storm, thrumming in his chest, flooding his groin with a pulling need for her. "A kiss should suffice."

She leaned forward as though sharing a secret they would keep from the orb. "Should we kiss here and now?"

"Here, Josie—" Gideon threaded his fingers through her hair, cupped the back of her head and drew her close, savored the nearness of her mouth, her quick little breaths against his jaw, the surge of anticipation, touching his lips to her temple, her cheek—

"Does this—oh, that's wonderful, Gideon. Yes, right there. Oh!"

She leaned lightly back into the cradle of his hands, tilted her chin, offering her lips, closed her eyes. "—count as a kiss?"

"Ah, Josie!" Starved for the taste of her, he covered her mouth with his, kissing her fiercely, plunging and plying, drawing a mewling moan from her that set his skin on fire. Next thing he knew, she was wrapping her arms around his neck, pulling him closer with kisses of her own. Hot and wet, touching his face with her soft fingers.

Until his kiss became hers, and he was lifting her into his arms where she fit so deeply and deliciously. Long, lingering moments passed, exploring her, enjoying her taste, her touch, until she was giggling and raining kisses all over his face, and he wanted nothing else in the world but to take her for his own. Forever more.

"Did you hear that, Gideon?" she finally asked against his neck when all he could hear was the pounding of his heart.

Then an annoying thump on the thick door and a voice, "That's the all clear, Miss Josie!"

She pressed her fingers against her secret smile, touched the softness where his lips had just been playing.

"I guess I'm wanted." She spread her fingers across the middle of his chest and stepped backward.

"Clearly, Josie." Wanted like he'd never wanted anything or anyone.

She straightened the collar of her shirt. "Do you think the kiss worked?"

He felt himself smiling like a fool. "It did for me."

"But for the orb? Do you think it sensed disinterest?"

He frowned as though he cared. "I'm not sure."

She caught her lower lip with her teeth. "I'm not sure, either."

"You go, Josie." He winked, couldn't wait to see her again. His very own enchantress with a mythical birthmark that needed exploring. "I'll lock up on my way out."

She pressed the key into his palm, closed it inside his fist and dropped a kiss on his knuckles. "Tomorrow night, in the library?"

"I'll try, Josie. I promise." Though his schedule shifted with the needs of the Operational Base and the other seemingly-senseless draws upon his time.

She got all the way to the door, turned and ran back to claim another kiss, then left Gideon standing in the cellar full of lush scents and very old spirits.

CHAPTER 10

"Tere you are, Miss Josie," Mrs. Peak said the moment Josie entered the parlor where the Knit for a Knight ladies were packing away their work, "we feared you'd gotten lost in the raid."

Thoroughly lost, thoroughly kissed. Good grief, did it show? She could still feel the heat of him, the taste of him. Her cheeks were flushed as though she'd run a mile and she wondered if the women suspected that the reason was Gideon.

"I was just seeing to the stragglers, Mrs. Peak." To hide her blush Josie held out a brown jumper by the shoulders. "It's beautiful! Who knitted this?"

"I did the arms," Vera said, "and Myrna did the body."

"Forty-four jumpers in all," Mrs. Peak said dropping a pile of folded knitwear into a box, "and six dozen scarves."

"My dear ladies," Josie said, looking around at their earnest faces, "I know I don't say it enough, but I'm so very proud of you and all the work you do for the war effort. Our men in uniform will be so grateful come winter to be wearing one of your lovely creations." The jumpers were expertly constructed, every knit and purl made with love toward a complete stranger.

"If it weren't for your gift for talking people out of their donations, Miss Josie," Vera said, shaking a ball of yarn pulled from the woman's own reclaimed cardigan, "we'd not have wool enough to make a single knit cap."

Josie smiled. "Let's keep collecting yarn and knit goods wherever we can beg them. We'll meet here again next week, after the Spitfire Fete. Fingers crossed there's not another air raid!"

It took another hour but Josie finally managed to send the members of the other committees on their way home to the village, and didn't finish meeting with the Land Girls until nearly midnight.

Francie had hinted at having seen her escaping with Gideon to the wine cellar, but Josie brushed off the comment with a patently ridiculous story about taking inventory and accidentally breaking a bottle, and having to clean up, and—

"Oh, la! I'd let the colonel take my inventory any time."

Josie hid her blushing guilt by joining in their laughter and a bit of racy girl-talk, until they were all giddy with scrumpy and began dreaming aloud about Errol Flynn and Cary Grant and Clark Gable.

Three romantic stars of the silver screen that couldn't hold a candle to the man who had just kissed her so deeply. Her brain was still in a tumble over Gideon when she finally dropped into bed, as exhausted by air raids and committee meetings and the endless war work as she was exhilarated by this new peace she had made with him. Still felt his fingers threading through her hair, the warm feel of his mouth on hers.

And then it was morning again. She rose early, bathed quickly, actually primping in front of the mirror before going to breakfast in the dining room, hoping to meet Gideon there, hoping not to meet him. After all, what would they say to each other after a kiss that had been meant to prove to the orb their disinterest in each other when she had felt his unmistakable male hardness against her belly? Had lost herself in his embrace, melted against him when he gathered her into his arms and plundered her mouth, her senses.

What would they speak about when next they saw each other?

Not at lot, as it turned out. There was hardly any time to spare. Their meetings in the library were postponed with cryptic notes from Gideon left on her desk in the afternoon, and always with a promise to meet the following night. But only one of those meetings ever managed to happen.

Not in the library or the wine cellar, but briefly, in the most wildly romantic, impromptu embrace on the backstairs. Gideon catching her up in his arms on his way up, whispering against her ear as he strung his hot kisses along her neck. Releasing her to continue her way down the stairs, only after turning her legs to jelly and leaving her breathless and wanting so much more.

The next few days flew past, with her rushing from one emergency to another, and Gideon as elusive as ever, with deliveries of construction materials arriving nearly every morning and disappearing into the military lorry that afternoon.

The new evacuee children arrived from Bristol, as filthy and disheveled as the first group had been. This time Josie and the household staff made a game out of changing into 'country clothes' after a good scrubbing, followed by a hearty meal with the other children, bread with butter and berry jam, then a hike down to the lake with Godby to feed crusts to the mallards. So far, so good.

She was at her desk in the farm office on the morning of the Spitfire Fete, dividing change among the various tills when she looked up to find Gideon smiling at her from the doorway. He was dressed as she'd seen him of late, in khaki work trousers, sleeves rolled to his elbows, the muscles of his forearms bronze and flexed and fine.

"There you are, Josie," he said, entering the office with a smile that melted her knees. "I've stopped in a few times, but you've been busy the past few days."

"You've been out late, Gideon."

He smiled, his eyes bluer than she remembered. "Too late for our meetings in the library, much to my regret."

She would hear him and the other men come up the stairs well after midnight, heard running bathwater, their low conversations and quiet laughter, and then nothing at all until well after she was gone in the morning. "I take it you're out there constructing your chain of anti-tank islands between here and Taunton."

"Official secrets," he said putting his finger to the side of his nose as he sat on the edge of the desk, close enough to touch. "What have you got there?"

"Tills and ticket rolls for the Spitfire Fete. One each for the game and food stalls, and one for the main donation stall. We're expecting quite a crowd, from all over the county. You're coming, of course?" She'd been hinting at it for the past week. Had come right out and told him that he should at least put in an appearance for the sake of the Home Guard.

He studied her for a long while. "Can't ever be sure what the day will bring, can we?"

"The fete has everything, for everyone! A jumble sale, a fortune teller, a helter skelter ride, a Punch and Judy show, a field full of games, free ice-cream coronets for the kids, a dance band for the adults and a Have-a-Go lane, if you'd care to learn to knit or throw a hand-grenade."

"Turns out, I already know how to do both." His gaze was honest and true, a sure sign that he wasn't jesting.

"Then I might tempt you with the coin-drop. It's a canvas tarp laid on the ground, with the outline of a full-sized Spitfire drawn on it in red."

"Why is that?"

"So people can fill it with coins. Gives everyone a chance to contribute to the fund, no matter their circumstance. Come see for yourself, if you can get away."

"I'll admit to curiosity about how a village as small as Balesborough goes about raising enough money to purchase an entire Spitfire."

"Penny by penny, Gideon, just like most worthwhile things. One step at a time." Though patience had never been Josie's strong suit. "So you must come and see the village in action; you might even be moved to add a penny or two to the outline yourself. Even better, come to the central donation stall and purchase a Spitfire lapel badge from me."

"A badge?"

"We've created a special brass and enamel pin-badge, oval with the figure of a Spitfire in flight across a field of blue. Will you promise to try to attend?"

"I'll try, Josie." His eyes never left hers as he lifted her hand—as sad-looking and work-worn as any farmer's, and brought it to his lips for a kiss that made her heart flail about in her chest, a blush creep up out of her shirt.

She leaned close, then his lips met hers, hungry and heated, his breath brushing her cheek as he kissed the corners of her mouth.

Not the sort of behavior that would convince the orb of their disinterest. He cupped her chin, deepened his kiss. Her pulse rocketed around inside her chest, striking the breath from her.

"I've miss you, Josie," he said against her ear, then mumbled something she didn't understand, that brought her back to her senses.

"The orb, Gideon, have you seen it?"

He kissed her nose, then shook his head slowly, his eyes locked with hers. "Not seen a glow anywhere."

"Neither have I." A good thing, wasn't it? Exactly what they had both wanted. "Do you suppose it's finally given up on us?"

He slipped a strand of hair behind her ear, his fingers gentle and warm. "Would you like that, Josie?"

"I—well, of course. It's for the best, isn't it?" What a silly twit she was becoming! She smiled at him like a fool, found him smiling back and yanked her hand out of his, went back to counting pennies into the three tills, just as a rap sounded at the open office door.

"Busy?"

Her father, wearing a smart British Army dress uniform, from the last war. "Where did you find that? In the Stirling costume shop?" Or had he been digging about in the attics?

"Thought I'd find you here, Josie Bear!" To make a point of some sort, he gave Gideon a capacious wink, then a salute that whiffed of camphor. "Afternoon, Colonel."

"Edward," Gideon said, standing and returning the salute as her father remained at attention. "Quite impressive, sir."

"Brought it with me from Stirling House, though I don't know why. Thought I'd wear it to the fete since I haven't a proper Home Guard uniform." He removed his cap and tucked it under his arm. "Fits me damn well after twenty-odd years in mothballs. But egad, Daughter, surely you're not wearing those dungarees to the fete."

"Some of us are still working, Father." Blushing to her toes as both men appraised the rusticated state of her clothes. She spared a glance at the long case clock in the corner. "It's eleven. I've two hours to finish, dress and be ready to open the fete."

"I'll let you go then, Josie," Gideon said, offering only a nod. "Enjoy the fete, Edward." Her heart sank as he shook hands with her father and left her with only the most enigmatic smile.

"Father, do you remember Aunt Freddy's Orb of True Love?"

"How can I forget? Damn thing nearly drove your Uncle Anthony crazy before he landed the love of his life." He canted his head, like Winnie on the scent. "Why? Has it returned? Have you seen it? Has it fixed its cupid's glow on you and Gideon?"

The man was too sharp by half. "Never mind, Father. Forget I asked."

"Not likely. I quite like that young man. And you do, too."

"Father!"

"No time for a heart-to-heart, my dear. I'm off to meet my comrades in arms before the fete. As you very well know, the

Home Guard is manning the Have-a-Go at Throwing a Mills Bomb stall. A brilliant idea of yours to use conkers still in their burr jackets instead of live grenades." He stepped behind her desk and kissed her on the cheek. "See you there, girl. And, pray God, not in those dungarees."

Grateful to be alone once more, Josie finished the bookwork for the tills, loaded them into the back of Bess and secured them among boxes bristling with Union Jacks on sticks, banners and strings of pennants, along with the estate's donation of six crates of Nimway Scrumpy and four of Nimway's Top-Drawer Honey to add to the WI stall.

An hour later, she had managed to bathe, lingering in the bathroom long enough to wash her hair, smooth over her freckles with a bit of foundation powder and soft pink rouge, brighten her lips with a subtly deep red and, for the first time since the war began, brush her lashes with a dash of mascara.

Last evening's rain shower had threatened to dampen attendance at the fete, but the morning had dawned bright and cloudless, improving by the hour until the early afternoon sun became unseasonably warm enough for Josie to wear one of the dresses Aunt Freddy had brought her from Paris the year before the war.

Cap-sleeved and floral with a sweetheart neckline and matching belt, its skirt draped in swinging gabardine; Josie felt grand and feminine and powerful. She would wear the dress in solidarity with the women of Paris, who were surely suffering untold indignities now that the German forces occupied all of France.

She'd also wear the dress for the two men in her life who had just censured her everyday dungarees, as though she had forgotten how to dress like a lady.

Wear it especially for Gideon, in case he decided to attend the fete. He was a delight to be with and his kiss had sent her to the moon. A journey she longed to take with him again. The orb be damned.

But her mind needed to be occupied elsewhere than Gideon this evening if she was to pull off the fete, as well as her more pressing obligations.

~

It was nearly one o'clock by the time Josie pulled Bess up to the back of the WI stall in the field behind Balesborough's village hall. She unloaded Nimway's honey and cider donations, delivered the flags and banners to the decorations committee and soon the grounds began to flutter with color and excitement. She dropped off the tills to the volunteers covering the three ticket stalls then walked the lanes of food and market vendors, toured the games, watched a test ride on the helter skelter, and double-checked the bandstand schedule.

The fete was spread out across the unused cricket pitch; come February the pitch and the fields around it would be plowed under and planted in sugar beets. But for now the canvas marquees and brightly colored stalls lent a feeling of victory and hope for the war effort.

To guard against becoming a target for bombers, come night-fall, the fete would move into the village hall, where the music would continue and the dancing would begin.

By two o'clock a crowd of nearly a thousand had gathered around the outdoor stage to hear Mayor Wharmsley's opening speech.

"Our own Balesborough Parish Spitfire already has a propeller and a tail! Now let's us dig deep into our pockets tonight and buy our lady a proper body to go with them. To that honorable end, I hereby open this Fete to one and all! Victory!"

Josie took her place alongside Mrs. Peak and her teenage daughter at the main information and donations stall, greeting people as they streamed by, flogging the lovely Spitfire badges and rattling the tin donations box, unable to resist watching all the while for Gideon.

The badges were an easy sell, and she had just returned to the front of the stall to pick up a few more when Mrs. Peak patted her hand and nodded behind Josie.

"Look, Miss Josie, there's the colonel. Isn't he handsome in his dress uniform?" Mrs. Peak was so very wrong; Gideon Fletcher wasn't handsome, he was breathtaking.

And he came! Was walking toward Josie through the shifting crowd, the picture of command, his stride measured and heading straight for her.

Looking at her with unmistakably hungry eyes that made her heart leap and her pulse race even before he took her hand. "Good evening, Josie," he said, just between them. "You look quite beautiful."

"Out of my dungarees, you mean?" Oh, damn, she didn't say that aloud did she?

"In your dungarees or out of them, Josie, you take my breath away." His eyes sparkled blue, his gaze drift downward to the risqué neckline of the dress she'd worn just to entice him.

How the man could continually make her stammer and blush like a faint-hearted schoolgirl was beyond her understanding. Made her wonder if the orb had begun to stalk them again, though they were well away from the grounds of Nimway Hall.

"Yes, well," she finally managed, thoroughly flummoxed, holding tightly to his arm as she led him through the streaming crowd to the counter of the donations stall, recovering enough to say, "We're delighted you decided to attend, Colonel. You'll be an inspiration to the Home Guard when they see you."

"I don't know about that," he said, tucking her hand into the crook of his arm, "but I could hardly pass up your invitation. And my staff and the sappers were quite eager. We walked here from the Hall and the lot headed straight for the carnival games with fists full of tickets."

Mrs. Peak clapped her hands. "Balesborough will be so pleased to see them join in the fun. Your men have been ever so gentle-manly to the village."

"I'm gratified to hear that, Mrs. Peak, I'll note it in my daily report."

Josie gave Gideon's arm a gentle squeeze. "Colonel Fletcher tells me that he would be delighted to purchase a Spitfire badge. Would you please do the honors?"

"I'd be glad to." Mrs. Peak peered over the counter. "How many, Colonel?"

"Just one will do, thank you." He dropped two pound coins into Mrs. Peak's hand and received the badge from her moon-eyed daughter. "I've instructed my officers not to return home tonight without each sporting a badge of their own."

He turned the badge over, examined the pin, then handed it to Josie. "Will you help me? I'm quite bad at this sort of thing."

"My pleasure." Josie managed to keep her fingers from shaking while she pinned the badge to the flap of his left breast pocket, gave it a pat. "There, Colonel, in the traditional place of honor."

Before she could move her hand, he covered it with his own, gazed down at her. "Can you get away for a stroll sometime later?"

"I'd love to, Gideon, but I can't for a while yet." Too much on her plate, too many obligations. "I'm to manage another stall in a few minutes, and another after that—won't be free until after seven when the fete moves indoors. Can you stay until then?"

"I'll do my best, Josie. But if not here at the fete, let's meet tonight in the library."

She knew she was grinning madly. "I can't wait. Oh, and, Gideon, do be sure to walk past the outline of the Spitfire. I expect you'll be amazed!"

"I'll do that. Ladies." He touched his hand over to the brim of his cap, nodded, then strolled off into the crowd, leaving Josie feeling bereft.

"Don't get much more handsome than that man, Miss Josie."

"You have me there, Mrs. Peak." Which made them both giggle like a pair of schoolgirls.

Half an hour later Josie gathered her satchel from behind the donations stall and headed for her next assignment, the very popular Coconut Shy. The elaborate red-and-white striped marquee, was closed on three sides and open for competitors at the front, where they would stand outside the boxed-in area that was enclosed by a low wall on three sides. Inside the stall, a half-dozen large cups had been attached to the top of three-foot tall posts, which were anchored in the grass. Each cup held a coconut.

The crowd seemed a living thing, a magnet for men and boys and even a few girls. Among them, all eight evacuees from Nimway Hall, each more excited than the next. And thankfully, Mrs. Tramble was riding herd.

Lucas was standing at the children's throw-line inside the box, grinding the ball into his palm as he drew a bead on the coconut directly in front of him. He reared back, threw the ball and his shot hit dead on, knocking the coconut off the cup before arching to the side and nearly hitting the one next to it.

"That's three for me!" Lucas shouted. The crowd cheered him and Mr. Tully from Lower Farm presented a ecstatic boy with a six-inch model of a Spitfire. The boy turned and saw Josie, ran to her and showed off his winnings then went "burrrrrrring" off making engine noises, the Spitfire held aloft as he negotiated the crowd and disappeared.

"Thank you for your courage, Mrs. Tramble," Josie said to the woman as she went smiling off after the children. who were now following the new pilot. The last she saw or heard of them for the rest of the fete was the woman's cry of "This way to the ice cream, children!"

Josie checked her wrist watch and decided it was time to take her place at the Coconut Shy beside the other volunteers from the Nimway estate. She slipped around the barrier at the side of the gallery and donned the heavy canvas apron Mr. Tully handed to her, filled the large apron pockets with a half-dozen of the heavy balls and was so quickly absorbed in the spirit of the game she hardly ever thought of Gideon.

Certainly not his kiss.

~

"Look there, Colonel, isn't that—"

"Miss Stirling, yes, Crossley." Slender sinewy legs, trim ankles and a waist he could span with his hands. "I'll see you gentlemen later."

He'd left his men and had nearly made a fool of himself when he saw Josie waiting for him in front of the donations stall, eager and flirting.

He smiled at the memory. Made a promise to himself to meet her tonight in the library.

With more than an hour before he needed to be in place for the live drop, Gideon took a moment in the bogs to move the Spitfire badge from his left pocket, where Josie had so charmingly pinned it, to his right, where Arcturus would expect to see it as confirmation that he was Invictus.

Next, to honor his promise to Josie and curious as hell how the outline of the Spitfire was faring, Gideon made his way to the huge canvas outline, its corners anchored to the grass by croquet hoops.

"Remarkable," he would have said to Josie, had she been standing beside him. Nearly every square inch inside the profile was covered in copper pennies and other coins. A short-legged wooden pier bridged the entire width of the fuselage just aft of the wings, giving access to the center of the airplane, while a volunteer encouraged donors of every age onto the bridge.

"These are for my da, from me, my mum, and my baby broth-er," a little girl said as she held onto her mother's hand and tossed three coins toward the propeller. "He's a navalgator."

Clearly, a young family living in hope that their beloved father would make it home from the war, a wife who must know that the chances were heartbreakingly low.

He recognized two men from Balesborough's Home Guard unit; father and son electricians he planned to draft into the Auxiliary Unit, if their names weren't already on the list that Arcturus was to hand over to him today. They stood for a moment in silence at the center of the bridge before adding their coins to the rest.

"Colonel Fletcher!" With only Molly's shout for a warning, Gideon was suddenly surrounded by Nimway's own evacuees, his loyal cadets and the four new ones he'd not yet had time to muster into their band.

"We're donating our rosehip money, Colonel," Molly said, standing at his elbow, proudly rattling a chocolate tin, coins that Josie had paid them for every ounce of wild rosehips they brought to her for the herb cabinet.

"I'm proud of you all!" He was, that and so much more as he watched them race to the bridge, all the little hands tossing coins and squealing in delight. Children who had fallen lucky into the arms of the lady of Nimway Hall.

With a half-hour until the live drop, Gideon spotted his men in the field, laboring mightily at their end of a tug-of-war rope, pulling against a team of fliers from the air station. After two more wins, they came away filthy with mud and roaring in triumph. Admiring their fighting spirit, Gideon bought a round of beer from the tap stall, then excused himself and made his way toward the live drop.

According to his message from Arcturus, the drop would happen near the Coconut Shy. He was to be in the general area by six, wearing a Spitfire badge on the right side of his jacket. He expected no more information than that. A live-drop was, by necessity, a malleable event; anticipating too many details in advance left no room for an agent to react to amend or even abandon a plan.

He only had to wait, watch, to appear to be a natural part of the goings on. Shouldn't be any trouble if he needed to have a go with the Shy. He was an ace marksman with a rifle, could land a live grenade inside a tea cup and, by the age of eleven, he'd been banned from every fete in east Kent for the power in his arm and the accuracy of his aim at a coconut.

The Shy seemed quite popular, with spectators two-deep, and every throw drawing groans or cheers. He stood on the perimeter and watched the action, certain that Arcturus was here, wondering how he planned to make the hand-off.

His senses were always heightened surrounding a live drop, sounds more distinct, shadows and sunlight more stark, smells and movement more discernible. Rather like having Josie nearby; made him deeply aware of her scent, her laughter, her kiss.

Another cheer went up and a new contestant stepped to the throwing line. The crowd to shifted in and out of the perimeter, wagers were made and paid, and Gideon adjusted his position for a better view over the heads of the father and two young sons who were standing in front of him, leaving him an unobstructed view of the marquee, the line of mounted coconuts, the new contestant who was warming up his arm in great wide circles, the spectators watching from the sidelines and the four volunteers working the stall.

He recognized one of Josie's tenant farmers, Tully, the man's two grown sons and—as though Josie's Aunt Freddy's Orb of True Love had followed them to the fete—Josie herself, holding three balls in her hands, and wearing a red-and-white striped apron that reached nearly to her knees.

She saw him at the same time, smiled shyly across the distance and waggled her fingers before dutifully turning her attention to the next contestant.

Three wind-ups and three misses later, Gideon scanned the

crowd for anyone who might be his contact, saw no one and left the perimeter to wait for Josie at the edge of the stall.

"Are you stalking me, Gideon," she asked as she approached him, slipping the balls into the large pockets and wiping her hands on the apron.

"Just idling while you work, Josie."

She was laughing brightly, freely, her gaze glittering as she looked up at him. "You'll have-a-go at the coconuts, won't—" she had been smoothing her warm hand across his chest, stopped suddenly, swallowed hard before she continued, laughing lightly "—won't you, Gideon? Raising funds for the war effort, you know."

Pennies to buy a Spitfire; he was ashamed to doubt her. "I've a pocket full of tickets. I just may have to."

"Good." Her smile had weakened, a line of worry creased her brow, her breathing shallow and quick. "Then...well, I'd best be getting back to the stall before they miss me."

"Will you be free at seven?"

She exhaled deeply, offered another wan smile. "Yes, Gideon. It turns out that I'll be free." She started back into the stall, then turned back, seemed sad all of a sudden, different. "Where will I find you?"

"I'll find you."

"I look forward to it," she said with a shy wink that caught him in the heart as she returned to her place in the stall.

He watched her for a time from an open space where Arcturus surely could see him, could catch his eye or pause beside him long enough to slip a message to him inside a propelling pencil or a cigarette lighter.

"Join us, sir!" Easton said, with a tug at his sleeve. "Let's all have-a-go at those bloody coconuts!"

"Miss Stirling's there at the side of the stall, Colonel!" Durbridge's grin was wide, the front of his shirt still streaked with mud. Come along, show her what you've got!"

Why not? A half-hour had passed without contact. Arcturus could be any man connected to the fete, someone local with the ability to move among a variety of people and not be noticed.

And who better than Mr. Tully, from Lower Farm. Nimway's orchardist, a veteran of the Great War, a clear-headed member of the Home Guard, and his occupation allowed him access to regular delivery routes throughout the county.

And there was the very man, running the Coconut Shy, scanning the crowd, taking tickets from all comers in exchange for a trio of balls, his hands repeatedly dipping into the huge pockets of his apron. What better cover for a live drop than that?

Gideon watched Crossley and Durbridge wage their own personal tournament, until Tully finally called them off and handed three balls to Gideon along with a wink.

"Best of luck, sir."

He needn't have worried that his arm had lost its teenage accuracy. Tried not to think about the woman who was watching from the stall, failed miserably at that, but threw harder and faster and more accurately than he'd ever done as a youth. Actually cracked all three coconuts and sent one arcing into its neighbor for a record-breaking four-count.

While the crowd roared and his officers gave him a thumping good razzing, he realized that in his attempt to impress Josie with his prowess, and to convince himself of the rapid progress of his recovery, he had wrenched the injured muscle of his thigh with enough force to break open the incision at its weakest point.

Not painful enough to worry about now, the familiar dampness at his knee easily ignored until he could tend to it in the privacy of his own quarters.

Just now he was wondering what the devil had happened to the live drop. He'd been so certain he had found Arcturus in Tully's exuberant handshake and backslapping congratulations, that Gideon had expected to come away from shying coconuts with more than a model Spitfire. Tully could have easily slipped the list of names for the Aux Unit into his hand as he surrendered his game tickets or with the balls. Nothing.

Arcturus was an expert in tradecraft, wise enough to abandon a live drop if he sensed trouble. Always frustrating and concerning. But the safety of both agents was always the top concern. Even above the operation itself. Another day. Another drop.

He took himself away from the Coconut Shy, in case there had been a breach in security and his cover was compromised. The sun would be setting soon and the fete was already being moved indoors by an army of volunteers.

He'd promised to find Josie, but had lost her in the shifting crowd and the fading light and assumed she would be meeting somewhere with the organizing committee.

His knee was beginning to stiffen and swell, the open incision scraping against the wool of his trousers, forcing him to move like an old man toward the village hall, where the music had begun behind to seep from the shuttered doors and windows.

He drew aside the blackout curtain and stepped through the vestibule into the lighted hall. The fete had indeed been brought inside, the flags and banners and bunting, the food and drink stalls, the music and dancing.

And Josie. He'd found her deep in conversation with an older man who was sitting at the cashier table. Pencils and pages flew as they seemed to be tallying columns of figures and entering the totals into an account journal.

Rather than interrupt them, Gideon purchased two pint glasses of Nimway Scrumpy, claimed two places for them at an empty table and was about to go fetch her when he turned to find Josie moving toward him, her hair like spun gold, skirts playing against her shapely legs.

He felt anchored to the ground, beguiled, as she held out her hand and took his when she reached him. "I saw you come in, Gideon. I'm so glad you stayed."

"I said I'd find you."

Her eyes were misty and studied him a long time. "Yes, but did you find me, or did I find you?"

"Shall we call it a draw?"

"A draw, then." She took his other hand. "Colonel Fletcher, I know I'm a woman and it's not my place to ask of a man, but would you care to dance?"

He felt the music thrumming beneath his shoes, the pulse of his wound throbbing more sharply than it had in months, the pleasure of holding her in his arms too enticing to refuse her anything. "I haven't in long while. Not since college."

"Then you'll have to trust me, sir, to make decisions for the both of us." She led him out onto the dance floor among the other couples and he lost himself in her enchantment.

CHAPTER 11

*G*ideon Fletcher was *Invictus*!

Josie was still reeling, still couldn't believe it was true! Even as she waltzed with him among the other dancers, as he held her close and smiled down at her with his beguiling blue eyes. As she smiled back at him, her heart racing with dread, and tried to pretend that nothing had changed between them.

The live drop with Invictus should have been the simplest of operations. She'd completed more than a dozen since joining MI6 at the beginning of the war, in far more complex locations than her own village. She would have identified Agent Invictus by more than just the Spitfire badge he'd be wearing on the right side of his coat. She'd have known him by his intent, the exchange of glances, an almost imperceptible nod of confirmation. Followed by the precisely choreographed dance of the trade, further confirmation; passing and circling each other in the smallest increments, finally settling into an unremarkable position on a bench or in the press of a crowd. They might even have exchanged pleasantries, or commented on the weather. Ordinary.

She had planned the live drop with Invictus as she would have with any other agent, in broad daylight, in the midst of a crowd of spectators. Any other agent would have marked her intent, noticed her glances then would have either met her in the wing of the Shy for a face-to-face transaction or allowed her to pass the note to him when they exchanged his ticket for the wooden balls he would throw at the coconuts.

Simple. Professional. In any other situation, with any other operative, except this one.

She'd smiled and waved at the man from the stall only because he was Gideon and he was smiling back at her, and he'd kissed her that morning as though he couldn't get enough of her. She'd been delighted, flattered, when he came to chat her up in the wings, couldn't keep her hands off him.

And then she'd put her hand on the Spitfire badge and realized, like a devastating bolt from the sky, that he had shifted it from his left pocket where she'd so blissfully pinned it, to his right.

Realized, too, that he'd only found her because his gaze had been sweeping the crowd for Arcturus, that he'd come to the Coconut Shy to make the live drop, that of all the men at the fete today, only Gideon Fletcher could be Invictus.

Feeling gut-punched and too stunned to proceed, she'd called off the live drop in the next breath. Not because it would have been awkward or dangerous to continue, but because Invictus had dismissed her out of hand, had never once in his misogynistic expectations ever considered that she, Jocelyn Regina Stirling—a woman—might just be the Arcturus he was searching for.

Now that she'd had time to consider the situation, the fact that Gideon Fletcher was Invictus made perfect sense; the clues had been plain to see since the moment they met. A highly experienced intelligence officer of the SOE posted to a farm in rural Somerset. Hadn't she even remarked to him that his posting seemed unusual?

His disappearances at all hours, even when his staff had been in the Hall. Good grief, she'd been exchanging messages with Gideon at the dead drop all this time.

And now, with soft music playing to the beat of her heart, as she gazed up into his eyes, blue and lit by an inner fire, as he held her close against his chest and smiled down at her with those fine lips, she wanted nothing more than to kick him in the shins. Or higher.

"You surprise me, Gideon," she said instead, to this man of way too many surprises, "you dance very well for not having done so since college."

"You're too kind for saying so, Josie, considering." He was actually a very careful dancer, held her close but didn't travel far with her in his arms, rarely turned, and then only slightly. A sheen of perspiration had begun to collect at his temples and on his close-shaven upper lip.

"Are you feeling all right, Gideon?" He was pale, blinking and breathing deeply.

"Not getting enough sleep."

"You and your men do come in late every night. Stomping up the backstairs."

"Sorry about that. Night work suits us for security purposes."

There was the gaping breach between them. "Tiring work, keeping secrets from civilians."

Whatever dodgy excuse Gideon had been about to make was interrupted by the arrival of her father, looking fresher, smarter this evening that he'd been when she'd seen him eight hours before. Where did he get the energy?

"Care if I take a turn around the floor with my darling daughter, Colonel?" Her father seemed in a fine mood, had checked in on her from time to time during the fete and now spun her away from a smiling Gideon, who gave her such a conspiratorial wink she wanted to haul him aside and tell him exactly what she thought of him and his bloody prejudices.

"Everything splendid between you two, Josie? Gideon seems

off his feed and you're looking—can't say exactly how, but I've seen you happier."

She had been *blissfully* happier—not that long ago. "Let's just say that I'm feeling invisible at the moment."

He laughed. "Impossible, my Josie Bear! You are the center of every circle, the spark that makes that man's heart keep beating."

"I doubt that, Father," she said as the mayor stepped onto the stage, "and it looks like it's time to sit." She took his hand as the music faded and the other dancers began leaving the floor.

Gideon was waiting for her at their table. His staff officers were standing about in their boisterous good cheer as she approached with her father.

"Lt. Colonel Fletcher," her father said, with a click of his heels as he offered Josie's hand to Gideon, "I return your partner to you, none the worse for our foxtrot."

"You put us all to shame, Edward." Gideon's gaze lingered softly on Josie, though his smile seemed almost forced.

"But now I must join my fellows at the Home Guard table. You're all a bit stuffy for the likes of us."

Gideon and his men seemed to adore her father and always made room for him in their company, sought him out for games of chess, and bridge, and visits to the pub. Men as fine as Gideon. She'd shared many conversations with his officers over the past weeks, mostly in passing, but had enjoyed their wit and banter, learned about their homes and families, their adventures in the war, and yet she felt older and much wiser than any of them.

Gideon himself was oddly quiet, standing bolt upright behind the chair he'd kept for her, smiled as he held the back and gestured for her to sit, which she so badly wanted to refuse. She was his colleague, his equal in all things. Yet, in his single act of rejection, she'd been reduced to being his date.

It was impossible not to sense him behind her as she sat and they listened to the mayor present prizes for the 'best' and the 'most' and the 'biggest.' Impossible not to feel the searing heat of his hand through the gabardine of her dress as he caressed her shoulder. Very hot, clammy, as though he'd become over-heated.

"And now, ladies and gentlemen of Balesborough Parish, it's time to announce the sum raised today for our Spitfire campaign." Lots of cheering, hooting. "And who best to make the announcement than the organizer of the fete, our own Miss Josie from Nimway Hall."

She disliked this moment at the end of every local event, when she was recognized for doing exactly what anyone else would have done in her position as lady of the Hall. Which nearly everyone in the parish did every day of this terrible war—they willingly gave their all.

Gideon bent down to whisper, his large hand on her shoulder, hot as before. "You've got a major success on your hands, Josie. Let them love you for it." He gave a brief squeeze to her upper arm then let her go.

"Thank you, I will—" as though she needed his approval or direction! Wanting nothing more than to call the man out for his chauvinism, Josie left Gideon without looking back and made her way toward the stage, winding through the tables and across the dance floor where the children were all seated.

"A miracle of a day, Miss Josie," Mayor Wharmsley whispered, grinning madly as he handed Josie the slip of paper from the fund-raising committee. A quick glance at the total told her the reason!

Josie thanked the fete committee for their tireless work, the donors of so many goods and services, and her friends and neighbors "—for so generously opening your hearts and emptying your pockets for the war effort."

Which seemed to delight the crowd and made Josie very proud of them all.

"Now to the figure you've all been waiting to hear. Due to your generosity and hard work today, we have added £4,388 and thruppence to Balesborough's Spitfire Fund Campaign."

The audience began to applaud and the band struck up a tune, but Josie raised her hand and the sound stopped.

"Before the drumroll, gentlemen, can any of our brilliant young students seated below me add that sum to our current total of—" she checked the slip of paper "—£878?"

Almost instantly Molly raised her hand and shouted correctly "—£5,266!"

"And thruppence!" added Lucas. Making the crowd roar and Josie's heart swell with pride.

The mayor waved his arms to quiet the tumult. "Ladies and gentlemen, we have bought a Spitfire!"

The band struck up a blaring tune and the dance floor filled again, scattering the children and swelling the hall with the noise of celebration.

Josie had purposely not spared even a glance in Gideon's direction as she made the announcement, hadn't wanted to witness his disbelief.

But as she stepped down from the stage she saw him whisper something to Crossley, then slip out the backdoor. The bloody coward! Couldn't even wait long enough to face her 'I-told-you-we-could-buy-a-whole-Spitfire!'

Well, good riddance to you, Colonel Fletcher. The fete hadn't been the time to reveal to him that she was Arcturus. There would be time enough in the next day or two.

Josie worked her way through the press of dancers and well-wishers, taking her time returning to the table where Gideon's men were tucking into plates of cabbage, sausage and potatoes.

"Congratulations, Miss Stirling!" Crossley stood with the other men, raised his spoon in salute. "What a roaring success!"

"Look there—" Durbridge pointed to five model Spitfires sitting in the middle of the table. "We bought enough game tickets and scrumpy to fund an entire squadron."

"We'll be giving those to the children at the Hall," Easton said, inspecting one of the toys. "The colonel said he watched our little evacuees donate their rose-hip money to the cause."

"Did they?" And did Gideon take time to watch them?

"He also asked if we would pass along his congratulations to you," Easton said, raising his pint to Josie. "His leg was giving him fits, so he thought it best to head back to the Hall."

"His leg?" Had the girls been right about Gideon's injury?

"Didn't bring his cane with him to the fete and I think he came to regret it, especially after the Coconut Shy." Crossley shared a nod with his comrades, then lowered his voice. "Was in gobs of pain when he left here just now, though he'd never let on, not even to us. Wouldn't limp in front of strangers, if it killed him."

But they had become so much more than strangers. "How did it happen, Lt. Crossley? Has he said?"

"Not a word to us. But we do know he was seriously wounded on a covert intelligence operation last spring, nearly didn't make it home."

Gideon, nearly killed in the line of duty, a chance that they would never have met. A chill settled on her heart as she turned away and noticed what looked to be a smear of oil on the wooden floor where he'd last been standing. She brushed it with her fingertip and came away with blood.

"How was the Colonel getting back to the Hall?"

"Walking, I assume. Wouldn't ask for a ride."

Foolish, prideful man!

"Thank you, Lt. Durbridge. Gentlemen." She grabbed her things and raced through the near-dark to where Bess was parked beside the deserted WI stall. She slammed the rear doors on the stacks of empty crates, slid into the driver's seat and sped off west through the village toward the lane that turned up to the Hall.

When Gideon wasn't there, she knew exactly where he would be heading—to the dead drop at the back wall of the churchyard.

And there he was, in the pale light of her headlamps, standing outside the lych gate, her Invictus, checking the gate post for a signal from Arcturus.

It's not there, you exasperating dolt!

Josie pulled alongside and honked Bess's horn. "Get in!" she shouted out the driver's window.

"Josie?" He turned, sheltered his eyes from the light. "Is something wrong at the Hall?" His pace was slow and upright as he approached the passenger side, his pain as poorly disguised in the dim light as his unsteady gait.

"You're bleeding, Gideon." Josie got out of the van, went round to the passenger side and opened the door. "Leaving a trail that any child could follow, let alone an enemy agent."

"Enemy agent? Don't be absurd."

"Get in, or I'll throw you in."

"Josie, please leave me be. I'm fine. Go back to the fete."

"Don't tempt me. And you're not fine. Get into the van and I'll drive you to the Hall where you can continue bleeding all over the marble floors, if you'd like. Or you can let me see this gaping wound you've been hiding from me, and I'll staunch it. I know how. I'm trained in first-aid."

"I don't need your help—"

"But you do need a ride." She gave him the slightest nudge toward passenger seat and he dropped in, frowning as he turned to face the front.

Josie dismissed the feeling that she had just bagged a live tiger, and with it the worry about his temper when she finally let him loose.

No matter that he was a thick-headed lout, was stubborn and too handsome for his own good, Gideon Fletcher was a fallen colleague and it was her duty to take him safely off the field of battle and see to his wounds before another minute passed.

The showdown between Arcturus and Invictus would have to wait until the man could at least stand upright.

~

Bloody hell, if he hadn't been showing off like a schoolboy for Josie, he wouldn't have re-injured his leg at the Coconut Shy, wouldn't have risked the live drop which had doubtlessly sent Arcturus back into hiding.

He'd been so damn proud of Josie when she announced the success of the fete, astounded by her faith and determination. She had proved that a village like Balesborough could bind together to buy an entire Spitfire.

By that time his knee was nearly blinding him with pain; he couldn't dance, couldn't stay and didn't want to ruin her celebration with questions about him.

And he'd been hoping that Arcturus had left the fete after abandoning the live drop and managed to slip the intended message with the Aux Unit names into the dead drop. He'd been beyond disappointed not to find a chalked signal on the lych gate post.

And, though he would never admit it to Josie, he was beyond grateful to her for insisting she drive him back to the Hall.

What had begun as a noticeable wrench deep inside his knee when he'd heaved that last ball at the coconut had grown into a throbbing, near-blinding ache. The blood on his trousers could only have come from the raw-edged surgical incision, was more dramatic than life-threatening. Still, the pain was like an inferno and he'd wondered how he would have made it back to the Hall on foot.

He held on tightly as Josie flew up the lane and into the drive, stopping long enough for the young sapper on guard at Nimway's gate to peer into the van, salute Gideon and wave them on. Minutes later she pulled up to the rear of the darkened house, grabbed her electric torch from the glove box, then met him on the passenger side as he was opening the door to get out.

"Gideon, are you sure you can do this on your own?" She caught his elbow as though he were an invalid.

"I'm sure." He wasn't sure at all, swallowed a gasp as he swung around in the seat and stepped out with his left leg, didn't even try to stand until he was square on his right, then braced himself upward with his hand on the back of the seat and stood upright. "There."

"Not even close, Gideon." She seemed impatient and angry as she slammed the door behind him, raised the bonnet and removed the rotor arm. "Everyone is at the fete for the next hour. We'll go in through the pantry and then back to my office."

"I'd much rather go up to my room–"

"I need to fix that—" she flicked on the torch and shined it on the stain on his trousers "before it worsens."

"It won't."

She ignored him, caught his elbow and headed toward the kitchen stairs, fixing the beam of light on the hard-packed gravel just in front of him. "The Land Girls told me weeks ago that you had a limp and walked with a cane. I don't know how I haven't noticed in all our time together. But I see now how you've been able to mask the pain."

"Have you, then?"

She left him and watched carefully from the top of the kitchen steps, the same way she must do when one of her livestock went lame. "There. A hitch, as you rise on your right, your left leg slightly stiff. Carrying the pain in your shoulders as well. Over-working your right leg."

Winded, he stopped when he reached the top and braced his weight on the wall. "Do you mind?"

"Can you bend your knee fully?" She held the door wide as he hobbled through.

"Not at the moment, unless you want me to bleed all over the pantry."

"No, but can you normally bend your knee fully?"

"With effort on a good day, nearly impossible today." He steadied himself for a moment on the edge of a sink. "I'd like to thank you for the lift, Josie, and for a most marvelous day. But, if you'll excuse me, I'll retire and take care of th—"

"No, Gideon, I won't excuse you; you're not getting rid of me until I have seen this wound of yours in the flesh." She scowled. "And blood."

"It's nothing, really."

"'Nothing' doesn't leave a trail of blood. Doctor Wealty is in town tonight for the fete—it's either me or him."

"Josie, it's an old injury. I'll not bleed out." Though he could feel new blood seeping down his leg.

"The first aid supplies are in my office. It won't be but a minute for me to take a close look and see what's needed."

"A minute then." Even so, he refused to hobble as he followed her through the kitchen, resisted propping himself against the worktable when the pain jarred him.

"This way, Gideon!" she called from her office, wheeling her chair to the side of her desk by the time he entered. She turned on the lamp and crooked the light toward the seat. "Sit here. I'll get your shoes off. I don't think you can reach your left one."

Wary of every comfort she was offering, Gideon lowered himself into the swivel chair and extended his left leg, exposing the patch of blood, dark and clotted, at the knee of his trousers.

"I don't mean to be fresh, Gideon," she said as she knelt and unlaced his shoes.

"Go right ahead—" he leaned forward to be nearer, "takes my mind off the pain."

"Very well." He caught her in a brief smile as she slipped off his shoes and set them aside, then gently slid his trouser leg upward toward his knee "—hold this, please."

She left him holding the hem, went to the workbench sink, ran water and returned with a damp towel. His left sock was stuck to the top of his calf where blood had congealed with hair and the knitted wool.

"Were you just planning to bleed to death?" She dabbed the wet towel against the crusted blood, wetting his leg and the ribs of the sock.

"That was my plan, yes."

"I know this is an old injury, but what happened? How did you re-open it? Did you fall?"

"No." I was showing off for you, Josie. "I just stepped badly."

"And did all this damage?" She was still wearing her shapely dress from the fete. Looked even more lovely now than before. When she bent to pull off his socks, her neckline gaped, revealing more than he ought to be taking in, her breasts soft and round and promising. The birthmark she spoke of so lightly, hiding just out of sight over her lovely shoulder.

He'd never been undressed by a woman. It was always the other way around. Not that the number of women was great. Certainly none lately, save for the parade of stern-faced nurses who had raised him from the dead and then sent him home to be nursed by his mother. But in his misspent and unrepentant youth, there had been a few.

None came close to matching the heart of the woman kneeling before him, not in grace, devotion, wit or intelligence, not to mention beauty.

"Fair warning, Gideon, this might—" she yanked his sock down his calf, pulling out hair that was still dried to his sock "—hurt."

"It didn't." Barely distracted him from the throbbing in his knee, the spasm in his back.

"I can't see much of the wound itself for your trouser leg, but at least it's not still bleeding." She stood, pointed to his trousers. "Time to take them off."

"Take what off? My trousers? Really, Josie, you're straight-forward."

"Can you make it upstairs to your room? I'll follow shortly with my first aid bag. But I warn you, if you're not out of your trousers and in your dressing gown when I arrive, I'm straightforward enough to take them off for you."

She handed him his shoes and socks and he made his way up the backstairs to his room, his knee stiffening with every step. The blasted woman was right, he did need her help with his wound, at least tonight.

He'd let her patch up his knee tonight then take better care of it himself as he'd done for months now. He'd grown tired of applying surgical tape over a bandage, over a dressing. The incision had mostly healed, the sutures long gone but the healing had left a mighty fierce looking pirate scar that was still weeping, and bled when he wasn't careful.

He hobbled through his sitting room into his bed chamber and dropped his shoes and socks on the floor beneath the wardrobe. It took every bit of concentration to drop his trousers over his throbbing knee, to balance on one leg as he removed his braces, tie and dress shirt, leaving him standing in his olive-drab military-issued knickers and vest.

He was just tying his sash around his dressing gown when she gave two raps on his door and entered carrying an enormous veterinarian bag, an enamel pitcher and basin. She stopped and stared, bold as brass.

"Ah, good, you've changed."

"You've changed as well." Into a pair of khaki work slacks and a slim-fitting, white cotton-knit Henley shirt. Every inch the country vet.

"My calving uniform."

"I remember." An unforgettable night, assisting her with the birth of Jill's calf. "But you needn't do this for me, Josie. If you leave a few bandages and a dressing, I can take care of it myself. I've done it before on the battlefield, for myself and my comrades."

"You're not on a battlefield, Gideon." She set down the bag and basin on his dressing table, then made for the bathroom that adjoined his sitting room, talking all the while. "You're in Nimway Hall. I have no idea what the orb thinks of this moment but I imagine its influence can't possibly hurt." She returned with the pitcher full of water and a stack of towels tucked under her arm, gave the room a quick scan. "I think you'll be most comfortable if you sit there on the bench at the foot of the bed.

"Good Lord, woman I'm not giving birth."

"No, but you've made as big a mess with whatever you did to your leg—" she yanked aside the left side of his robe and peered at the wound "—bloody hell, Gideon."

"It is a mess, isn't it?" He hadn't dared look closely at the damage he'd done, until now. The incision was ten inches long, was again oozing blood and fluid.

"This needs a dressing at all times, Gideon, until it's fully healed."

"Seemed to be doing well enough lately, so I stopped using the gauze bandage and dressing."

"On doctor's orders?" She raised her brows at him, waiting for his confirmation. "As I suspected. Now sit on the bench and tell me how you did this."

"Do you mean today's incident, or originally."

She moved a set of pillows to the end of the bed. "Both would be helpful to know."

Seeing no point in resisting her any longer, Gideon backed up to the bench, caught his hands behind him and lowered himself onto the tufted silk, relieved to see the left panel of his dressing gown slide off his left leg and the right panel settle modestly between his legs. That the woman had stopped breathing as she watched was far more arousing than was safe. He was wearing knickers, but they were hardly a barrier to his erection, so he hunched forward, straightening his injured leg.

"I broke my fibula, this bone, in my calf—" he pointed to the left side of his left leg "—near the top, and tore up my knee at the same time." Took a bullet in his right arm and right calf, but they had long ago healed.

"How, Gideon?" She was on her knees, peering closely at the gory mess that would daunt most other women. "It takes a lot of force to break a leg bone."

It was a long story that he wasn't free to tell. "Let's just say it happened in an ambush on a snowy precipice."

She sat back on her heels, her eyes wide and worried. "So you were on the ground in Norway with the SOE operation back in early April, before the invasion."

How the devil would she know about the SOE in Norway; not many did. But then she seemed to be involved in numerous local defense organizations, could easily have heard through channels. To ask how she'd learned of the operation in Norway would be to confirm the information.

"Let's just say it was dark and I fell–"

"Off the snowy precipice?" She slipped his hand between both of hers, soft and warm and healing. "That would make sense, Gideon, a fall like that could easily break a bone. Did you take anyone with you, I hope? Off the precipice, I mean."

"Three Germans went with me into an icy stream. We fought, they lost."

"Three against you?" He hoped it was admiration for his prowess that pinked her cheeks. "And then what?"

"I managed to climb back up the cliff side to my unit—"

"In the dark, with that horrible broken leg? How?"

"Doesn't matter how. Only that by the time I reached them, we had lost two of our fellow officers in a fire fight and then another during our escape." Images he could never erase. Would never want to.

"I'm sorry."

"So were the dozen bastards who ambushed us. We brought out our fallen comrades, made it back to the fishing boat before we were spotted, and only there, in the chaos of leaving the pier did someone notice that my leg seemed to be broken."

"Someone else noticed? Not you?"

He'd suspected that something was wrong when he landed below the cliff, but he'd been trained that if he could move through the pain, it wasn't serious. "Too busy, I suppose. Too damned cold to feel much of anything."

"Hmmm... if you say so." She finally released his hand, sorted through her supplies for a wad of gauze, then upturned a bottle of tincture of iodine and dribbled a few drops onto the pad. "Keep talking, Gideon."

"I don't have many memories of the fishing boat—it was a British intelligence asset." She began dabbing the pad against the trail of blood that had run down the side of his calf, working her way upward toward the wound itself. "Apparently, I caught a fever early on and wasn't fully conscious again until I woke up in an evacuation hospital somewhere in Kent. Woke again in still another hospital ward and discovered that my surgeon had given me that ugly thing when he opened my leg and reconnected my fibula to my knee."

"It's a thing of beauty, this incision." She smiled up at him from her gentle tending, had placed a warm compress of mint and lemon over the entire length of the incision. "I hope you thanked him."

"For ensuring that I'll never again see the front lines? I did not."

"Bugger that attitude, Gideon! The man gave you back a normal life. Your knee will heal."

"Well enough to keep me posted here in the hinterlands, alongside the rest of the stay-at-home army, waiting for an invasion that will never come, paddling around like ducks in a pond."

"How dare you!"

"I dare, Josie, because it's the truth. My truth. I'm a soldier by trade, that's all I know, all I want to know. I'm trained in special operations behind enemy lines, not writing reports and approving engineering drawings."

"And I'm just a duck, paddling around in a pond? You still believe that?"

He wasn't sure what he believed. Only that his leg had begun to feel better within minutes of her touch, the wound cleansed and looking less inflamed. "I believe that you are a miracle worker, Josie. But all the surgeons and all your tender nursing can't mend me well enough to send me back to the front lines where I want to be."

"Have you even tried?" She was frowning hard as she began dabbing the raw flesh dry with a gauze pad, as efficiently as any duty nurse.

"Over-tried, ouch!"

"Sorry, Gideon." She gentled her motions, then inspected the entire length of the incision. "Over-tried? What does that mean?"

"Tried to rush my recovery, according to the surgeon, my mother, the rehabilitation unit nurses then the private physical therapist hired once I was recovering at home with my family."

She narrowed her eyes at him. "That would have been during the evacuation of Dunkirk."

"It was." Drained by the memory, he dropped back on his elbows against the end of the bed, soothed by Josie's gentling touch against his skin as she dressed and wrapped the wound in gauze, secured it in surgical tape. "Yet, the closest I could get to the action was a few hours spent watching from the terrace of one of our cliffside farms near Broadstairs. Fishing boats and steamers heading toward Margate, passing under my position on their way to and from Ramsgate, returning with all those soldiers, more than three-hundred thousand saved by—"

"—the stay-at-home Navy?"

He felt his chest flush with anger, shame. "All I could do was sit and watch."

"That was your assignment at the time, Gideon." She rose

suddenly, rested her knee on the bench beside him, hovered in her umbrage. "To let others do their best for the war effort when they were called up."

"I should have been there." He sat up, feeling exposed, besieged by Josie and his own anger.

"How? With your leg like this? You'd have been a liability. Or do you mean that those fishermen and yachtsmen, the fireboat pilots were less brave than you would have been, less patriotic because they hadn't commissions and weren't wearing combat uniforms?"

"That's not it, Josie." Wasn't exactly his meaning. "Of course, I admire and respect their miraculous achievement. I do. Their Dunkirk Spirit."

"But you could have done better, is that it? Because if that's your thinking, that you must do it all, Gideon, then it explains why your body is wracked with tension."

"I'm fine." He actually felt more relaxed than he had in months.

"You're not. Lean back. I'll show you." She pressed her hand into the middle of his chest, able to force him backward against the bolster of pillows only because she was kneeling over him, enchanting him, smiling softly, her hair falling around her shoulders. "Will you lie still?"

"Probably not." He propped himself on his elbows, wary of the challenge in her smile. "What do you plan to do?"

"I promise not to hurt you." She backed off the bench and carefully braced his good leg across the seat of his dressing table stool.

"I'm not in the least worried about you hurting— Oh, gad, Josie!" He sat upright, would have rocketed off the bench had her hands not been encircling his thigh, kneading the muscles above his knee, sending waves of pleasure straight to his groin. He clamped his hand over hers, stopped her from moving any higher. "What the devil are you doing?"

"Showing you that all your hitching around on your bad leg just to prove something to yourself, has made every muscle in your body as hard as a rock." Seeming to demonstrate, she flexed her fingers beneath his hand—creating a jolt of rawboned lust that would have brought him to his feet with Josie in his arms, but she had managed to pin him down in the only way possible. His good leg on a stool, his bad leg useless, and the luscious woman standing between them.

"That's enough!"

She straightened, her hands on her fine hips. "Do you see what I mean? How much tension you're living with?"

A dangerous woman, that's who he was living with. "I do see, Josie, very clearly."

He stood, caught his sash around his waist and stepped away from the woman's little infirmary.

"Where are you going?"

"We're finished here, Josie. I appreciate you dressing and bandaging my injury. It much feels better. Now, if you tell me where you keep that kit, I'll do it myself next time."

She pulled the stool to the center of the room. "Plasters and surgical tape might protect your incision, but that won't help with your biggest issue."

"Which is?"

"Sit here." She patted the seat of the stool. "I'll show you. Or don't you trust me?"

"Give me a single reason why I should." He could count them in the dozens. In a few short weeks the woman had turned his life upside down.

"Because I can see from here that every muscle and tendon in your body aches like fire. Am I right?"

Damning himself for a besotted fool, he closed his eyes, took an instantaneous inventory of his limbs and torso, and found no part of himself that didn't ache. Only cramping spasms radiating from his injured leg, shooting into his back and shoulders, his arms, his chest. She was staring at him when he opened his eyes, her head cocked as though she'd been listening for his pain.

"Suppose you're right, Josie, and I do ache all over; what can you possibly do about it?"

Her smile grew soft and kind, the wry slant of it thrilled him. "Sit and I'll show you."

Knowing full well that he was walking toward his doom, Gideon sat carefully on the stool, bracing his bad leg in front of him. He listened to her puttering behind him, was fine until she slipped his dressing gown off his shoulders.

"What are you up to back there? Ohhhh—" Her fierce thumbs found the knotted muscles on the ridge of his shoulders, knot on top of knot, the exquisite pressure hissing the breath out of him like fire and ice.

"Good, yes?"

"Yes." So good. So unlike the hands of any therapist he'd consulted. Hers were warm and fluid, followed through to his deepest pain, lifted it, dispelled it with her magic.

"This works best, Gideon, if you relax each muscle as I address it." Her breath brushed against the back of his neck. "Feel this knot?"

"I do." And the warm shifting of her breasts across his back as she moved her kneading pressure down his left arm, leaving him growling and sighing like a beast. His bare arm hung limp in her skilled hands and yet quickened with energy as though she were resurrecting his limbs. By the time she finished his right arm he was hunched over his knees, boneless and nearly incoherent when she took away her touch.

"You're not finished?" He didn't want her to be, not yet, not ever.

"I just need you to take off your vest. I'd do it myself, but my palms are full of liniment."

He turned, only one eye willing to fully open, found her standing close, both hands raised like a surgeon's before a procedure. "What do you plan to do with those?"

"Massage your back, and then your arms again."

He groaned at the thought of the pleasure. "I won't be able to walk."

But he shucked out of his vest and gave himself over to her healing generosity, steeled himself against her touch, the rhythmic movement of her chest against his back as she pressed her thumbs along his spine, followed every rib all the way down to the band of his knickers.

He wondered suddenly at this particular talent, upon whose aching muscles she had learned. Which man she had treated with such intimacy? "Do you do this sort of thing regularly?"

"Why?"

"Because you're very good at it. At getting right to the—ahhh, the spasm, the knot of things. How did you learn?" He hoped his question sounded casual, when he was beginning to resent whoever this other man was.

"Promise you won't laugh?" She came around and knelt in front of him.

"Old Godby?"

She laughed, touched his good knee. "I leave that to Mrs. Godby. No, my only patients have been lame horses—"

"That stuff is horse liniment?"

"Medicinal herbs from our own garden, concocted in our own kitchen by Mrs. Lamb to ease the aches and pains of man and beasts of Nimway Hall." She pulled a blanket off the end of the bed and covered the spread. "Now. stand up and lie here on your stomach so I can do the same to your legs. The muscles of your back were a jumble of knots and gnarls, your arms nearly as bad, but your legs have been taking all the punishment as you compensate for your injury."

The only sense he'd made of her explanation made him ask, "You want me laid out across my bed?"

Her smile, her eyes, the perfect rise of her breasts, more worldly than virginal. "I'd not put it that way, Gideon, but yes, I do."

CHAPTER 12

*G*iven her disillusionment and fury when she discovered that Gideon was agent Invictus, Josie had never expected this night to end with him standing, bronzed and glistening and nearly naked in front of her, bandaged and bruised. Hadn't anticipated the lush feel of his skin beneath her fingers, the feral power of his muscles against her palms, the brush of her nipples across the sinew of his shoulders. His unmistakable arousal at her touch or when he looked at her just that way, a durable tumescence that she wanted to fondle, to explore.

But now he was looking sleepy as he staggered toward the bed, an enormous bear shambling toward his winter cave, dangerous, because he might snag her for one last meal before settling down to sleep until spring.

"Can you make it to the bed, Gideon?" She caught his forearm, the hard-shifting power beneath his skin confirming that he had forced himself through a program of rehabilitation in the months since his injury, targeting every muscle and bone in his body, including his beleaguered leg. "How does your knee feel when you walk on it?"

"Hardly any pain at all."

"Here you are. Just slip onto the bed, on your stomach, please. That's it." Like leading a child toward his nap.

He mashed his face into the pillow, then turned out to her, eyes half-lidded. "If you were an enemy agent, I'd suspect you drugged me with your liniment."

"You found me out. I treated my bare hands with the antidote before massaging the sleeping drug into your bare skin. Do you want the antidote?"

"Not ever." His voice had grown low and groggy.

Josie retrieved her jar and set it on the bedside table, trying to ignore the heap of man sprawled out across the mattress, dwarfing the bed, the bolster and the bank of pillows. His broad shoulders relaxed, rising and falling as he breathed.

Her "live drop" in the flesh.

Damn the man and all his faults. He was perfect for her, perfect all around. Honorable and witty, opinionated and intelligent, handsome beyond all thinking. He loved children and dogs and birthing calves, was charmed by Nimway Hall and her beloved wood. Had even come to accept her word that the Orb of True Love was a strange family legend and not a threat to world peace.

But he would never accept that she was, and needed to remain, Arcturus, and she dreaded his scorn when he discovered the truth. The clock was ticking on their idyll, the war was about to intrude in a way she could never have anticipated when he arrived at Nimway.

He groaned and muttered when she began kneading the hard-packed muscles along the back of his good leg, her hands aching to range freely over his firmly-shaped, muscular backside beneath his knickers, but that would lead to an eventuality she had longed for but could no longer afford.

By the time she finished with his massage, he was snoring softly into his pillow, his breathing steady and deep. She would have risked pressing a kiss on his temple, but that might wake him and break her heart completely.

Best to keep a professional distance while she was still able. She was about to slip the message capsule out of her trouser pocket when she realized his eyes were half-open and he was looking at her.

"Have I been asleep?"

"You still are."

"I thought so, Josie. You've always been my dream. Or have you been here all the time?"

"Both."

"Then come, love, join with me." He beckoned her with his curled finger and she knelt on the rug beside the bed, couldn't help herself any more than she could stop herself from loving him. He sifted his fingers through the hair at her nape, his eyes half-lidded and smoky as he drew her close. Kissed her softly, deeply, nibbling and crooning, his gaze wandering over her face. "You are a wonder to me, Josie Stirling, Guardian of Nimway Hall. Commander of the Orb of True Love." He kissed her once more and settled back against the pillow. "What shall I do without you?"

"Are you going somewhere, Gideon?" she whispered.

His answer was a long, deep breath and a soft snore.

Hers was a quiet sob.

Because the truth was immutable. She was Arcturus. He was Invictus. The country was at war and needed them both equally. In the most hopeful part of her heart she knew that Gideon was wise enough, perceptive enough to accept her as his peer. But would he be able to invoke that fairness in himself when he learned the truth?

If he couldn't, he would just have to apply to the SOE for a new posting, a new partner. She damn well wasn't going to resign just to soothe the man's brittle pride.

She loved him, would have proudly served their country along side him, gladly spent the rest of her life with him. But, if all that happiness was the sacrifice she must make to help win the war, then so be it.

Her heart broken and aching for what she was about to do, Josie packed up her first aid gear and removed it to the sitting room. By the time she returned, Gideon had rolled onto his back, one arm crooked over his head on the pillow, the other resting at his side, fingers flexed and relaxed.

Never in the realm of tradecraft had there been a more perfect example of a live drop than Arcturus delivering the message into the closed fist of Agent Invictus while he slept.

Her next moment would set in motion a cascade of consequences which would cloud the rest of her days and prove to the orb once and for all that she and Gideon were not compatible and would never be.

She drew the capsule from her pocket, still warm from its hiding place. Overcome by an aching heart, she pressed it to her lips then easily slipped it into the cradle of his palm, his fingers still relaxed and curled, as though he'd picked up the dead drop, only to be bewitched by a spell that had sent him to sleep before he could read it. And perhaps he had been.

But he would read the message in the morning, would realize in an instant that she was Arcturus and come looking for her.

And just in case their paths didn't cross during the day, as so often had happened, she'd added a note to the back of the Aux Unit list, instructing him to meet Arcturus tomorrow night in the cider mill.

Then Heaven help them both.

She carefully settled a blanket over him, her dear, handsome, intractable Gideon. He slept on in his dreams, his chest rising and falling in a rhythm she would have loved matching with her own in some fairy tale future, drifting to sleep every night to the sound of his steady breathing, waking every morning wrapped in his arms.

That kind of peace between them was not meant to be. The

morning would bring the end of all things. And she hardly slept a wink.

~

But it was clear to Josie the next morning as she was standing at the workbench in her office sorting seeds for next winter, that Gideon had slept hard and awakened late, as furious as a hungry grizzly. She assumed all this about him when she heard his door slam above her, the rush of his footsteps down the backstairs, his sharp knock on her door—then the man himself was standing at the doorway, shirtless, shoeless, in a clean pair of uniform trousers, his vest and a pair of leather braces.

"Josie!" He was breathing like a steam engine.

Here it comes—in a blaze of anger and accusations. How could she possibly have predicted that the end would begin with Gideon looking so wickedly handsome?

"Yes?" Let him make the first strike.

"Did you—" He stopped and shut the door, came to stand next to her, gently turned her chin with the tip of his finger and looked deeply into her eyes. "Did anyone come into my room last night after you left?"

"I'm sorry?" She couldn't parse his question, or place the emotion in the fierceness of his gaze. "What do you mean?"

His smile was lop-sided. "I quite remember your—" he made a sultry sound in his throat, lifted the hair away from her ear and whispered "—your touch, Josie. The fleeting pain of your healing hands, the pleasure you lavished upon my aching flesh."

"Oh, my—" He brushed his warm lips against her nape, slipped his fingers along the ridge of her collar.

"You see, I remember that much."

"As I do." Would never forget that moment. Or this.

Or that the puzzling man might be setting her up for a shattering fall. She stepped away to the tray of seed cups on the table.

"Now, what is it you were asking, Gideon?"

"Yes, of course." He seemed to gather his senses, leaned back against the workbench and folded his arms across his chest. "I wanted to confirm that you were the last to leave my room last night."

She was ready for his accusation, would answer his questions without equivocation. "As far as I know, Gideon. You were fast asleep when I left. I turned out the lights in your room and the sitting room, closed both doors. Were you expecting anyone?"

"Not exactly." He rubbed his stubbled chin with his thumb and forefinger. "Not then. Certainly not in my bedroom."

So that was his conclusion? Damn the man! Of all the narrow-minded, unimaginative, dim-witted pillocks! She had just admitted to being the last person in his room the night before. The message from Arcturus was probably tucked into his trouser pockets at this very moment, written in her own hand. And still he couldn't possibly fathom that it was she who'd made the drop while he was sleeping.

What a bloody pleasure to be reeling out just enough rope for the lout to hang himself. "So, Gideon, I take it you were expecting someone. Just not in your room. When was the meeting supposed to happen, then? Where?"

He shook his head, still mulling over the answer that was standing right beside him. "Can't get into that, I'm afraid—"

"Official Secrets Act, of course."

"It's just that I found something I wasn't expecting to find."

"In your room? What did you find? Where was it?"

He looked down at the palm of his hand, clenched his fist. "Can't discuss that either."

Exasperated beyond her ability to remain polite, Josie turned to him and plastered on a smile. "How can I help you, Gideon?"

He made a sound in his throat then pushed away from the workbench. "Frankly, you can't help me, Josie. Not any more than you have already, than you did for me last night with your tender care." He turned toward her with a smile that melted her heart, then cupped her face between his large, capable hands and kissed her again, deeply, fully.

She closed her eyes and kissed him back, slipped her fingers through his dark hair, tugged him closer, relishing this final moment of intimacy with the man she loved with all her heart.

He laughed softly against her mouth, and set her away. "I've much to do today, Josie. And I see that I've interrupted your—" he gestured to the workbench.

Josie took a steadying breath. "Seed sorting—"

"I'll be sure to know that next time. Now I must return to my room and finish dressing."

"Other plans for the day?" She couldn't help asking because she knew exactly how his day would end.

"Nothing of note. Though I do hope you and I can meet tonight in the library. I've missed our time together."

"So have I."

"Half-ten, then," he said with a smile and so charming it took all her restraint not to toss a trowel at his head on his way out the door.

In any case, the die was cast. Arcturus and Invictus would meet this evening in the cider mill, come hell, high water, or an air raid.

Gideon raked his fingers through his hair as he tromped up the stairs to his room, trying to make his way through the herb-scented fog of his memories of last night and yesterday. No matter which path he followed, each ended with Josie. Her hands kneading his aching muscles, soothing his aching flesh, working his tendons until she had molded his pain into a pleasure so fathomless he could hardly keep his eyes open, despite his yearning to enfold her in his arms and make love with her through the night.

He'd heard nothing after that, and had slept like a stone until nearly eleven, had awakened flat on his back in his knickers, his knee much improved. It wasn't until he had sat up and swung his legs over the edge of the bed that he realized he was clutching a dead drop capsule in his hand.

He'd assumed at first he must have gotten out of bed after Josie left, encrypted a message to Arcturus for the morning, prepped the capsule with his reply, then had somehow returned to bed with it and fallen back to sleep. Why else would he have awakened holding a drop capsule?

It was only after he'd unscrewed the cap and read the message, that he knew the capsule wasn't his. Couldn't be. The rolled slip of paper was the list of Aux Unit recruits Arcturus was supposed to deliver during the live drop.

Yesterday. At the fete.

How the hell had it gotten here in his room? Who had put it into his hand? Arcturus? Had the man entered his room in the dead of night, come close enough to slip the capsule into his hand and not wake him?

A head full of questions had sent him, half-dressed, downstairs to Josie's office. Just the sight of her standing at her workbench had thrown him off balance again, set his pulse racing. Her uncommon beauty, the rose of her mouth, the fragrance of sage and apples that wreathed her hair. She'd become everything in his life, his respite from the war, his reason to feel hopeful.

Not wanting to spook her, he'd hesitated to bring up last night's egregious security breach, the significance of an agent—enemy or friendly—gaining access to Nimway Hall, let alone to his bedroom, undetected. After all of his early blustering about her laxness, one of his own men had failed to protect them!

But he'd learned little from Josie's recollections of the previous night, had stolen kisses from her and made a promise that nothing would stop him from meeting her in the library tonight.

Gideon returned to his suite more troubled than ever, more outraged, because it was clear to him that someone—Arcturus, at best—had deliberately penetrated an intelligence operation without first signaling his intent. He investigated every inch of his sitting room and bedchamber, the common area in the corridor, looking for evidence of a breach, points of entry, detritus on the carpet, papers moved on his desk, drawers rifled.

A quarter hour later, he'd found nothing out of place, out of the ordinary, only the mint and lemon scent of Josie's liniment.

Having wasted time that he couldn't afford, he dressed for the day, snagged a late breakfast of buttered toast and jam from the redoubtable Mrs. Lamb then took his tray to his desk.

He found Crossley and Easton at their drawing boards, Durbridge at the far end of the worktable, bent over the materiel lists for the Operational Base.

"You're looking spry this morning, sir," Easton said with an approving nod. "Shook Miss Stirling to bits when she learned you'd banged up your leg again."

"I'm fine, Easton, thank you," Gideon said, wondering suddenly, impossibly, if one of these three men was Arcturus, hiding in plain sight. Nonsensical in this case, but not unheard of for the SOE to plant two intelligence agents in the same department without them knowing about each other.

"She caught us when she was coming out of your room last night with her medical bag," Crossley said, holding his protractor to the light. "Asked if we'd let you sleep in this morning, said it would do your knee a world of good."

"It has, Crossley. Thank you." Of course, his staff was quartered on the same floor as his suite. "By the way, what time was that? When you saw Miss Stirling?"

"Just before eleven," Durbridge said as he pulled open a file drawer. "The fellows and I closed the fete at ten, had a quick pint afterward at the Hungry Dragon—"

"Did any of you hear anything later? See anyone upstairs who shouldn't be there, that you didn't know?"

"Hell, no!" Crossley stood and stretched. "Would have tackled the fellow and alerted you, for certain. Why? Was something stolen?"

"No. Just curious." He left the matter where it stood and joined Crossley and Easton at the drawing boards, discussed the interior layout of the OB. The plumbing and electrical risers, the wall of bunks, storage shelves for food and munitions, dining table, chairs, a latrine carved into the limestone–for a cave it was bloody well-appointed. The trapdoor entrance carved into the ceiling was so well camouflaged on the forest floor he wouldn't have been able to find it, even in the daylight, had he not known it was located immediately above the original collapsed door to the icehouse.

"Everything to plan, as you see, sir," Easton said. "We should be at the next Operational Base in Chard in two weeks."

"Everything to plan," Gideon said, heading for his desk, adding under his breath, "except recruiting and training the Aux Unit."

He retrieved the list from his trouser pocket and carefully uncurled the slip of paper until it looked like a normal note, rather than a secret, encoded communication from a stealthy, not-to-be trusted fellow agent. With little enough time to contact the candidates and assess their skill sets, Gideon began creating individual evaluations cards for each name on the list.

He finished in the late afternoon, had already made appointments to meet with three of the twelve men—four, if he counted Edward. Satisfied with his progress, he was about to ball up the slip of paper and toss it into the fire when he noticed a line of uncoded writing on the reverse.

Cider Mill Cellar-7P

"Bloody hell!" he said under his breath. "Back in a few minutes, gentlemen."

Gideon left the office, crossed the great hall and entered the darkened library, the windows still shuttered, the blackout curtains closed. He went directly to the Speed map of Nimway and flicked on the sconce lights.

"The Cider Mill?" He hadn't been there, hadn't seen it on the map of the grounds they had used to site the OB. He ran his torch across the face of the map, but found nothing.

The estate must have a cider press somewhere; Nimway Scrumpy had been on sale at the fete. He drank it every day. And who better to point the way than the lady of Nimway Hall.

Hoping Josie was still in her office, he left the library through the service hall and found her still bent over her collection of seeds.

He hadn't gotten two steps into the office when she turned and smiled and asked, "What can I do for you, Gideon? You look lost."

"Do I? I guess I am." In more ways than she could ever know. But how to ask about the mill without sounding suspicious? "The Speed map in the library. I was looking for something—can't seem to find on the map and frankly had never heard about—the cider mill?"

"Ah." She swept him with her gaze, as calm as he was on edge. "Are you in need of a pint of Nimway Scrumpy, Gideon? Because Mrs. Lamb keeps a keg on hand in the kitchen."

"It's not that. Just curious about the mill. Do you mind showing me, please?"

"Not at all." He followed her into the library and stopped along side her. "Trouble is, Gideon, the cider mill doesn't fit on the map."

"Where then?"

"I was about to say that if it were on the map it would be out here on the western edge of the orchard, at the end of this lane. There's a road beyond that we use for deliveries to Balesborough and beyond." She smiled, slipped her hand inside his, taking his breath away. "Do you want me to take you there?"

"Ah, no, Josie. But thank you. I just—Crossley is cataloging the remaining undocumented structures on the estate grounds and we all realized that we'd never seen the cider mill that produces such delicious scrumpy." He could not have sounded more implausible if he tried.

"Thank you for the compliment. I'll pass it along to our cider master. This is his busiest season, of course. I'm sure the press will be working overtime."

"Tonight?"

"From five in the morning until the crew finishes up about five this evening." She slipped her hand out of his and straightened his tie. "Now, Gideon, I'd like nothing more than to spend the rest of the day with you in the library, but that will have to wait until tonight."

Yes, tonight, my dear Josie. After tangling with Arcturus and setting the man straight about boundaries and honor and professional lines that should never be crossed.

Gideon spent the remainder of the afternoon attending to his everyday duties: approving Durbridge's equipment lists for the OB, signing purchase orders, organizing the training schedule for the Aux Unit recruits, finally composing that week's report for Capt. Fenwick at Operational Section headquarters in Bridgwater, a constructive week that showed his men and their abilities in the best possible light, and made him proud.

By six o'clock he had determined that none of his three officers could possibly be Arcturus, and dismissed them for the night with his permission to trounce their rivals from yesterday's tug-of-war in a game of darts at the Hungry Dragon, scheduled, significantly, for seven. He took dinner at his desk and a half-hour later it was time to leave.

Gideon gathered up his rucksack and slipped out of the Hall, unnoticed by anyone but Winnie, who caught up with him as he stepped into the garden, and trotted along side.

"Then come along, girl," he said, charmed by her canine smile and the energetic wagging of her tail as they started down the hill toward the lake.

Having no idea from which direction Arcturus expected him to approach the cider mill, he cut short around the lake, with Winnie in the lead as though she knew where he was bound. They followed a deer track north through a stand of timber until it crossed the commercial road, which eventually ended in the well-traveled lane that led up through the thickening twilight into the cobbled mill yard and its tidy complex of buildings.

A warehouse, a brew house, three wagon loads of apples waiting in line to be pressed. And at the center, what looked to be the oldest of the buildings, the two-story stone cider mill, perched on a slope that fell away into the shadows behind the building.

Winnie sniffed her way through the deserted compound, the cider makers gone for the night as Josie had predicted. He felt no sense of danger, of being watched. He was ten minutes early, perhaps Arcturus hadn't yet arrived.

Feeling entirely at ease, Gideon went up the stairs of the cider house, told Winnie to stay outside, then opened the door and entered the main room, its air rich with centuries of pressed apples and fermented cider. In the shadows, he could see three hulking presses of varying sizes and ages in three separate alcoves, the ceiling crisscrossed with timbers and pipes, pulleys and ropes. A maze of unfamiliar equipment, silent as a stone, the works appearing to have been cleaned and abandoned not ten minutes before.

He found the open gallery to the cellar and took the set of worn stone stairs down to the landing and the closed door. Prepared to meet anyone on the other side—Arcturus or enemy agent, Gideon listened a moment, readied his electric torch and his side arm then carefully lifted the latch and pushed the door into the soft darkness of what appeared to be an open storage area for all manner of cider making equipment. Long shelves of jars and jugs, baskets and funnels, piles of folded burlap, bales of straw and an empty wagon parked in front of a pair of large sliding barn doors.

An odd place for a live drop, a new one on him. Unique to Somerset, to Nimway Hall. Deciding against calling out to alert Arcturus, he closed the door behind him and switched off his torch to allow his vision to adjust to the shadows.

Only then did he notice—through a forest of hanging ropes—a small clapboard room tucked into the back corner, a pale yellow glow seeping around the edges of a door, and a voice, staccato and low, followed by the faintest set of clicks.

Arcturus—at last.

He made a silent, studied approach born of his training and stopped at the door to listen. The murmur of the same voice, another round of clicking. The frizzle and buzz of a radio dial searching out a frequency.

Had Arcturus been operating all this time from the grounds of the Nimway estate? Was he the cider master, or Tully, the orchardist, after all? And why hadn't he been informed by HQ of the radio transmitter?

It was long past time to confront the man and make this bloody live drop happen! Gideon yanked open the door, expecting to find Arcturus at the radio—

Not Josie! But there she was, perched on the edge of a stool, headphones covering her ears, elbows propped on the tall table, her left hand twisting a knob on the transmitter, her right hand holding a pencil, poised above a code book.

She turned and smiled at him as though she'd been expecting

him, eyes bright and excited as she listened to whatever sounds were coming through her headset.

He could only watch in dumbfounded silence as Josie, his love, read out a set of numbers into the microphone as though she'd done so a hundred times. She listened intently, touching the tip of her pencil to the code book, counting number by number, paused and then said, "Roger. Johnnie-Sugar-One. Out."

"Josie." Her name was the only thought in his head. *Josie-Stirling-One.* Was she a Special Duty civilian observer, along with everything else? "What are you doing here?"

She turned on the stool, hooked a heel on the crossbar and pulled off the headset, her eyes glinting in the pale light of the single shaded bulb hanging over the radio.

"Have you really not figured that out, Gideon? After all the clues I left you last night and yesterday, last week and the week before?"

"Clues?" He was having trouble not gathering her into his arms, his marvelous Josie. "I don't understand."

"Yesterday at the fete—I was so surprised! I wasn't expecting you, any more than you were expecting me."

"After kissing me, imploring me to come? You invited me, Josie." He'd been so torn, wanting to escort her, having instead to meet his contact, afraid suddenly, in this fracturing moment, that he'd misunderstood her feelings for him. "Don't you remember?"

"Gideon, you're not hearing me. *Josie* invited you to the fete." She stepped down from the stool and took his hand, held it fast, as though afraid he might turn and leave in the next breath. "But it was *Arcturus* who arranged the live drop between us."

"What do you mean?" Her words roiled inside his head, making them difficult to follow.

"At the Coconut Shy, just after six. We would find each other as agents do, I would hand-off the list of the Aux Unit names then we would go our separate ways, unremarked by anyone but us."

His heart slowed, his brain too. "You're not making sense, Josie. How could you know about—"

"And how could you *not* know, Gideon. I am Arcturus. Why can't you understand when the evidence is so very clear?" He glanced away from her silly chatter, but she caught his cheek with her soft hand, found his gaze and trapped him in her story. "That after I'd dressed your leg and massaged your aching body, you kissed me and fell asleep and I left my own dead drop capsule in your hand."

"You couldn't have." Surely, someone else—

"I told you this morning when you asked me that I was the last, the *very* last person in your room, and yet you didn't believe me."

A night of magic that must still be holding him in its enchantment, muddling his thoughts.

"And yesterday, you waited nearly an hour at the Coconut Shy for Arcturus to approach you. But the live drop never took place, did it? Because I called it off."

"You?" She couldn't have. How could she have known what was about to happen between him and Arcturus?

"Because when you came to flirt with me at the Shy, you were wearing the Spitfire badge on the right side of your jacket, not on the left where I had pinned it earlier."

He spread his fingers against his chest where she'd touched the badge, the memory of her warm palm and her odd reaction, her sudden distance and melancholy, beginning to settled on his heart like a dark web.

"You see, Gideon, I knew in that single moment that you were Invictus, the agent I had been waiting for."

No. "But that would mean you are—"

"Arcturus? Yes. I am. And there I was, standing in front of you at the Shy with the message capsule in my pocket, ready to hand it off to you, waiting for you to recognize me as Arcturus. But you didn't. You were looking right at me, Gideon, looking *for* me, so blinded by your narrow-mindedness that you couldn't possibly see me as your equal. Your fellow agent of the SOE. Your partner."

Not his partner. "Not possible."

"Certainly not possible after tonight, Gideon."

A chill swept through him, the life he'd begun to imagine with Josie at his side vanishing beyond his reach. She'd made him love her for her generosity, trust her with his heart, believed in her ideals. And now she had turned her exacting mirror on his shame, revealed to him his own fanciful reflection of himself, a man no longer whole, no longer invincible.

"You're right, Josie—or whoever you think you are." He took a deep breath to temper his outrage, filled his lungs with the warm scent of apples and autumn and this woman of illusions. "We are dangerous together."

"How can you say that?"

Because she had changed him, unfocused and diminished him. "I'll stay at Yeovilton tonight and make arrangements for a transfer in the morning. We are done here."

"Just like that, Gideon?"

Just like that. No other way. "I'll report to headquarters that we weren't a match, as we must be in order to be partners."

She was looking at him with watery eyes. "Which will hurt me more than you could ever imagine. Because I love you, Gideon. I will to the end of my days. For your uncompromising courage, your compassion and your sense of honor."

The receiver crackled and a thin voice squawked through the headset.

"Yes. Well, Josie. Then it's done. Take care of yourself." She'd chosen a path he could not follow.

"And you, Gideon." Her voice had already turned away from him.

He shut the door on the intimacy of her hushed words spoken into another man's ears and left the cider mill, his decision easily made.

~

The night was as dark as Gideon's mood as he drove the Austin along the country road away from Nimway Hall toward the air station. He'd left the cider mill and called ahead to Todd, who had been eager to learn of his sudden interest in a new position in the SOE. Not behind enemy lines, but given the condition of his knee, that path now seemed forever closed off to him.

Whatever came of it, he couldn't remain at his current post; working alongside Josie every day would not only be a threat to the operation, but an indictment of his principles.

You were looking right at me, Gideon, looking for me, so blinded by your narrow-mindedness that you couldn't possibly see me as your equal.

Bloody hell, Josie was all he could see at the time, was far more than his equal, all the good he could imagine, their lives together stretching out into a future filled with love making and honey and loads of children. Even now, as he sped away from her as quickly as he was able through the darkness, putting as much distance between them as possible, she was calling him back to her with her nonsensical logic.

Different battlefields, certainly. Different weapons, different enemies, but, farming and soldiering are equally critical to winning the war.

Bloody woman and her bloody notions about the prosecution of the war. Warfare was an ordeal of violence and gore, the darkest of human strategies played out upon a landscape of death and horror, and survived only by the strongest. No place for romantic ideals. This war would not be won on the home front. Not with Spitfire fetes or ration books, or by village ladies knitting jumpers for the troops.

Not by Josie, who believed herself to be invincible.

Damn and blast! He hurried along the narrow lane, the only light available to guide him over the corrugated roadbed was the slitted spread of the car's shielded headlamps. Not even the faintest illumination to mark the farm houses that he knew were set just off the roadway.

Nothing to illuminate the interior of the car but the soft glow of the dials on the instrument panel, which seemed stronger than he remembered, suspiciously blue-white and bright enough to throw its reflection into the center of the rear seat.

A vexingly familiar glow that he was certain he'd left behind forever at Nimway Hall. Convinced that his eyes were playing tricks on him, he slowed to a crawl, adjusted the rear view mirror to focus into the backseat where the glow was brightest, and nearly swerved into the hedge.

Josie's orb! He stomped on the brake and stopped in the middle of the road, twisted in his seat. The bloody thing was still there, pulsing blue and white, its center swirling, agitated, as though wanting to speak its mind.

It's pushy and rude and thinks it knows best—

As though such an object could actually think!

"What the devil are you doing here?"

Just as Gideon realized he was demanding an answer from a bloody stone, the yellow beams of a lorry came into view behind him. The hulking vehicle came to a halt and blew its horn. Feeling the fool, he pulled forward into a lay-by and listened to the string of colorful curses and grinding of gears as the lorry lumbered around him before continuing on its way.

He'd watched until it disappeared beyond a curve, hoping the incident would clear his mind of Josie and the backseat of his unwelcome passenger. But there it sat: the Orb of True Love, pulsing and shimmering and, yes, rocking all on its own.

"You're not supposed to be away from the Hall, you bloody thing." Must be a madness of some sort: to be chiding a stone for breaking the house rules and hitching a ride with him. Not that distance from the Hall seemed to matter. He'd driven the Austin well clear of the Nimway estate, nearly to the A37, fifteen minutes short of the air station where he would be free to choose his own path.

But like any stone, anywhere, it said nothing. So he reached between the front seats and grabbed the orb, opened the window and held it outside, ready to toss it to the verge and drive on, let it find its own way home.

Home to Josie.

Are you in need of true love, Josie?

She'd blushed and stammered at the time, answered with one of her distractions. *Besides, I'm fairly sure that the orb changed its mind about us.*

Then the marvelous woman had set about proving just the opposite, by ravishing him with her kisses, enchanting him with her magic, inviting him into her heart. To live there. To love her.

But if she was Arcturus, then who was he? Who was Invictus? Who could they possibly be together?

I love you, Gideon. I will to the end of my days.

Invictus. Unconquered.

Josie!

CHAPTER 13

*W*e're done here, whoever you think you are.

I'm Josie Stirling, you pompous, pigheaded, prig! My code name is Arcturus, and will remain so, until the war is won! With or without you!

Oh, to have thrown that and so much more at Gideon before he'd had a chance to stalk off! But why waste her time, or her breath, on a man who would never change, who cultivated wrong-headed opinions about everything and everyone, himself especially?

He had every right to be angry, to feel deceived and manipulated. So did she. Angry at whoever decided to make them partners and not inform them from the start. Next time she spoke with Fenwick at HQ she'd wring the name of the culprit out of him and make sure it never happened again.

But the real and sharpest ache that had settled like a stone in her heart, was that she had been so right about Gideon's reaction when he finally realized she was Arcturus. Dismissed her and her intelligence work as though she'd highjacked the code name from a more deserving agent. Her allegiance and experience held no more value to him than a toast crumb settled on his sleeve, brushed away and easily forgotten.

So be it, Colonel Fletcher. I wish you well.

It was nearly half-eight by the time she completed her radio transmission duties, locked up the cider mill and finished her final rounds of the estate. For once it was blessedly quiet in the Hall, the children in bed, not a single meeting, her father on an all-night training patrol with his Home Guard unit, the Land Girls attending the cinema in Shepton Mallet.

And Gideon would be in Yeovilton by now, expediting his transfer, with no plans to meet her in the library at half-ten tonight, or any night in the future.

Weary and heartsick and angry to the marrow, she sat at her desk in her office as she'd done every night of the war and encoded her intelligence observations, planes spotted, Home Guard patrol reports, messages sent and received, the radio transmission and, tonight, the disheartening quarrel with Gideon. Hardly a quarrel, a quarrel would have meant a debate with the man, a heated exchange of ideas, followed by a logical compromise of one kind or another. But Gideon's answer was to dissolve their partnership on the spot. No discussion. No room for discourse.

No room to keep stewing about the impossible man. So Josie logged the farm's output into her daily journal, acres plowed and planted, eggs collected, gallons of milk and fat percentages, petrol consumed, barrels of cider pressed—

Exhausted and hoping to keep thoughts of Gideon at bay by reading herself to sleep, she took a bath, dried her hair and had just finished slipping into her flannel pajamas bottoms and jersey top when Winnie began barking at something outside, beyond the wall of the kitchen garden.

Winnie had never been an idle barker, her alerts usually meant business, especially at night. So Josie slipped sockless into her loafers and her oversized Mackintosh, left her office with her electric torch and hurried through the service hall to the outside porch then out into the light rain.

She tracked Winnie's voice along the kitchen pathways, up the stone stairs and through the garden arch, found the dog easily, her head and shoulders stuck deep inside a low hedge of shrubby cotoneaster, barking and snuffling, tail curled and wagging wildly.

"What is it, girl?" Fairly certain Winnie's target wasn't an enemy paratrooper, Josie shooed her from the hedge, then flashed her torch beam down through the branches just as one of Mrs. Higgins' white Leghorns charged forward with a cackle, flapping her wings and diving between Josie's legs before she could catch the accursed thing.

"Oh, no, you don't, little lady!" She chased the indignant hen through the flower garden, was finally able to scoop her up in the middle of a bed of spent buddleia. The rain had slickened the cobbles, but she made it to the chicken house, popped the unhappy escapee through the top of the nesting gallery and dropped the lid on a chorus of squawking.

As soggy as the angry old hen, Josie hunched the hood of her Mackintosh over her head and hurried back through the rainy darkness to the covered porch and into the service hall, looking forward to climbing into bed and pulling the covers over her head.

Josie shut the door, stepped out of her muddy loafers, threw off her wet Mackintosh and hung it on the hook. Cold and nearly as wet as Winnie, she was starting toward her office in her bare feet when the dog let out a woof then loped around the corner into the darkened corridor that serviced the Hall's public rooms.

"Winnie, quiet! You'll wake the house!" She followed with her electric torch, ready to give chase before the dog could race up the stairs and into the children's room. But Winnie was waiting for her in front of the service door to the library, tail wagging.

"Sorry, girl, not tonight or ever. He's gone. I'll have no more meetings with the colonel." No more imagining a future with him. "Come, let's go to bed."

But Winnie only sat swishing her tail across the floor, staring intently at the door—and the sharp beam of blue-white light streaming through the keyhole and striking the brass bowl on the console table on the opposite side of the dark-paneled passage.

Just to be certain the light wasn't coming from her torch— which at best was only ever a sorry spread of yellow, she flicked it off, set it on the console table, then stood there staring at the soft limning of silver that framed the library door, and knew it could only mean—

The orb! Oh, how wrong you were about me and Gideon, you vicious old thing!

Finished with the man and romance and the whole Nimway True Love nonsense, Josie yanked open the door, not caring what she might find on the other side, or how she was going to rid herself of the family curse.

There it was! The abominable orb, beaming away on the table between the two reading chairs where she and Gideon used to sit in front of the fire during their companionable meetings. Where they would share the workings of their days and try to chart their tomorrows, would tease and banter, where he would lift her into his arms and kiss her, warm her with a blanket when she arrived, wet and muddy and at sixes and sevens.

Here in her beloved library, where the orb had first tried so fiercely to bring them together.

And now glints of silver and blue were shimmering within the depths of the moonstone, bright bits of starlight breaking on its surface between the golden talons, whispering—

I love you, Josie. I will to the end of my days—

Promising the impossible—

Beckoning her to believe, to embrace its radiance with all her heart, until she was reaching for the orb on the table, bearing its hopefulness, its happiness in both her hands, hot tears welling in her eyes for all that could have been.

"You're too late!" she said, stifling a sob.

"Dear God, I hope not, Josie."

"Gideon?" She caught the orb against her chest and looked around for him, for his shadow in the darkness beyond the brightness in her hands. He couldn't be here. Shouldn't be! The lout was out of her life for good. The orb must be playing tricks on her again, tempting her to believe he'd returned.

"It's half-ten," Gideon said as the mantel clock chimed once, his silhouette stark against the flames dancing in the fireplace. "Right on time."

"For what, Gideon?" She held fast to the orb, a shock of anger rising from her chest and flushing her cheeks. "You said you'd be staying the night in Yeovilton. You said we were done."

"Ah, Josie—" He blew out an unsteady breath and stepped toward her from the shadows into the incandescence of the orb, his shoulders broad and strong as he looked down at her, his brow dark and furrowed as he captured her gaze. "I said a lot of regrettable things tonight."

Her heart beat happily to feel him so near, was bound to be broken again if she allowed him inside. "Is that supposed to be an apology?"

He smiled to himself and then at her as he scrubbed at his jaw with the back of his knuckles. "A confession."

"That you're a turn-tail as well as a boor? I already know that, Gideon. So, if that's all you've come to say, then we *are* done here, as you said."

"Oh, I'm all that, my love, and more. Scornful, pretentious, parochial—"

"Don't forget pompous and pigheaded." *Wait.* His love? Is that what he just said?

"And quite full of myself, yes, I know." He smoothed his hand over hers where she was holding the orb, the pressure of their shared touch lighting little fires against her palm where it met the silky smooth stone. "Then you came into my life, Josie. And I became even more so."

"More full of yourself?"

"Full of you. The challenge you set for me: to be a better man than I'd ever imagined I could be."

"I don't know what you mean by that, Gideon." Or why he was here in the library when he had been so determined to leave the Hall. She covered his hand with hers. "But what ever you think of yourself, Gideon, you're a good man. I would never believe, never say otherwise."

"There. You challenge me even now." He cupped her face between his hands, tipped her chin with his thumbs so their mouths were inches from meeting. "Because the one thing I didn't say at the cider mill, Josie, the one thing I should have said, and I hope to say every day for the rest of our lives together, is that I love you."

"You—" What? Oh, God no! It's happened! Though his gaze was fierce and earnest, he couldn't have just told her that he loved her, not of his own accord. It was the wicked machinations of the accursed orb that was compelling him to thread his fingers through her hair, to smile softly at her as though bewitched.

"My beautiful Josie." He bent toward her mouth, and his kiss would be—

—heavenly! "No, Gideon, don't!" She clutched the orb tighter and backed away from the kiss that she would have cherished forever, suddenly protective of the lout. Afraid that he'd become enchanted and was being held against his will by the orb. Was saying such tender and lovely things to her when he'd been so clearly repelled at the idea of her being his partner.

"Sweet, your hair is wet. You're shivering." He slipped his warm arms around her, touched his lips to her temple. "Lost in the woods again tonight?"

"Yes." No. Lost in his embrace, in their private fairytale, in the eddies of warmth pouring off his chest. "In the garden. Winnie found her. The Leghorn."

He lifted her chin with the crook of his knuckle, his smile relaxed and teasing. "Are you talking about a chicken? Is that how you got wet this time?"

"I am. I did. Yes, Gideon. My war work, I'll have you know." Josie blinked at him, willing herself to take control of her senses, though she was shaking from the cold.

"Chasing chickens for the war?"

"Wherever I'm needed, thank you very much." Suddenly remembering that she must get rid of the orb before it could do any more damage to their lives than it already had, so Gideon could leave on his own, she circled out of his embrace and started toward the door. "Now if you'll excuse me, I need to—"

"You need to be warmed, Josie." Two strides and he'd cocooned her inside a hearth blanket, carried her to the fireplace like a mummy, and stood her on her bare feet, her back to the fire, the carpet heating her toes.

She would have objected to his manhandling, but her teeth had begun to chatter and his neck smelled so deliciously of his soap, bay and ginger, the heat of him stealing her power to protect the foolish man from further influence by all this Nimway witchery. Distance from her, and the orb that she was still clutching against her chest, and the whole of the estate was the only way to save Gideon from himself.

"What were you going to do with the orb, Josie?" He propped her upright with his strong hands, leaned down and peered into her eyes as though he couldn't get enough of her.

"I'd rather not say." But she had to get rid of it quickly. Something powerful must have happened to Gideon since the cider mill. He'd left her like an enraged dragon bent upon destruction, he'd returned as though he was enraptured with her.

Yes! That was it! The orb had loosed Nimue's and Merlin's

passions against him, had afflicted him with some kind of powerful love spell.

"I want you to know, Gideon, that I haven't seen the orb since you and I kissed in the wine cellar. I don't know how it got here in the library tonight!" Of all nights!

"I do." He was smiling as he smoothed his hand over her cheek, whispered against her ear, "I brought it."

"You brought the orb? From where?" He'd gone daft, of course. Was in thrall to it, spellbound and believing its romantic tales. "Where did you find it?"

A smile teased the corners of his eyes as he turned her toward the fire and added a pair of logs to the dancing flames. "The orb found me."

"It found you where?" Fearful for his sanity, she clutched the blanket at her neck with one hand, cradled the orb in the other and lowered herself onto the upholstered stool.

"About a mile north of the A37, on the Lottisham Road." He seemed to be smiling at some memory as he watched the sparks snap and soar up the flue.

"A mile from the A37? That's not possible, Gideon! I know that road, it's well south of the boundaries of Nimway Hall. How could the orb have found you there?"

"I wondered that, too, after it appeared and I realized how far I'd driven from the Hall." He sat down on the stool opposite her, leaning toward her on his elbows, taking both her hands. "But then I concluded that if Nimue was once the ruler of Avalon, her holdings must have enclosed every hectare of Somerset. Am I right?"

"I suppose so." This engineer, this man of logic had succumbed to citing local legends to support his theories. Oh, dear.

"Then why shouldn't the orb decide to hitch a ride with me in the Austin?"

"The orb hitched a ride? You didn't take it with you when you left the Hall?"

"Good God, Josie, why would I have done that—in the bitterness I felt when I stormed out of the cider mill? I was on my way to Yeovilton. To a new job. I never wanted to see the bloody orb again. And yet, there it was."

"So, to be clear, Gideon—" God knew she was having trouble keeping up with his story "—the orb was sitting in the middle of the road when you—"

"No. It was sitting in the middle of the backseat of my staff car."

"That's impossible, Gideon!" More evidence of his enchantment.

"Big as life, my love, glowing back at me as though it planned to ride all the way to the air station."

"A moment, Gideon, please. I'm having trouble understanding how the orb—" the moonstone in its golden talon which was settled gently on her lap, its pulse in rhythm with the beat of her heart "—ended up in the backseat of the Austin without you having put it there. I mean, really!"

He laughed, caught her chin and kissed the end of her nose. "I've no idea how it came to be there, Josie. Doesn't matter in the least. Because I'm certain that I know *why* it did."

"You do?"

"Because the orb thinks you and I should to be together."

"You believe that?"

"With all my heart. You are the love of my life."

"The love of your life?"

"My beautiful Josie." He dropped to his good knee, became the whole of her world as he knelt above her, caressed her chin and smoothed his thumb across her lips.

And then he kissed her, blissfully, thoroughly, hotly, plundered and played, until she was breathless with need for him, as wildly enchanted as he must be.

She wrapped her arms around his neck and pulled him close, began kissing him as fiercely, tasting every place she could reach, unable to get enough of him, his lips, his brows, his throat, the lobe of his ear until he began making growling sounds in his throat and suddenly pulled away and looked into her eyes.

"Together, Josie. Always."

"Together—" just as the orb wished for them. Oh, no! "Gideon, you must tell me what you did after you found the orb."

"Turned around on the Lottisham Road and came back here to meet you in the library."

"Yes, but, please, tell me exactly what made you decide to turn around."

"Exactly?"

"Yes, please, Gideon. It's very important."

His eyes were alight with passion and promise. "You, Josie."

"Me?" Oh, that was fine, then. He decided on his own, wasn't persuaded by—"

"And the orb, of course." He grinned, a giddy lift to his brow that made him look more than a little mad. "We had a talk."

"The orb spoke to you?"

"In its own way."

This wouldn't do at all! Damn the orb and all its wickedness!

"Gideon, I must ask you something quite serious—" tears stung the backs of her eyes, but she had to be sure, took his hands in hers, so large and kind and masculine. "And you must promise to answer as honestly as you've ever answered any question put to you, by anyone."

"This sounds serious indeed." He narrowed his eyes, looked down his handsome nose. "Go ahead."

"Are you enchanted?"

"Enchanted?" He laughed, his eyes glinting in the firelight as he smiled and cupped her face with his fine hands. "Completely, my love! You have enchanted me beyond rehabilitation."

"Oh, no, Gideon, I was afraid of that!"

"Afraid?"

"That you've been bewitched by the orb, and you don't know it."

"Bewitched by you, my love." He dropped his voice between them, low and sultry, smoothed his forefinger across her lips. "And I'm very, very aware of it."

"No, magically bewitched by the Hall, Gideon. And the orb. These outlandish legends of love and desire! How can either one of us be sure you've not been beguiled into believing you love me when you don't?"

"But I do love you!"

"You left here barely three hours ago as though I had tainted your honor. Said that we were done. Finished!" She stood, felt the orb slip off her lap onto the carpet at her feet. "And then the orb appears in the backseat of the Austin, and now, here you are in the library, kissing me as though nothing has changed."

"Much has changed, Josie. Myself most of all. Inside, where it counts most." He smiled and stood, then lifted her into his arms, blanket and all, and started for the library door. "I told you before that I'm an engineer, a soldier. I know truth from fantasy. And you are my truth."

"But the orb, Gideon?" How could she be sure?

"A reminder of how little my life would mean without you in it. A reminder that I'm a bloody fool."

"And that I'm Arcturus?"

He stopped in his stride and stared at her, as though still disapproving of her intelligence work. And his approval would make all the difference to their future, because, enchantment or no, they couldn't remain together without mutual respect.

"That I was an idiot. Clearly. When I returned here to throw myself on your mercy, I called Todd to tell him I wasn't coming tonight after all. He had news that involves us both, you and me." He'd gone suddenly serious, businesslike.

"About?"

"Seems I'm to head up a new research section for SOE."

"Where?"

"Here in Somerset. Southill House at first, then Yeovilton once the air station is operational."

"You're staying here?"

"Is that an invitation?" He grinned and continued toward the door. "Because your Aunt Freddy's Orb of True Love was right all along. You and I belong together. I want you to marry me. Have our children. We'll spend our lives making scrumpy and planting barley."

A life of bliss and fulfilment.

"Which changes nothing in the meantime, Gideon. Not where my work for the war is concerned. I'm an agent for His Majesty's most secret service. And so are you."

He stopped at the door, his smile deepened and darkened, as though he was brewing an exotic secret between them. "And so are *we*, my dear Arcturus."

"Oh, Gideon. Invictus. I love you." Loved their secrets. She slipped her arms around his neck. "And I'm so very glad the orb hadn't stolen your wits, that you don't actually believe in the bloody thing."

"But I do believe in its power, Josie. The most powerful force the world has ever known."

"Love?"

"Simple as that." He kissed her as he carried her through the door to the service hall. "There you are, Winnie—" kept kissing her all the way into her office "—see that we're not disturbed, there's a good girl—" and into Josie's bedroom, where she'd left a lamp burning low on her bedside table.

The bed, tall and testered, the bedclothes plush with a thick down spread, a bank of pillows against the headboard. She'd never thought of taking a man to her bed, but now that was the only thought in her fevered brain.

This man, in her bed, making love to her. The marvelous man of secrets and honor who was standing with her in his arms in the middle of her room, plundering her mouth and stealing the breath from her. A shiver ran through her that had nothing to do with being wet from the rain.

"Take me, Gideon. Make me yours."

"Take you, Josie?" Gideon raised his mouth from hers and knew from the sultry look in her eyes that he was in deep trouble. Deeply in love and wanting the woman in his arms like flame needed oxygen, burned to slide his hands over her silky skin. "Where?"

"All the way, please." She snuggled her lips against his ear, nibbling and tugging.

"All the way, Josie, to what?" His plan was to kiss her quickly, bid her a good night and leave her safely in her room. Alone.

"All the way to bed. To wherever this wonderful feeling will take us tonight."

"Not a good idea, my love." Not trusting either himself or the lusty woman in his arms who was trying to kiss his neck and unbutton his shirt. He caught her hands to stop her exploring and managed to stand her on her feet. "Not yet."

"When, then? Soon? Father won't be home all night."

Good God, she was serious and even more beautiful when she was pouting, her rosy lips full and damp. "Not until we are married."

Hoping to distract her from the dangerous direction she was heading with her fondling, he left her to lock the door against her surprising immodesty, then flicked on the lamp on her dressing table. When he turned back she was still standing in the center of the room, the blanket in a pool at her feet.

"That won't do, Gideon." She was wearing the most god-awfully beguiling pair of formless, over-sized flannel bottoms, gathered at the waist, the hems overhanging her bare feet. The top presented a lusciously different prospect. Long-sleeved, knit, military-issued silk jersey, ivory, that followed every curve and offered his aching fingers a placket of four buttons that stopped just below her breasts.

He swallowed hard, barely breathing, barely able to think. "What won't do, my love?"

"To wait. There are things in a marriage that must be tested first."

"Things?" He was painfully aware that his erection was fully engaged, ready for the woman. "What sort of things?"

Her smile was lopsided, worldly and innocent. "Love-making. Those very important things."

"You've seen for yourself, Josie, that my 'things' work perfectly well."

"I can see that." She was doing a poor job of hiding her smile. "And did last night."

"Yes, last night." Not so very long ago. And yet a thousand years.

"But you were in your knickers at the time. Which doesn't really count."

It counted for everything. "My knee hurt like the devil and yet you aroused me with your touch."

"I couldn't help but notice." Her eyes widened with her smile. "And oh, how I wanted to touch you everywhere."

"Good grief!" He looked down at her fingers that were working the front of his shirt again, caught them before she could continue. "What are you doing?"

"Proving to you that I've been well-trained in all subjects." She smiled up at him. "I know you still doubt my skills as an intelligence agent."

"I don't, Josie. Truly. My reticence speaks only to my fear for your safety." He lifted her chin and kissed her, realized only then what she had said and that she was tugging his shirt tails from his trousers. "Well-trained for what exactly?"

"For every eventuality." Out came his shirt tails.

"Josie." He caught her hand as she went for his belt, tipped her chin again and looked into her eyes. "What training are you talking about?"

"Special operations." Said with a highly provocative wink and a wriggle of her shoulders. "Coleshill."

He could only blink back at her, trying not to imagine the kind of training she meant. He knew of MI6 officers who performed 'special duties' when necessary for a particular operation: infiltrations, kidnaping, the occasional 'removal' of a threat, but—

"How special do you mean, Josie? And where did you receive this training?" The training that allowed her to unclasp his belt buckle without him realizing.

"Special intelligence training, given just to women. Weapons of Espionage for the Femme Fatale." She gave a tug and his belt zipped through the loops at his waist, came off in her hands and in a flash she'd reached around and corralled him with it, pulled him tightly against her, her hips against his thighs, his erection against her belly. "Using anything at hand to subdue one's male target."

"Male target? Josie, no!" Horror shook him, the full panorama of the danger she was in. His Arcturus. His dearest love. He lifted her off her feet, carried her to the bed, pressed her back against the bank of pillows and trapped her knees with his bad knee, supporting himself above her on the good one.

"What kind of training have you been given? Where in God's name are they planning to send you?" Here is where he would draw the line, sharp and deep.

"It's not like that, Gideon." Her smile softened as she looked up at him, her eyes bright and damp.

"But you've been trained in this?" She was an agent. She damn well better have been trained. By whom? To do what? Jealousy warred with fear for her.

"Of course, I've had a good deal of training over the past year. Radios and wiring and such. But not seduction."

"Are you sure?"

"What do you mean, 'am I sure?'" She shoved him away and came forward onto her knees, arms crossed over her chest, just under her perfect breasts. "I think I would have noticed had my homework assignment been to seduce a handsome fellow agent."

She was beautiful in the shadows, the amber of the bedside lamp making a halo of her hair as she knelt in the middle of the bed like a forest nymph who'd sneaked indoors on a whim. A wave of heat and delight swept over him, that Josie loved him.

"*This* fellow agent would have volunteered as your practicum."

"I would have chosen you. My Invictus." She slipped off the bed and ran her fingers through her hair, loosened the long golden tendrils to fall behind her shoulders, causing the dark peaks of her breasts to press against the tight fit of her jersey, beckoning his hand to caress them, his mouth to taste her. "Lt. Colonel Gideon Fletcher, you are my superior officer when it comes to this sort of training, experience-wise, I assume. And I suspect you've a lot to teach me about the most effective methods of seduction."

"You were doing quite well on your own, my love. Too well." Too rousing. He ought to leave right now, shut the door behind him and sleep until the clear light of day when his head would be clearer, his hunger for her not so fierce.

But she was walking toward him, hips swaying beneath those capacious pajama bottoms, her long, golden hair hanging free around her shoulders, hiding the curves he longed to explore.

"I know this much, Colonel, that your shirt goes first."

And so he let her peel him of his shirt and stood breathing like a stag in rut, certain he couldn't last through her tutorial, but willing to try.

"As you wish," he said, kissing her neck, working free the buttons of her jersey, nuzzling the warmth in the V between her breasts, caught her as she leaned back and opened to him. He pulled aside the fabric and took her nipple into his mouth, nearly bursting with his need for her when she moaned, the sound lingering like a howl.

"Oh, Gideon! Yes, there! Oh yes!" His wild partner ground her hips against him, his erection hard and throbbing. "Please!"

"These go next, my love." He fit his hands to her hips, stuck his thumbs into the elastic waistband of her pajama bottoms and had them off her a moment later.

He stood away to look his fill at the woman who had lifted him out of himself and set him down in the middle of her life, her jersey hanging loose around her naked breast, the fair patch at the cleaving of her thighs, her legs bare and her fists clenched.

"I want you, Gideon." She lifted her shirt up and off over her head, tossed it across the room. "And if you know what's good for you, you'll let me have you."

"You remind me of the orb." He shucked out of his vest and his trousers as she watched. Struggled to shuck his knickers around the fierceness of his erection. Finally stood as naked as she, unmoving for fear of ravishing her on the spot.

"The orb, Gideon?" Her smile was languid and lovely as she came toward him. He drew in a long, shaggy breath as she placed the palm of her hand on the middle of his chest. "Why do you think that?"

Aching to form his hands to the shape of her breasts, to stray further to the curls he knew would be damp with wanting, he held back, knowing that to act would be the end of his restraint. "Because you're pushy and rude and think you know best."

"Yes, I do know best." She grazed her hands down to his hips, the silk of her palms arousing enough to shatter his patience, but when she bent on her knee in front of him, he caught her elbows and raised her swiftly.

"What are you doing, woman?"

"I know what I'd like to do, Gideon." She looked down at his very erect penis, then back up into his eyes, mischief alive in her smile. "But I was just going to check the dressing, before we ravished each other in my bed."

"I did as well as I could with the dressing after my bath." When she knelt again, he was startled enough to let her look, to let her touch both sides of his knee with her fingertips. "Looks fine, quite fine, in fact." She rose with that same smile and wrapped her arms around his neck, whispering, "The dressing looks good too. Now, please, Gideon, can we continue my lesson."

Bloody hell, could a man be more lucky?

"At your service, my love." He drew her against him and kissed her, meeting her tongue in a dance of fire, plunging and probing, collecting her moans of pleasure, his hands never still for wanting all of her, his arms quaking.

"To the bed, please," she whispered, rising on her toes and climbing eagerly into his embrace. She wrapped her legs around his waist, and he caught her backside, holding her against him, her desire a soft and slick heat against his belly. Oh, how he wanted to play there. To taste her.

"To the bed, my love." He carried her there, to the center of the bank of pillows and winced when he bent his bad knee to kneel beside her.

"You'll not be able to use that knee anytime soon, Gideon." As though she'd found a cure, she reached for his erection and took in a breath when she found it, held it. "It's lovely!"

He caught her hand to his chest. "Oh, God, no, Josie. Not tonight. I won't last. Perhaps it's for the best. We shouldn't."

"Why not. I don't mind at all that you can't mount me in the usual way. I've read that there are other positions. Female superior."

"Good God, Josie." He kissed her palm, rolled as far atop her as he could, hoping to still her for a moment. "It's for the best that I can't the regular way. Shouldn't anyway. I can, absolutely. You can see for yourself."

"I do." She closed her eyes and circled her hips beneath him. "But not tonight."

"Why not? You've asked me to marry you."

He had. And realized, "But you haven't answered."

"I haven't?" She smiled, caught his backside and in a single movement that defied the laws of physics, rolled with him so that he was on his back and she was straddling his hips.

"What are you doing?"

"I'm saying yes, Gideon, I'll marry you and love you and bear your children—"

"When?"

"When will I bear your children?" She braced herself on all fours, raining kisses across his face, down his throat. Then she was reaching for his penis, embraced it like a marvelous pulsing glove and fit its head against her slick heat, smiling down at him like a Cheshire cat. "After we're married, of course."

"Dozens?"

"Oh, yes. And I like you here, Gideon."

He could hardly find a breath, held tightly to her hips, to keep himself from plunging. "When will you marry me?"

"Tonight, if I could, my dear Gideon. Demand a special license and be married at midnight in the churchyard beneath our yew tree."

"My Josie." His pagan bride, dancing naked and beribboned in the moonlight, among the tall flowers and approving spirits of her ancestors. "If only we could."

"This Christmas, then." Her face was flushed with love for him, with her wild desires, her caress encircling his erection, an exquisite torture.

"Not sure I can wait that long."

"Let's not, then." She took a long breath, met his mouth in a fury of plunging kisses, then lowered her hips and pressed him past her silken folds, rocked her hips to take him deeper and deeper until she met her final barrier and could wait no longer.

"Together, my love." He rose up, spread his hands across her bottom then thrust sharply through her tightness, paused to hear her sweet moan against his ear, then groaned and carried himself all the way home. Deeply. Sweetly. Rabidly, measure by measure, as she began to rock with him, kiss him, sighing and soughing and whispering his name.

"Oh Gideon, you are—" Josie couldn't help moaning shamelessly against Gideon's cheek, couldn't seem to control the throbbing rhythm of her own hips, the need to drive him deeper and deeper inside. "You're... very... large!"

Her whispers seemed to draw a long feral groan from the wondrous man straining beneath her. The sculpted sinew of his chest, bronze and slick with sweat. "And you, my sweet, are tight and warm and so—oh, God, so—'

"So mad for you, Gideon! Oh, yes!" Her handsome beast was breathing like a bull against her breast, bracing her above him with his hard-muscled arms as he nuzzled a searing path to her nipple, tugging and laving and nibbling, the heat of him building a coil of pleasure that tightened her insides around his marvelous shaft and centered on the spot where she joined with him.

"Ride slow, my love," he said, his nostrils flaring, his fingers splayed across her bottom, kneading, pressing her closer, his voice a low rumble that echoed through her belly, "ride steady."

"So lovely!" So languid, like floating on a warm sea, with Gideon as her raft, warming in the sun, leaving her wanting more of him, all of him, taking him deeper, onward toward a licking fire that would surely consume them both.

"Too soon, my love—" His breath thundered out of him as he restrained his thrusting, anchored her hips against his, his eyes wild and bright, lit with a desire that mirrored the mists that swirled inside the orb.

"I love you, Gideon. Can't seem to stop this squirming against you." Feeling free and open to his gaze, she sat upright and began rocking, gasped when he sat up and wrapped his iron-bound arms around her.

"Then squirm, my love. I'll bear up for you."

"My partner, my soul." Josie sighed and arched backward in his arms, exposed herself to him utterly, trusting his heart, his very maleness, shuddered and cried out when, at the same time, he took her nipple into his mouth and found the heat of her between her legs where they were coupled and wet and so very warm.

"I love you, Josie!" In the next moment, Josie was lying on her back amidst the pillows, looking up at the man she loved with the whole of her heart, her legs spread wide to encourage the power of his thrusting, as he watched her, smiling, straining, pumping until the world around and above her suddenly stopped—

"Ooh, Gideon, together!" The quake of pleasure came hard and hot, swept over her with a shattering, convulsive wildness. Wave after wave of peaks and valleys, bits of starlight and whole constellations, ripples upon ripples of ecstasy until she thought she would die of it, of him.

Of her dear Invictus. The remarkable man who'd become the light of her life, was poised above her on his outstretched arms, growling her name between thrusts, plunging ever deeper and surer, until every muscle in his body seemed to still except the hard shaft buried inside her that pumped on its own, his seed like molten life pouring into her furrow.

"Josie!" He shuddered and thrust again and again, then, as though sliding back to earth from the cloud they shared, her handsome secret agent finally lowered himself onto his elbows, kissed and nuzzled her neck, a conquering smile in his eyes. "Not the way I thought this night would end, my love."

She kissed him. "But a better welcome to Nimway Hall than I gave you on our first meeting."

"Now that would have a been a greeting for the ages!"

"Do you think the orb had any part in this?"

He laughed and raised his head like a mythical beast sniffing the air, looked around. "Where is the bloody thing, do you suppose? Do you think we've proven that we're no longer in need of its assistance?"

"The orb?" Josie nipped at his chin, bent her knee, braced her foot on the mattress then rolled him onto his back where she could perch on his chest and look him in the eye. "Last I knew it was sliding off my lap onto the carpet in the library when you were kissing me."

"Back into Nimue's cave?" He skimmed his fingertips down her back, trailed them over her bottom.

She grinned at him. "I like to believe it will linger in the library where we found it."

"For our stubborn daughter to find one day when she's Guardian of Nimway Hall and is in desperate need of her own true love."

"Our daughter will be stubborn?" Josie made a show of being shocked.

"As stubborn as her mother, and our sons will be as pig-headed as their father."

"What a romantic man you turned out to be, Gideon Fletcher."

"And what a very fine intelligence operative you've turned out to be, Arcturus. Arthur. Guinevere. Merlin. Nimue. Could I have been more dense? I should have known who you were that first day in Balesboro Wood and in the wine cellar. All that talk of King Arthur. You blinded me with your faith in everyone around you, your unwavering faith in me. Made me understand that my life had been saved so that I might rise and fight again."

"My love, my champion." How could he have ever thought himself otherwise? How she loved him!

"And you are my Josie. The best of me."

"But now you have me wondering, my handsome, brave hero, can you really rise and fight again so soon." Josie flexed her fingers over his resting penis and thrilled to feel it fill her hand almost immediately. "Indeed you can!"

Josie enfolded them inside the down coverlet and made a closer inspection of the man and all his magnificence. They teased and kissed and came to each other again until they were lying together, spent and spooning, Josie snuggled against his chest, his hand cupping her breast.

He kissed her ear, whispered, "I've enjoyed tonight's meeting more than any other we've had."

She covered his hand with her own. "Most productive of the lot. So in keeping with our agenda, I will ask: What are you up to tomorrow, Colonel?"

"Tomorrow I ask your father for your hand in marriage."

She laughed. "And he'll ask what took you so long. My father agrees with the orb."

"Wise man." Another kiss that stirred her fires and struck the breath from her. "And what of your day tomorrow?"

"Indeed." She wasn't sure where they stood with Gideon's new position, what that meant for the two of them. "I plan to report to Fenwick that Arcturus and Invictus have successfully established a live connection."

"Haven't they, though?" His lips followed his fingers along a trail of bliss. "Invictus can't seem to keep his hands off Arcturus."

"And vice versa, though I won't tell him that detail. Wouldn't want to shock the man." Needing to be serious for a moment, she caught Gideon's hand. "But I will be assigned a new partner. Continue our mission."

"If you'd like. Or you can assist me in this new venture with the SOE. Lots of opportunities to expand your influence in the war effort. I'll know more in the coming week."

She couldn't leave the farm, but how thrilling that he should want her for her expertise. "Would you be my superior, then? Will I have to work under you?"

He arched a rakish brow, was fondling her in the most intimate of places. "I'd hardly call this work. But looking ahead, my love, I see an assignment for us at Christmas time. Very official. Involves a license and flowers."

"And music and a church? Oh, Gideon!" She was ready and aching for him again.

"But first—" He rose up on his elbow, settling her against the pillow and turning her away. He touched his fingertip to her back near her left shoulder. "There it is! Your legendary birthmark."

"Do you mean the pale oval?"

"Shaped just like the orb. It's quite lovely. I've been wanting to kiss you here since the moment you mentioned it."

"Do, then. Please do!" He kissed her shoulder, toyed with her nipple, making it difficult to answer. Or care. She sighed and reached her arms around him.

"The mark of the Guardian—" he kissed her shoulder again, then covered her with his fine, warm body. "Perhaps that's where the glow of the orb will live until it's needed again: inside your heart."

"And yours, Gideon! My true love."

THE END

≈

≈

Dear Reader,

I hope you enjoyed the story of Josie and Gideon — *1940: Josie*, the fourth in *The Legend of Nimway Hall* series. Bringing these two people to life and getting to know them was an enormous pleasure for me.

Learning about the English Home Front during World War II was as delightful as it was harrowing. I set the story in September and October of 1940 because it was the early days of the war, the

Blitz was raining terror on the British people, food rationing was increasing, the men were in uniform and the women were waging their own war in the kitchen, the fields and the factories.

I loved the idea of bringing the war to Nimway Hall and to Josie, the ancient estate's courageous Guardian. As the story opens, we find her knee-deep in evacuee children, Land Girls, the local Home Guard, a much-reduced estate staff, two cranky tractors and her widowed father she has just rescued from the London Blitz. Her days and nights are chock-full of wartime charity fund raisers, meeting the strict requirements of the Ministries of Agriculture and Food, organizing knitting circles, leading her local Women's Volunteer Service, tending the acres of orchards, the mill, and fields of grain.

Most amazing to me is that Josie's is just one of the many millions of women and men on the English home front who worked their normal jobs by day and served as civilian soldiers by night, often with no sleep in between. The threat of invasion was real and on-going, and I have only the deepest respect for the brave and devoted members of that generation.

My own mother was a 'Rosie the Riveter' on the American home front, my father was a radioman on a ship on the Pacific front.

Indeed, the Greatest Generation. This is their story.

Come find me at my website where you can sign up for my newsletter, linger over my booklist, and learn of my many adventures!

Enjoy!
Linda

ABOUT LINDA

I began my journey on the road to romance writing in 1972 with an overcooked Thanksgiving turkey and my nose buried in a delicious copy of Kathleen Woodiwiss's first novel, THE FLAME AND THE FLOWER. Reading had always been one of my favorite obsessions, but Woodiwiss had for the first time fused the sweeping majesty of history with the sensual power of romance, and from that moment the romance novel industry went into high gear and was changed forever. I was desperately hooked on historical romance and soon after began secretly writing my own romance novel. I had a lot to learn!

Nearly 25 years after that fateful Thanksgiving weekend of 1972, my unpublished manuscript, FOR MY LADY'S KISS won 1st place in six romance writing competitions, 2nd and 3rd place in six other competitions, and the 1995 Romance Writers of America's Golden Heart for Long Historical. Two months later the book sold, along with a one-line proposal for a second book, EVER HIS BRIDE, to Avon Books, and, in February 1997, my first novel—FOR MY LADY'S KISS was released to my great delight! More books followed, with five hitting the USA Today Bestseller list.

Of course, like every author, I started writing in early grade school, as soon as I realized that I could put my own words together to make my own stories, just like the authors of my favorite childhood books–BEAUTIFUL JOE and HEIDI and the Nancy Drew mysteries.

My love for storytelling eventually led me to a bachelor's degree in Theatre Arts at California State University, Dominguez Hills where I gained a deep understanding of character development, dialogue, scene-shaping and plotting techniques. I'm also a playwright, one of the lucky ones who have had full productions of their works—seven full length musicals, four revues and two full-length plays.

I write full-time from my home office near Portland, Oregon. And when I'm not writing, I've been known to direct plays and musicals, garden 'til I drop, hunt mushrooms, spoil my two grandkids, take extended research treks with my hero husband and blaze trails through our 5-acre woodland with Pippa, our Portuguese Water Dog who holds numerous titles in the new canine sport of Nose Work.

https://lindaneedham.com/